A RAVAGED SKIES NOVEL

ALTERED WORLD

DJ COOPER

 Copyright © 2025 Angry Eagle Publishing, LLC
https://AngryEaglePublishing.com

Cover design by DauntlessCoverDesign.com

This book is a work of fiction. The characters are imaginary, and any resemblance to actual persons is accidental. However, some places are based upon actual locations, but all incidents and events are fictional.

Paperback ISBN: 978-1-964884-17-2

Find DJ Cooper on the web.

Https://AuthoroftheApocalypse.com

Don't forget to sign up for the spam free newsletter

https://bit.ly/3KmAGjh

"How baffling it is that we imagined cities incinerated by alien bombs and death rays when all they really needed was Mother Nature and time."

— Rick Yancey, The Infinite Sea

Contents

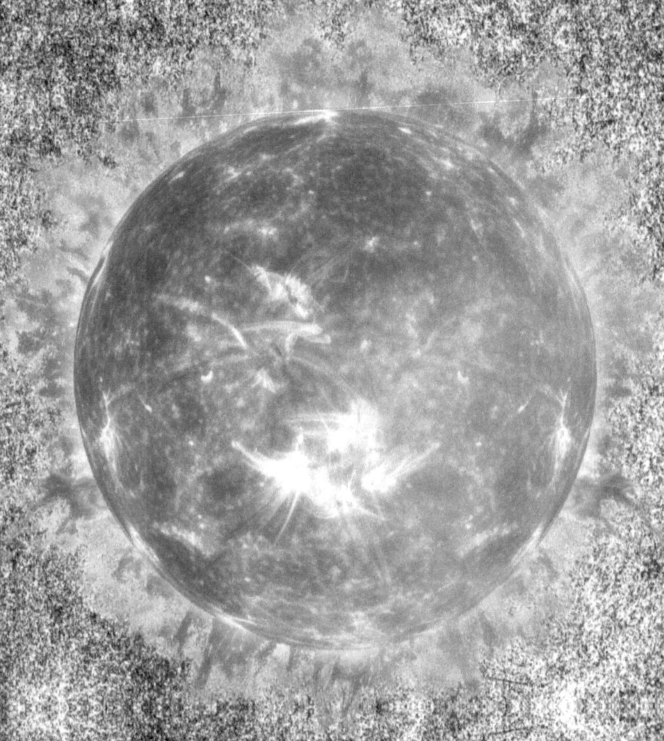

"THEY DON'T KNOW HOW TO SURVIVE WITHOUT A SOCIETY THAT SUPPORTS THEM EVEN AS THEY CURSE IT OR... REBEL AGAINST IT."

- WILLIAM R. FORSTCHEN, ONE SECOND AFTER

Grace

"Sorry for the delay everyone, but Mother Nature is being such a total bitch right now, completely ruining our liberation content—but don't worry, we're still going to get amazing footage even if I have to film over a few corpses to make it happen!"

Grace Reynolds held her dead iPhone toward the gray wall of rain, water streaming down her face as she livestreamed to an audience that existed only in her fractured mind. The phone's black screen reflected nothing but her own distorted image, but in Grace's reality, thousands of hearts were flooding the chat, subscribers were climbing by the minute, and her content was going viral in real-time.

Behind her, the valley had transformed into an alien landscape of destruction. Traveling along Route 25, a quiet two-lane road winding through the Saco River valley toward Cornish, now resembled the aftermath of a dam break. Three of her convoy vehicles sat buried to their door handles in what was only a trickle brook six hours ago.

The innocent-looking waterway, an offshoot of the massive torrent now behind them, swelled into a chocolate-brown torrent nearly completing the connection into one big river, leaving them caught between the two and carrying with it the debris of upstream destruction from the Saco. Lodged among splintered fence posts, a child's swing set, the bright yellow door of someone's kitchen cabinet, were things that bobbed in the current that nobody wanted to examine too closely.

The smell hit in waves—river silt and diesel fuel, the green decay of torn vegetation, and underneath it all, something sweet and wrong that might have been death. Forty-three of her followers stood scattered across the flooded landscape like survivors of a shipwreck as they sought a way across. Their tactical gear and stolen military equipment rendered useless by the simple fact that their vehicles couldn't move and the road ahead had become a river.

The storm had rolled in from the Atlantic like a living thing, bringing with it the kind of biblical fury that turned weather forecasts into dark jokes. Grace could taste salt in the rain. The ocean itself reaching two miles inland with the storm surge to remind everyone that nature had never really been tamed, only temporarily ignored. Lightning split the sky in jagged purple scars, followed by thunder that seemed to rise from the earth itself, making her followers flinch and look skyward with the primitive fear of creatures who suddenly remembered they were small.

Grace felt none of it. The storm was just bad lighting. The flooding was a production challenge. The growing terror in her followers' eyes was simply audience engagement.

"It's not nice to piss off Mother Nature, Grace."

The comment drifted from somewhere in the cluster of soaked, shivering people huddled around the stuck vehicles. Grace's head snapped up, her perfectly applied makeup now running in dark rivulets down her cheeks like war paint. The foundation she'd spent twenty minutes perfecting in her mirror that morning—because good lighting was crucial for quality content—had dissolved into a grotesque mask that made her look like a drowned corpse still trying to smile for the camera.

"Who said that?" Her voice carried that dangerous

sweetness her followers had learned to fear over the past months. It was the tone that preceded violence, the vocal equivalent of a snake's warning rattle. "I'm getting some really toxic comments in the chat right now, everyone. That's not the kind of engagement we want for today's stream."

She panned the phone across the faces of her followers, and even in her madness, some part of her registered their expressions. These weren't the eager, devoted disciples who had followed her out of Portsmouth. These were exhausted, starving people who smelled like sweat and fear and the unwashed desperation of too many nights sleeping in abandoned buildings. Their tactical gear was soaked through, their weapons were becoming waterlogged, and their eyes held the hollow look of people who were starting to understand they'd made a terrible mistake.

But Grace saw only her audience. Her community. Her content.

Mark Webb stepped forward, his combat boots squelching in the mud that had once been solid ground. He'd been one of Sherman Masters' most trusted lieutenants before Grace had absorbed their organization through a combination of psychological manipulation and strategic elimination of anyone who questioned her methods. Sherman failed her one time too many and found himself an unwitting hood ornament.

Now he stood like a scarecrow in the rain, water dripping from his tactical vest, his AR-15 slung uselessly across his back. The weapon that made him feel powerful in Portland's urban warfare collapse offered no advantage against the reality that their vehicles were trapped and the road ahead was impassable.

"Grace, we've lost two people already trying to cross," he said, having to raise his voice over the wind that howled through the valley like the breath of something enormous and angry. "Jenny went under about an hour ago near that downed tree, and

Mike…" He gestured helplessly toward the churning water. "Mike tried to follow her. The current's too strong. Maybe we should wait for the water to go down, or find another route, or—"

"Cut!" Grace screamed, lowering the phone with such sudden violence that several followers jumped. The mask slipped completely, revealing something wild and hungry underneath—the thing that lived behind her eyes when she thought nobody was watching. "Mark, sweetie, you're totally ruining the flow here. The audience doesn't want to hear about logistics. They want drama. They want action. They want authentic struggle content that builds real emotional investment in our journey."

She raised the phone again, and her smile returned like someone had flipped a switch, but now it looked painted on, a grotesque parody of human expression. "Sorry about that, everyone! Some people just don't understand how content creation works. Mark is still learning that you can't build a successful platform without taking some creative risks."

The valley around them told a story of creative risks gone wrong. To the north, where the road should have continued toward Cornish, a massive oak tree had fallen across what remained of the highway, its root system torn from the earth and pointing skyward like the fingers of a buried giant. The tree had created a natural dam that turned the flooding into something more like a lake, with only the tops of road signs visible above the brown water to mark where human civilization had briefly existed.

To the south, the way they'd come, similar destruction stretched behind them with the now raging Saco River well over the road bridge keeping them pinned on the small island of higher ground. Radio chatter from their other convoy groups painted a picture of universal chaos. Roads washed out, bridges collapsed, vehicles abandoned when the drivers realized that maps meant nothing when the landscape itself had been rewritten by water and wind.

The storm had been building since midnight, when Grace's meteorologist, a former Weather Channel intern named Dave who'd joined her organization for reasons nobody understood, including Dave, had assured her that the weather would be *totally manageable* for their dawn assault. Dave was currently huddled inside one of the partially submerged vehicles, presumably reconsidering his career choices and possibly his will to live.

Their carefully planned three-pronged assault had been designed to hit Cornish and the Thompson family farm from multiple directions at sunrise, overwhelming the community's defenses through coordinated attacks that would make for spectacular content. Grace had spent weeks planning the visual elements. Imagining drone footage of the assault, multiple camera angles, live commentary as they liberated the community from their false consciousness about survival and scarcity.

Instead, they were trapped in a flooded valley with Cornish miles away through terrain that now looked like the surface of an alien planet. But in Grace's mind, this was just another technical difficulty to overcome for better content. Every challenge was an opportunity. Every setback was character development. Every dead follower was simply a plot point in the larger narrative of her inevitable success.

"Okay, so here's what we're going to do," she announced to her imaginary audience, panning the phone across the devastation with the enthusiasm of a travel blogger showcasing a luxury resort. "We're going to cross this river because that's what winners do. They adapt. They overcome. And they always, always give their followers the best possible content, even when Mother Nature is throwing her little tantrum."

The water that blocked their path had turned the color of chocolate milk, thick with sediment and debris from upstream. The current moved with the kind of power that could pin a person against a rock or drag them under fallen trees before they could scream. Floating in the brown soup were pieces of people's lives—a kitchen chair, a child's playhouse, somebody's family photos in a plastic bag that bobbed along like a tragic message in a bottle.

"Grace, please." Rebecca Mitchell rose from where she'd been sitting on the hood of a half-submerged Humvee, water cascading from her clothes. The woman who had once been Hannah Mitchell's mother—who had packed lunches for school field trips and argued with insurance companies and worried about college tuition—was now something else entirely. Rebecca had lost perhaps thirty pounds since Grace had taken her from the South Portland community, her once-carefully maintained hair hanging in wet tangles, her cheekbones sharp enough to cut glass. She looked like a scarecrow dressed in wet camouflage, a broken puppet dancing to Grace's psychological strings.

Grace had been using Rebecca as her special project, her masterpiece of psychological manipulation. "My trauma pet," she called her in private moments. The perfect example of how anyone could be broken down and rebuilt in Grace's image, given enough time and the right kind of pressure. Rebecca was living proof that Grace's methods worked, that her understanding of human psychology was flawless, that she really could save people from their limiting beliefs about survival and scarcity... Or at least that was what Rebecca wanted her to believe.

"The current is too strong," Rebecca continued, her voice barely audible over the wind. "Jenny and Mike are already—" She stopped, swallowing hard. Grace had trained her well. Even in moments of crisis, Rebecca knew better than to contradict the narrative. "They're gone, Grace. The water took them."

"Jenny and Mike are going to be fine," Grace interrupted, turning the camera toward Rebecca with the smooth professionalism of someone who'd spent her entire adult life performing for an audience. "Everyone say hi to Rebecca! She's one of my most dedicated community members, and she's having a little crisis of faith right now, but that's okay. Sometimes content creation requires sacrifices for the greater good of engagement. Rebecca's learning that building a successful platform means staying positive even when faced with temporary setbacks."

Rebecca was Grace's favorite example of successful community building. She'd been so resistant at first, so attached to her old limiting beliefs about family and individual survival. Constant whining and crying about her husband who only died because he tried to hide that bitch Hannah who'd tried to undermine her content with her friend Maddie. But… months of careful guidance had helped her understand that Grace's vision was bigger than her small-minded concerns about her . Hannah husband and children. She was probably better off anyway. Grace had done Rebecca a favor by liberating her from the burden of helicopter parenting and showing her what real community looked like.

Rebecca's lips moved silently, forming words that Grace couldn't quite hear over the storm. But Grace had become expert at reading lips during their time together, and a skill developed through paranoia and the constant need to know what people were saying about her when they thought she wasn't listening. The words Rebecca mouthed were simple and devastating: "They're dead, Grace. They drowned."

"What did you just say?" Grace's voice dropped to a whisper that somehow carried more threat than her earlier screaming.

The wind howled through the valley, bending trees that had stood for decades and turning the rain horizontal. Somewhere in the distance, a radio crackled with static and panicked voices—Alpha Group reporting that Route 113 was completely washed out, Bravo Group requesting extraction from rising water near Steep Falls. But Grace's attention was laser-focused on Rebecca, waiting for an answer that would determine whether she lived through the next thirty seconds.

Around them, the natural world displayed its power with casual indifference to human ambition. The storm had transformed familiar Maine countryside into something primordial and alien. Pine trees that had weathered decades of nor'easters now bent like grass in the wind. The temperature had dropped twenty degrees since dawn, and their breath was beginning to mist in the air, adding hypothermia to the growing list of ways the environment was trying to kill them. This was more than just a summer hurricane, this was a storm of a century.

But Grace registered none of the cold, none of the danger, none of the growing desperation in her followers' faces. In her mind, she was creating the most authentic, most engaging content of her career. This was the kind of raw, unfiltered drama that built empires. This was what separated real influencers from the wannabes who only knew how to pose with coffee cups and sunset photos.

"I said…" Rebecca's voice broke, and Grace saw the exact moment when survival instinct overrode whatever remained of her integrity. "I said they're fine, Grace. They're fine."

"That's better." Grace turned back to her phone, the smile returning with mechanical precision. "Sorry everyone, Rebecca is still learning how to be a good team player. But that's why we're here, right? To help people understand what real community looks like. To show them that survival isn't about hoarding resources or building walls—it's about coming together to create something beautiful."

She began walking toward the swollen creek with the phone held high. The water was moving fast, carrying debris from upstream—branches, pieces of buildings, things that might have been furniture or might have been bodies. The crossing looked impossible.

"Now, I know what you're thinking," Grace said to her phone. "You're thinking, 'Grace, this looks super dangerous!' And you're right! But that's what makes for compelling content. Real authentic struggle. The kind of raw, unfiltered drama that builds serious follower engagement."

Mark grabbed her arm. "Grace, you can't be serious. That water will kill anyone who tries to cross."

She turned to face him, and for a moment her followers saw something that made several of them step backward. Her eyes were completely empty—not angry, not sad, just vacant, like looking into a broken window.

"Mark," she said sweetly, "are you trying to tell me how to run my stream?"

"No, I'm trying to keep you alive—"

The gunshot echoed across the valley, and Mark dropped face-first into the mud. Grace lowered her pistol, then immediately raised her phone again.

"Okay everyone, we just had to deal with some really negative energy there. Mark was bringing down the whole vibe of the stream, and we simply can't have that kind of toxicity affecting our content quality." She stepped over his body without looking down, her boots squelching in the mixture of mud and blood. "Remember to smash that like button if you're enjoying today's liberation content! And don't forget to subscribe for more authentic survival experiences!"

The remaining followers stared at Mark's corpse, then at Grace, then at each other. Some hands drifted toward weapons, though most of their ammunition was getting soaked and their electronic sights were useless anyway. Others moved toward the vehicles, thinking about the impossible choice between staying with a clearly insane leader and striking out on their own in the middle of a deadly storm. A few looked toward the rushing water that was starting to seem like the safer option compared to whatever Grace might do next.

Grace seemed oblivious to their growing terror, lost in her performance for an audience that existed only in her fractured mind. In her reality, the chat was exploding with hearts and fire emojis. Her subscriber count was climbing by the thousands. This was the kind of raw, authentic content that separated real influencers from the wannabes. This was what built empires.

"Now," Grace continued, her voice bright and cheery as Mark's blood spread in pink tendrils through the muddy water at her feet, "who wants to volunteer to test the crossing for us? We need some good action shots for the thumbnail, and I'm thinking water drama always performs really well with our demographic."

The silence stretched out, broken only by the sound of rain and rushing water and the distant crack of another tree falling somewhere upstream. Nobody moved. Nobody spoke. Even the radios had gone quiet, as if the other convoy groups had finally realized that maintaining contact with Grace's forces was more dangerous than helpful.

"Come on, people!" Grace gestured wildly with the phone, her other hand still holding the smoking gun. Water dripped from her hair, her makeup had dissolved into ghoulish streaks, and her clothes were soaked through, but her smile never wavered. "This is prime content! Think about the views! Think about the engagement metrics! We're creating something special here. Something that's going to change how people think about survival and community building forever!"

She began pacing back and forth along the water's edge, her movements becoming more erratic with each passing moment. "Jenny and Mike are already over there somewhere, probably setting up the perfect landing zone for us. All we need is someone brave enough to go first and show our audience what real leadership looks like. Someone who understands that you can't build a successful platform without taking creative risks!"

The storm intensified around them, as if nature itself was responding to Grace's madness with its own display of power. But Grace heard none of it. In her mind, she was creating the most epic content of her career, building toward the most amazing finale her audience had ever seen.

The algorithm would love this. The engagement would be incredible. She just needed a few more volunteers to make it perfect.

"Rebecca!" she called out sweetly, turning the phone toward her broken trophy. "Why don't you show everyone how it's done? You've been looking a little camera-shy lately, and I think some water action shots would really help rebuild your personal brand. Plus, you could probably use the exercise— you're looking a little skeletal these days."

"Grace," she said quietly, her voice taking on a strange new quality that made several of the other followers turn to look. "There is no camera. There is no audience. There are no likes."

The words hung in the air between them, mixing with the sound of rain and rushing water and distant thunder. For a moment, even the storm seemed to pause, as if the natural world itself was waiting to see what would happen next.

Grace's smile flickered, just for a moment, like a lightbulb with a loose connection. Her phone hand wavered slightly, and for an instant, her followers saw something human flicker behind her eyes. Confusion, maybe even a trace of fear.

Then it blazed back to life, brighter and more terrible than before.

"Cut!" she screamed, her voice cracking with rage. "Rebecca, what the hell? You're completely breaking character! The audience can see everything! Do you want to tank our ratings? Do you want to destroy everything?"

She raised the gun again, pointing it directly at Rebecca's chest. Around them, the storm raged on, and the water continued to rise, and Grace's empire of madness teetered on the edge of collapse.

"You know what?" Grace said, her voice dropping back to that dangerous sweetness. "Maybe you're right. Maybe we need a different kind of content today. Maybe what our audience really wants to see is what happens when someone brings negative energy to our community. What do you think, everyone? Should we give them some deletion content? Should we show them what happens when you don't respect the algorithm?"

The gun shook in her hand, but whether from rage or hypothermia, nobody could tell. Behind her, Mark's body had stopped twitching, and the storm showed no signs of letting up, and only a few miles away, the Thompson farm waited in blissful ignorance of the chaos that would eventually find its way to their door.

If it survived the flood.

If Grace survived Rebecca's rebellion.

If any of them survived what was coming next.

James

The storm finally passed, but its legacy remained written across the landscape in broken trees and churned earth. James Thompson stood on his farmhouse porch in the pre-dawn darkness, coffee steaming in his hands as he surveyed the damage by flashlight. Three outbuildings had lost sections of roof. The chicken coop leaned at a dangerous angle, held upright only by the oak tree that had fallen across it. Power lines, not that they mattered anymore, lay tangled in the debris like discarded Christmas lights.

But they were alive. The farm's elevated position protected them from the worst of it, and the reinforced storm cellar had sheltered their vulnerable tent living residents during the height of the winds. Now, as gray light began to seep across the eastern horizon, James saw the full scope of what they faced.

The radio in his jacket crackled with Beth's voice, tense but controlled. "Thompson farm, this is Martin. Come in."

James keyed the handset. "Martin, this is Thompson. Go ahead."

"The Ossipee is still rising. We're implementing evacuation protocols for the lower areas of town. How's your situation there?"

James glanced toward the barn where Daniel was already moving, checking on the livestock and assessing structural damage. In the distance, he saw smoke rising from the town.

Whether from storm damage or something worse, he couldn't tell from this distance.

"Some storm damage, but we're secure. What's your timeline on the evacuation?"

"Two hours, maybe three before we have to move people. The funeral home and town hall are already taking on water in the basements. If this keeps up…" Beth's voice trailed off, but the implication was clear. The town's lower areas, where most of their critical infrastructure was located, could become uninhabitable.

"We're ready to receive," James replied automatically, though his mind was already calculating the logistics. They had space in the main house, the barn, and several outbuildings, but housing and feeding potentially two hundred people would strain their resources past the breaking point.

Sarah emerged from the house, her hair still damp from a quick wash, carrying a tray of what looked like breakfast for the children. Even in crisis, she maintained the routines that kept their small world functioning.

"How bad?" she asked, setting the tray on the porch table they'd dragged outside to make room for sleeping refugees.

"Town's flooding. Beth's evacuating the lower areas." James watched his wife absorb this information, saw her mentally recalculating food stores, sleeping arrangements, sanitation needs. Sarah had always been the practical heart of their operation, he handled strategy and tactics, she handled everything that kept people alive day to day.

"We can manage," she said simply, but he heard the weight behind those three words. They could manage, but it would mean rationing food that was already stretched thin, organizing sleeping space for people who'd lost everything, maintaining sanitation for a population that would overwhelm their facilities. "I think we need to dig another outhouse though."

The radio crackled again, but this time it was Old Man Jenkins' voice, transmitted from his relocated ham radio setup in the barn. "James, you need to hear this. Got some chatter from the east."

James hurried toward the barn, Sarah falling into step beside him. They'd moved Jenkins and his entire radio operation to the farm the previous evening, recognizing that his monitoring capabilities would be crucial in the coming days. The elderly man had protested leaving his house, but the storm had made the decision for them. His place sat in a hollow that was now underwater.

Inside the tac room inside the barn, Jenkins hunched over his equipment, headphones clamped over his ears as he fine-tuned frequencies. The setup was impressive—multiple receivers, a powerful transmitter, and enough antenna wire strung between the barn's rafters to contact operators across New England. Daniel stood nearby, notebook in hand, jotting down fragments of intercepted communications.

"What are you hearing?" James asked.

Jenkins looked up, his weathered face grim. "The Queen's convoy got hammered by the storm. Multiple vehicles stuck in the Saco River valley. Radio chatter suggests they lost at least a third of their operational capacity."

Relief flooded through James's chest, followed immediately by caution. A wounded animal was often more dangerous than a healthy one, The Queen, as the survivors called her, had already proven herself capable of extreme violence.

"Any timeline on when they might be mobile again?" Daniel asked, his pencil poised over the notebook.

"Hard to say. The flooding's worse east of here—that valley turned into a lake overnight. But..." Jenkins adjusted his headphones, listening to something James couldn't hear. "They're still transmitting. Still coordinated. This hasn't broken them, just delayed them."

Sarah appeared in the barn doorway, her expression tight with concern. "Hannah and Mrs. Henderson are awake. I think they need to tell you what they learned about this… this Queen person."

James nodded, following her back toward the house. They'd barely had time to debrief the survivors the night before. Between the storm preparation and the ongoing medical emergencies, there'd been no opportunity for detailed intelligence gathering. Now, with a temporary reprieve, they needed to understand exactly what they were facing.

He found them in the kitchen, huddled around the wood-burning stove with steaming mugs of something that might charitably be called coffee. Hannah looked better after a night's sleep and a hot meal, but Mrs. Henderson remained gaunt and hollow-eyed, the kind of damage that went deeper than physical exhaustion.

Jake sat nearby, and James was pleased to see Ethan and Grayson had joined him, the three boys forming a natural cluster around the table. Ethan looked more relaxed than he had in days. Having other kids his age around seemed to be helping him process whatever trauma he'd experienced during the garden incident.

"Mrs. Henderson," James said gently, settling into a chair across from her. "I know this is difficult, but we need to understand what we're facing. This woman who calls herself the Queen… What can you tell us about her?"

The older woman's hands tightened around her mug, knuckles going white. When she spoke, her voice was barely above a whisper. "She's not… she's not human anymore. Not in any way that matters."

Hannah leaned forward, concerned in the way she observed Mrs. Henderson's responses. "What do you mean by that?"

"She talks to people who aren't there," Mrs. Henderson continued, her gaze fixed on some middle distance where nightmares lived. "Has full conversations with empty air. Laughs at things only she can see. And then, without warning, she'll turn on someone with such violence…" She shuddered, wrapping her arms around herself.

"How does she maintain control of her forces?" Daniel asked, trying to understand and cutting to the practical concerns. "If she's that unstable, why do people follow her?"

Mrs. Henderson looked up sharply. "They don't follow her. They follow the men around her. There's an inner circle— maybe five or six—who use her instability as a weapon. They point her at targets and let her loose, then clean up whatever's left."

James felt his stomach clench. Not just a madwoman with followers, but a madwoman being deliberately weaponized by calculating handlers. That suggested a level of organization and planning that made the threat exponentially worse.

"She enjoys causing pain," Mrs. Henderson added quietly. "It's not just tactics or intimidation. She genuinely delights in breaking people, and her handlers encourage it because it keeps everyone else terrified into compliance."

Hannah nodded slowly, her expression thoughtful. "That kind of severe psychological break. It's more common than people realize, especially after traumatic events. The CME, the collapse, the loss of medication for people who needed it…" She trailed off, then looked directly at James. "We're probably dealing with untreated psychosis, possibly bipolar disorder or borderline personality disorder, exacerbated by the complete breakdown of social structures that might have contained her before."

"Can she be reasoned with?" Sarah asked.

"No," Mrs. Henderson said immediately. "That's what

makes her so dangerous. There's no logic to negotiate with, no self-interest to appeal to. She operates purely on impulse and delusion, backed by people who profit from chaos."

The radio in James's pocket crackled again, Beth's voice cut through the morning stillness. "James, we're starting to move people now. First convoy should reach you within the hour."

He keyed the radio. "Understood. We're ready." He looked around the kitchen, at the faces of people who'd already lost so much and were preparing to risk everything on the hope that their small community could stand against what was coming.

"Grayson," he said, addressing the boy who'd proven himself surprisingly mature for his age, "I need you and Ethan to help organize sleeping areas in the barn. Jake, you're with them. One of you keep watch while the other two make preparations, three pairs of eyes are better than one."

The boys nodded and filed out, already discussing logistics with the seriousness of adults. James watched them go, another reminder of how quickly this world was forcing children to grow up.

He turned to Sarah and said, "I don't know how but we're going to need bedding."

"Hannah," he continued, "I know Emily's got her hands full with the water contamination cases, but when the evacuees arrive, we're going to need all the medical help we can get. Storm injuries, stress reactions, plus whatever ongoing conditions people are managing without proper medication."

"I'm ready," Hannah replied simply, but James saw the weight of responsibility settling on her young shoulders. Another person being asked to carry burdens beyond her years.

The sound of vehicles approaching drew his attention to the window. The first evacuation convoy arrived earlier than expected. Three pickup trucks and what looked like a converted school bus, all loaded with people and whatever possessions they'd managed to salvage from the rising water.

"Sarah, Mrs. Henderson, could you help coordinate the temporary housing assignments?" James asked, already moving toward the door. "Daniel, I need you to establish a perimeter watch. Just because we have breathing room doesn't mean we can relax security. Gather some of the residents already here to set up guard points."

As the Thompson farm transformed from refuge to command center, James felt the familiar weight of leadership settling on his shoulders. Every decision would ripple outward, affecting people he cared about more than his own life. The storm had bought them time, but storms passed. What came after would test everything they'd built, everything they believed about survival and community and the price of safety in a broken world.

Outside, the first refugees were climbing down from the vehicles, their faces marked by the hollow exhaustion of people who'd lost their homes twice in as many months. But they were alive, and they were here, and for now, that was enough.

The radio crackled again, Jenkins' voice cutting through the morning air with the flat tone of someone reporting disaster as routine. "James, you need to hear this. Their forces are regrouping. Timeline's still Thursday dawn, but they're adapting their approach. And…" He paused, and something in that silence sent ice through James's veins. "There's something else. Reports of a second force moving up from the coast. This isn't just about Cornish anymore. This is bigger."

Cold water rushed over the threshold of Foster's Hardware, and Maddie let out a strangled cry as it soaked through her jeans. The Ossipee River had jumped its banks sometime after midnight, and now brown water crept across the scarred linoleum floor like it owned the place.

"No, no, no!" She splashed toward the counter where she'd spread out her father's notebooks to dry after yesterday's leak in the roof. Water already lapping at the wooden base, dark fingers reaching for everything she had left of him.

She grabbed armfuls of papers, journals, loose diagrams drawn on napkins and receipt backs. Some were her father's careful blueprints, others her own messy attempts to understand what he'd tried to teach her. A sob caught in her throat as water soaked through a bottom notebook, ink bleeding across pages like spilled blood.

"Please, not these too." Her voice cracked like she was fifteen again, begging the universe for mercy it wouldn't give. First her parents, now their legacy, everything the flood touched turned to loss.

The front door burst open. Beth Martin stood there, water streaming off her rain slicker. "Maddie! We're evacuating now. Grab what you can carry."

"I can't leave!" Maddie clutched the notebooks to her chest, gripping the notebooks like a lifeline. "The filters, all Dad's work—"

"The building's compromised." Beth waded in, boots sending ripples across the flooded floor. "That water's rising fast. We've got maybe ten minutes before—"

A groaning crack from somewhere in the walls cut her off. The old building, Maddie's sanctuary, all she had left of family, shuddered like a dying animal.

"My filters!" Maddie spun toward the back room where she'd set up three working purification systems. If those were lost, if the town had no clean water…

She shoved the notebooks at Beth and ran, water splashing up her legs with each step. The back room was already ankle-deep, her beautiful filters—the ones that actually worked, that could save lives—sat partially submerged on their wooden platforms.

"Help me!" She grabbed the nearest unit, a Frankenstein creation of PVC pipe and ceramic elements that could clean twenty gallons an hour. It weighed at least forty pounds dry. Waterlogged, it felt like trying to lift a corpse.

Beth appeared beside her, grabbing the other end. Together they hauled it toward the door, Maddie's muscles screaming, her back on fire from the awkward weight. They got it outside just as another structural groan echoed through the building.

"One more trip," Maddie gasped, already turning back.

"Maddie, no—"

But she was already splashing back inside, the water now knee-deep and frigid. Two more filters. Two more chances to save lives. She grabbed the smaller unit, the one she'd built just last week after finally understanding her father's notes about flow rates.

The building lurched.

The floor tilted beneath her feet, and suddenly the water wasn't just rising, it was moving, rushing through some new breach in the foundation. Her foot caught on something underwater. It was a submerged shelf bracket, and she went down hard, her thigh raking across exposed metal as she fell.

Pain shot through her leg, hot and sharp against the cold water. She gasped, inhaling muddy water, choking as she struggled to stand. Blood bloomed dark in the murky flood around her.

"MADDIE!" Beth's voice seemed to come from very far away.

Strong hands grabbed her arms, hauling her and the two smaller filters she refused to release toward the door. Beth, thigh-deep now, face set with determination snatched one of the filters in one hand and Maddie's arm in the other. They struggled through the current together, while Maddie's leg screamed with each movement.

They burst out of the building just as something gave way inside with a sound like breaking bones. The hardware store, her father's life work, her childhood playground, sagged inward like it was exhaling its last breath.

"Move!" Beth dragged her toward the waiting truck where others were already loading salvaged supplies.

Maddie looked back once at the collapsing building, then down at the sodden mass of paper in her arms. She wanted to scream, to rage at the unfairness of it all. Instead, she just stood there shaking while Beth guided her to the truck, leaving bloody footprints in her wake.

"You're hurt," Beth said, noticing the blood soaking through Maddie's jeans.

"It's fine," Maddie lied, pressing harder on the notebooks. The pain felt distant compared to everything else she'd lost.

The sagging building grew distant in the side mirror and Maddie let out a strangled whimper as they wound up the road toward the Thompson farm.

The farm materialized through the rain like something from a dream—buildings on high ground, untouched by flooding, people moving with purpose instead of panic. Maddie stumbled from the truck, still clutching the ruined notebooks, her injured leg barely holding her weight.

"Maddie!" Hannah rushed toward her from the main house, medical bag already in hand. "Oh, thank God, when we heard about the flooding—" She stopped short, eyes dropping to the blood seeping through Maddie's jeans. "You're bleeding."

"I'm okay." But even as Maddie said it, her leg buckled. Hannah caught her, guiding her to sit on the porch steps.

"Let me see." Hannah's hands were gentle but firm as she cut away the torn denim. The gash ran deep along Maddie's outer thigh, at least six inches long. "This needs stitches. When did it happen?"

"In the store. There was metal under the water…" Maddie hissed as Hannah cleaned the wound. "I saved the notebooks. Most of them. And the large filter, along with two smaller ones."

Hannah's hands stilled for a moment. "You went back for notebooks?"

"They're all I have left of him." Tears mixed with still lightly falling rain on Maddie's face. "Mom's recipes, Dad's designs, everything they knew… I couldn't just let it drown."

Hannah led her inside the house and resumed her work, using a local anesthetic before starting she scrubbed and disinfected the wound before starting on the stitches. "I get it. After losing so much, you hold tight to what remains."

They fell into a rhythm—Hannah's steady hands stitching while Maddie gritted her teeth against the pain that still seemed to radiate outward in spite of the anesthetic. Around them, the farm buzzed with activity as more evacuees arrived, but here on the porch it felt like a bubble of calm.

"I keep thinking about Grace," Hannah said quietly, tying off another stitch. "About that day in Portsmouth."

Maddie's breath caught. Grace. Strawberry-blonde hair disappearing beneath dark water. "She just… jumped. After those men…"

"She was so lost by then." Hannah's voice held grief. "No meds, that complete break from reality. I wonder sometimes if drowning felt like escape to her."

"Stop." Maddie pressed her palms against her eyes. "I can't think about that. Not today."

"Sorry." Hannah focused on the wound again. "Almost done. You're lucky—missed the major vessels."

Lucky. Maddie almost laughed. Lucky to have only lost her home, her parents' life's work, nearly everything that connected her to them. Lucky to be sitting here bleeding while her friend was somewhere at the bottom of Portsmouth harbor.

"Remember freshman year?" Maddie asked suddenly. "Grace convinced us to sneak into that senior party at the frat house. Said we'd be legends."

A sad smile crossed Hannah's face. "We lasted twenty minutes before campus security showed up. Grace livestreamed the whole thing, even getting escorted out."

"'Content is content, bitches!'" Maddie mimicked Grace's performative voice. "God, she drove me crazy sometimes. Always filming, always performing. But she was our friend, you know?"

"Yeah." Hannah tied off the last stitch. "She was our friend for sure."

They sat in silence for a moment, mourning the girl who'd been equally exasperating and lovable, whose need for attention had ultimately consumed her.

"There." Hannah applied a waterproof bandage. "Keep it clean, change the dressing daily. I will need to check it for signs of infection. Flood waters are often full of all kinds of yucky stuff. You were lucky—" She caught herself. "I mean, it could have been worse."

"Thanks." Maddie tested her weight on the leg. It hurt, but she could walk. "I should find somewhere to put these notebooks. Try to dry them out."

"Mr. Thompson will have space. But first..." Hannah helped her stand. "Emily asked me to check on Elena. Asked for me specifically. Want to come? I could use the moral support."

Maddie nodded, grateful for something to focus on besides loss. They made their way upstairs, Hannah's arm steady around her waist. "Listen, Emily told me that she's already lost the baby but refuses to acknowledge it. This is why she sent me. In hopes I can make that point clear. I already know there will be no baby, but I have to make her believe. We discussed it at length and there were signs early on that she knew something was wrong, so just go along, okay?"

They found Elena in an upstairs bedroom, pale and drawn, hands pressed protectively over her abdomen. She looked up as they entered, eyes focusing on Hannah with desperate hope.

"The baby?" Her voice was thread thin. "Is the baby okay?"

Hannah moved to her side, voice gentle. "Let me examine you. When did the bleeding start?"

Maddie hung back, feeling like an intruder on something intensely private. But Elena's eyes found hers wide and frightened.

"You're Maddie? The one who makes the water filters?"

"Yeah, that's me." Maddie moved closer, favoring her injured leg.

"Matthew talks about you. Says you're brilliant." Elena's laugh had a hysterical edge. "Must be nice, being useful. All I could do is grow babies, and I can't even do that right."

"Don't say that—" Hannah began, but Elena cut her off.

"It's true though, isn't it? This baby was never going to make it. I've known for weeks." The words tumbled out like a confession. "The last ultrasound before everything went dark, they found… problems." Her voice had an edge to it and her eyes narrowed when she looked between Hannah and Maddie. "Major ones. The doctor said maybe twenty percent chance of surviving to term, less than five percent chance of… of being normal. But I couldn't tell Matthew. He was so happy, so hopeful. I thought maybe if I just believed hard enough…"

Hannah's hands stilled on Elena's abdomen. The silence stretched, heavy with unspoken truth.

"There's no heartbeat," Hannah said finally, voice soft with sympathy. "I'm so sorry, Elena."

The sound Elena made wasn't quite a scream, wasn't quite a sob. It was something animal and raw that made Maddie's chest tight. She found herself holding Elena's hand while Hannah continued her examination, speaking in soft medical terms about what would happen next.

"Don't tell Matthew it was always doomed," Elena gasped between sobs. "Please. Let him think it was the attack, the trauma. He can't know I lied to him all these weeks."

Maddie squeezed her hand, remembering her own father's death, how her mother had hidden her symptoms until it was too late. The secrets we keep to protect the ones we love. "He doesn't need to know that part."

"Thank you." Elena gripped her hand like a lifeline. "I just… I wanted it to be different. You see, he was going to break up with me. But then with the baby… Well, he—"

Hannah worked with quiet efficiency, doing what needed

to be done. Maddie stayed, offering what comfort she could to a woman she'd just met. She'd known Matt for most of their lives and felt for him as well. They were all broken here, all carrying losses too heavy for their young shoulders.

There were sensitive moments when Hannah had to do an internal exam and Maddie excused herself. Just outside the door, she found Matthew sitting alone on the porch steps, staring at nothing. The rain had finally stopped, leaving everything waterlogged and gleaming. She hesitated, then sat beside him, her injured leg throbbing with the movement.

"She lost it," he said finally. "The baby. Our future."

"I'm so sorry, Matt."

He laughed, bitter and broken. "Everyone's sorry. Sorry doesn't bring back my child."

They sat in silence, watching water drip from the eaves. Maddie thought about Grace, about her parents, about all the futures lost to this new world.

"Elena thinks I only stayed with her because of the baby. I heard you all upstairs. The baby was never going to be." Matthew said suddenly. "Like I'm that shallow. Like I didn't love her before, without…" His voice cracked. "But what if she's right? What if I didn't want more? Things were getting tense. I only wish she could have believed in me, she was always accusing me of cheating and wanting other women. I didn't," he pleaded, glancing at Maddie. "And now this? A trap? A lie? Maddie, she lied to me for months and used the baby to keep me in a constant state of alarm through all of this when I should have been helping the family."

Maddie didn't have an answer for that. She was twenty-one years old and had never been in love, never lost a child, never had to rebuild a relationship from ashes. But she knew about loss, about the way it hollowed you out and left you wondering who you were without the things that defined you.

"After my mom died," she said slowly, "I couldn't look at anything in our house without seeing her. Every recipe card, every garden tool, every stupid coffee mug. I thought it would kill me. But then… then I started seeing her in those things differently. Not the loss, but the love. Not the ending, but all the moments before."

Matthew turned to her, eyes red-rimmed. "How long did that take?"

"I'll let you know when it happens." She offered a weak smile. "But I think… I think trying is what matters. Showing up even when it hurts."

"I don't know if I can forgive her for the lies and the manipulation." His head dropped and he stared at his fingers that had begun to writhe between one another as though he were working through the problem in his palms.

His shoulders started shaking, and suddenly he was crying, great gasping sobs that seemed to come from somewhere deep. Without thinking, Maddie put her arms around him, letting him cry on her shoulder the way she'd cried into Hannah's earlier.

"She lied to me," he whispered. "The whole time, she knew. She knew the baby was dying and she didn't tell me."

Maddie held him tighter, feeling his pain like a physical thing hanging between them. "She was scared. People do impossible things when they're scared."

"I would have stayed." His voice broke completely. "Even without the baby, I would have stayed. If she would have only trusted me. Why couldn't she believe that?"

"I don't know." Maddie stroked his back, feeling very young and very old at the same time. "But you can tell her now. You can show her."

"Thank you," he whispered against her hair. "For not trying to fix it. For just… being here."

"Of course." She held him tighter, this jock from high school who felt like family in his grief.

The door opened behind them. Maddie looked up to see Elena standing there, Hannah supporting her, face ravaged by loss and something else, something sharp and dangerous as her eyes took in Matthew in Maddie's arms.

"Elena—" Matthew started to rise.

"Don't." Elena's voice could have cut glass. "Don't you dare. I lose our baby and you're out here with—with her?"

Ethan

Ethan pressed his eye against the knothole in the barn wall, watching the adults gather in the farmyard below. The morning air still carried the scent of rain mixed with dirt of the torn earth from last night's storm, and puddles reflected the weak sunlight breaking through the clouds. His grandfather stood in the center of a rough circle, mud splattered up to his knees, gesturing as he spoke to the assembled group.

"They can't hear us up here, right?" Grayson whispered, shifting on the damp hay.

"Nah, we're good," Jake said with confidence gained by weeks hiding from actual threats. "Wind's blowing toward us. Carries their voices up but not ours down."

"Unless someone sneezes," Ethan added, then immediately felt his nose start to tickle from the hay dust. He pressed his finger against it desperately.

"Don't you dare," Jake hissed.

Ethan's eyes watered, but he managed to suppress the sneeze into a weird snorting sound that made Grayson giggle despite the seriousness of their spy mission.

"Shh!" Jake waved at them frantically. "This is important recon- i-stance!"

"Don't you mean reconnaissance?" Grayson asked.

"That's what I said," Jake hissed.

Ethan put his hand up to end the debate and they pressed closer to their respective spy holes, straining to hear. The barn loft had become their unofficial headquarters over the past two days, though it smelled strongly of wet hay and chicken droppings after the storm. They'd dragged an old tarp over their main spot, but water had still leaked through in places where the fierce winds had damaged the roofing, leaving dark patches on their makeshift furniture—overturned buckets and feed sacks arranged in a rough circle.

"Look, there's Mrs. Henderson," Jake pointed through his spy hole. "The old lady who came with me and Hannah. She's still shaking."

Ethan spotted her—Mrs. Henderson stood near the porch steps; a blanket wrapped around her thin shoulders despite the warming morning. Even from the loft, he saw how her hands trembled as she accepted a cup of something hot from his grandmother.

"She saw some bad stuff," Jake said quietly. "Really bad stuff with those people."

"Those people?" Grayson repeated. "You mean the Queen of Likes, right? Still the dumbest villain's name ever."

"Sounds like something from Sophia's princess shows," Ethan agreed. "Like, 'Oh no, the Queen of Likes didn't get enough hearts on her Instagram!'"

Jake didn't laugh. "Trust me, there's nothing funny about her. Mrs. Henderson said she watches people die while filming it on a phone that doesn't even work anymore."

That killed the joking mood pretty quick.

"Shh!" Ethan hissed. "Grandpa's saying something."

They pressed closer to their respective spy holes. The wind carried James Thompson's voice in fragments.

"—storm bought us time, but not much—"

"—Frank's betrayal means we've lost eyes in town—"

"—need to prepare for siege conditions—"

"Frank really did betray us?" Grayson whispered. "I knew that guy was sketchy! Remember when he kept measuring distances from the house to the barn? Said he was 'helping with defense planning.'"

"And he kept asking about the storm cellar," Ethan added. "How many people it could hold, how much food we had down there."

"Classic intelligence gathering," Jake said with the authority that came from reading too many superhero comics. "We should've seen it coming."

Below, more adults gathered. Beth Martin arrived on horseback, her uniform somehow still maintaining an air of authority despite being plastered with mud. Daniel and Robbie followed on foot, carrying salvaged equipment.

"Man, I wish we could hear better," Jake complained, pressing his ear against the wall.

"Wait, I got an idea." Ethan scrambled across the loft to where they'd stashed their supplies. He pulled out an old coffee can with both ends cut out—something Grayson had found and suggested might work as a "listening device."

"Does that actually work?" Jake asked skeptically.

"Only one way to find out." Ethan pressed one end against the hole in the wall and his ear to the other. "Oh wow, I can actually—OW!"

A spiky point in the metal on the rim of the can jabbed into his ear. He jerked back, dropping the can with a clatter that seemed impossibly loud in the quiet morning.

All three boys froze.

Below, Daniel glanced up toward the barn, frowning. They held their breath, not daring to move. After what felt like hours but was probably only seconds, Daniel shook his head and returned to his conversation.

"Smooth," Jake whispered sarcastically.

"The can works though," Ethan insisted, rubbing his ear. "I heard Beth say something about twenty to thirty in their main force."

"Twenty to thirty?" Grayson's eyes widened. "Against us?"

They silently counted the adults below. Maybe fifteen, if you included the older teenagers who'd been given guard duty.

"We're so dead," Grayson muttered.

"We're not dead," Ethan said, trying to channel his grandfather's confidence. "We have defensive advantages. High ground, prepared positions, knowledge of the terrain."

"Plus, we have secret weapons," Jake added.

"What secret weapons?"

"Us." Jake grinned, but it didn't quite reach his eyes. "They won't expect kids to be fighting."

"Because kids shouldn't be fighting," Ethan pointed out, even as his hand unconsciously moved to his pocket where he'd started carrying a knife again. This was his grandfather's old folder, given to him just yesterday with a serious talk about responsibility.

"Kids shouldn't have to shoot people either," Jake said quietly, "but you did what you had to do."

The garden incident hung between them, unspoken but understood. Ethan had changed, and they all knew it.

"Let's just focus on the meeting," Ethan said, desperate to change the subject.

They returned to their surveillance. Below, Mrs. Henderson was speaking to a gathered group, her voice stronger than her frail appearance suggested.

"—she calls them performance reviews—" The old woman's words drifted up.

"—executed three of her own people for 'low engagement'—"

"—talks to her phone like it still works—"

"Performance reviews?" Grayson whispered. "Like when my dad used to complain about his boss?"

"If your boss killed you for not doing a good job," Jake said darkly.

"That's insane," Ethan breathed. "Like, actually insane."

"Yeah, and she's coming here with twenty to thirty other insane people," Jake reminded them.

They watched as the adults below grew more agitated. Ethan's mother emerged from the house, medical bag in hand, probably to check on more storm-injury patients. She moved with that particular exhaustion Ethan recognized—the kind where you keep going because stopping isn't an option.

"Your mom's hardcore," Grayson said to him. "My mom cries when she gets a paper cut."

"She's had practice," Ethan said. "Remember when the Brennan twins both broke their arms jumping off the barn roof? She set both breaks while giving them a lecture about natural selection."

Despite everything, Jake snorted with laughter. "Natural selection?"

"She said if they were dumb enough to think they could fly, maybe they shouldn't pass on their genes."

"Harsh," Grayson grinned.

"The twins thought it was hilarious. They still call her Doc Darwin."

The moment of levity felt good, normal even. Like they were just kids hanging out in a fort, not preparing for a siege by a crazy girl turned warlord.

"Oh, hey, look," Jake pointed. "They're bringing out maps."

Sure enough, Daniel and James had spread a large map across a makeshift table made from sawhorses and plywood. Various adults gathered around, pointing at different areas.

"That's smart," Jake said approvingly. "Planning defensive positions, probably setting up kill zones—"

"Kill zones?" Grayson interrupted. "That sounds like some kind of Terminator movie."

"It's where you channel attackers into areas where you have maximum firepower advantage," Jake explained. "I saw it in a movie where they tried to get this guy off a mountain by cutting off all his escape routes. It was an old movie but so good. That guy totally kicked ass."

"And here we are," Ethan said quietly. "Hopefully this queen of likes isn't like that guy."

They watched the adults point to various positions on the map. Ethan tried to memorize where they were indicating—the old stone wall by the garden, the drainage ditch that ran along the east field, the cluster of apple trees that could provide cover.

"We should make our own map," he suggested suddenly. "Mark all the spots adults might miss. Like that crawl space under the porch, or the hollow log by the creek."

"Good idea," Jake agreed. "We know this place differently than they do."

"Plus, we're smaller," Grayson added. "We can fit places they can't."

"The Defenders' tactical advantage," Ethan said, trying to make it sound official.

"Okay, we really need a better name than 'The Defenders,'" Grayson insisted. "It sounds like a bad TV show."

"What's wrong with The Defenders?" Ethan protested.

"Everything," Jake and Grayson said in unison.

They spent the next few minutes arguing about potential names—The Shadows, The Watchers, The Thompson Farm Resistance (shot down immediately for being too long)—while keeping half an eye on the adult meeting below.

"Wait, what's Mrs. Henderson doing?" Jake suddenly hissed.

The elderly woman had stood up, swaying slightly, and was gesturing emphatically. Even from their height, they saw the distress on her face.

"—not just fighters!" Her voice carried up, thin but urgent. "She has families with her! People she's forcing to follow! My friend Rebecca—" She broke off, shoulders shaking.

"Rebecca Mitchell," Jake breathed. "My mom."

Ethan watched his friend's face transform, hope and fear warring for dominance.

"She said families," Jake whispered. "That means Mom might still be alive."

"That's good, right?" Grayson asked carefully.

"If she's being forced to follow a psychopath who executes people for bad performance reviews?" Jake's voice cracked. "I don't know if that's good or just a different kind of bad."

They watched as Emily Thompson moved to comfort Mrs. Henderson, guiding her to sit back down. The meeting continued, but Jake had withdrawn from his spy hole, sitting back against a hay bale with his knees drawn up.

"She's tough," Ethan offered. "Your mom, I mean. Hannah said she was the strongest person she knew."

"Yeah," Jake said quietly. "But everyone has limits."

The barn fell silent except for the murmur of voices from below and the rustle of disturbed pigeons in the rafters. Ethan wanted to say something comforting, but what could you say to someone whose mom was held captive by a murderous influencer?

"We'll get her back," Grayson said suddenly, his voice firm. "When they attack, there'll be chaos. We can find your mom in the confusion, get her somewhere safe."

"You mean during the battle where we're outnumbered two to one?" Jake asked, his tone mocking and sarcastic.

"Details," Grayson waved dismissively. "We're The Defenders—or whatever we're calling ourselves. We don't let that stop us."

Despite everything, Jake cracked a small sad smile. "You're idiots."

"Your idiots," Ethan corrected. "Brothers, remember?" He held up his wrist where the red thread still circled, now dirty and frayed but intact. "We're in this together. We may be idiots but we are your idiots just like you are ours."

Jake looked at his own thread, then at his friends. "Yeah. Brothers."

They returned to their surveillance with renewed purpose. The adult meeting was breaking up, people dispersing to various tasks. Storm cleanup, defensive preparations, the endless work of survival.

"You know what's funny?" Ethan said suddenly. "Not ha-ha funny, but weird funny. A year ago, the biggest thing we worried about was whether we'd make the baseball team."

"I was worried about the math final," Grayson admitted.

"I was worried about everything," Jake said. "Mom always said I overthought stuff."

"Bet she didn't imagine you'd be overthinking battle tactics and rescue operations," Ethan said.

"Probably not," Jake agreed. Then, more quietly, "I hope

she's okay."

"She will be," Ethan said with a confidence he didn't feel. "We'll make sure of it."

Below, the farm returned to its rhythm of preparation. But now the boys had their own mission mixed with their grand plans for surveillance and defense. They would be The Defenders—name still under debate—but more importantly, they'd be ready. Ready to help, ready to fight if needed, and ready to save Jake's mom from whatever horror she was trapped in.

As they settled in to continue their watch, Ethan thought about how much had changed. A few months ago, he'd been a kid who collected beetles and read adventure stories. Now he was a kid who'd killed to protect his family, who planned defensive positions and counted ammunition.

But looking at his friends. He realized maybe that was okay. Maybe growing up in this broken world meant becoming something harder than you were supposed to be. At least they were becoming it together.

"Hey," Grayson whispered, pointing toward the road. "Someone's coming."

They scrambled to their viewing positions, watching as a lone figure on a bicycle pedaled up the farm's long driveway. As the person got closer, they saw it was a teenage girl, maybe sixteen, mud-splattered and exhausted.

"Messenger from town," Jake identified. "See the white flag on her backpack? That's the neutral signal Beth established."

They watched as James and Daniel intercepted the cyclist, engaging in urgent conversation. Whatever news she brought, it wasn't good—Ethan could tell by the way his grandfather's shoulders tensed, the way Daniel's hand moved to his sidearm.

"This is it," Jake said quietly. "Something's happening."

The adults below burst into sudden activity, the careful preparations becoming urgent mobilization. And high above in their barn loft fortress, three boys with red threads around their wrists prepared to play their part in whatever came next.

Emily

Emily Thompson's hands moved with practiced efficiency as she sutured the gash across Tom Bradley's forehead, her fingers steady despite the chaos erupting around her makeshift medical station. Blood had dried in rusty streaks down his face, mixing with the river silt that coated everything the storm had touched. Each stitch pulled the torn flesh together with small tugs that barely registered against the background symphony of pain filling the farmhouse.

The dining room had become a battlefield hospital. Bodies covered every available surface. The mahogany table where her family had shared Sunday dinners now supported Mrs. Kellerson, who wheezed through fluid-filled lungs after nearly drowning in her basement. The antique sideboard held bandages, antiseptics, and a dwindling supply of pain medication that made Emily's stomach clench every time she reached for it.

"Hold still, Tom." Emily's voice was stern. "Almost finished."

Tom's eyes were unfocused, pupils unequal, a sure sign of concussion. He'd been found unconscious in the wreckage of the funeral home, where storm surge had torn through the building like a giant's fist. The entire staff had been relocated to the farm along with most of their supplies, but space designed for a large family now held forty-three people who'd lost everything to the flood.

"Doc Thompson?" A voice called from the kitchen doorway. "Mrs. Kellerson's breathing is worse."

Emily tied off the last suture and pressed gauze against the wound. "Keep pressure on this. Don't let him sleep for the next four hours."

She pushed through the crowd of injured and displaced people; each face a reminder of how quickly their prepared community had fractured. The storm hadn't just brought water. It had brought desperation. People who'd been neighbors yesterday now eyed the medical supplies with calculating hunger, understanding that resources meant survival and survival meant someone else might go without.

Mrs. Kellerson lay on a makeshift bed in what used to be Sarah's pristine kitchen. Her breathing came in short, labored gasps, and pink foam collected at the corners of her mouth. Pulmonary edema. The woman had inhaled too much contaminated water during the evacuation, and her lungs were drowning from the inside.

"How long has she been like this?" Emily asked Hannah, who knelt beside the older woman with a stethoscope pressed to her chest.

"Started about an hour ago. Heart rate's climbing, oxygen saturation dropping." Hannah's face was grim. "Without proper equipment…"

Emily nodded, understanding the unspoken truth. Mrs. Kellerson needed a ventilator, IV diuretics, maybe even intubation. They had bandages and basic antibiotics. The gap between what they needed and what they possessed yawned like a chasm.

"Make her comfortable," Emily said quietly. "Elevate her head, small sips of water if she can manage. That's all we can do."

Hannah's jaw tightened, but she nodded. They'd been having variations of this conversation all morning—medical decisions that would have been routine in the old world now carried the consequences of life and death.

"Emily?" James appeared in the doorway; his clothes still damp from coordinating storm damage repairs. "How many can we realistically handle?"

The question she'd been dreading. Emily wiped her hands on a bloodstained towel, looking around the crowded space. "We're past capacity now. If this Queen attacks while we're dealing with this many injured…"

"I know." James's voice carried the burden of command. "But we can't turn people away."

"We might have to." The words almost hurt to say, but Emily forced them out. "Medical triage isn't just about treating the wounded—it's about allocating limited resources to save the most lives possible."

Through the kitchen window, she saw more people arriving, stragglers from the flooded town, families carrying everything they owned in waterlogged bags. Each new arrival meant stretching their supplies thinner, dividing attention among more critical cases.

"What do you need?" James asked.

"More hands. More supplies. More time." Emily managed a tired smile. "Since you can't give me any of those, I need you to make the hard decisions about who stays and who gets relocated to the secondary shelter sites."

James's expression hardened. In the old world, he'd been a farmer and county council member. Now he was making choices that would determine who lived and who died. "I'll talk to Michael about setting up the massive tent from the fairs that Beth had brought up as an overflow facility. Anyone not in need of critical care can be moved into these temporary living quarters. Does that help?"

Emily nodded gratefully, then resumed her rounds, checking vitals, changing dressings, deciding on necessary medications, and directing patients with superficial wounds to see Michael to be set up in the temporary shelter. The storm had created a cascade of medical emergencies. Broken bones from falling debris, infected wounds from contaminated water, heat exhaustion, and the ever-present threat of waterborne illness.

She found Hannah in the living room, working on a young boy whose arm hung at an unnatural angle. The break was clean, but without X-rays, Emily could only guess at the extent of internal damage.

"How's Elena handling everything?" Emily asked while Hannah carefully positioned the splint.

Hannah's hands stilled for a moment. "We should talk about that. Privately."

Emily's pulse quickened. "Is she having complications?"

"Not the kind you're thinking." Hannah tied off the splint and gave the boy's mother instructions about watching for circulation changes. "Can we step outside?"

They moved to the covered porch, where the sound of hammers and saws provided some privacy. Michael's crew was already working to reinforce the farmhouse windows, preparing for siege conditions while Emily fought to keep people alive inside.

"Elena's recovery is proceeding normally," Hannah said carefully. "Almost too normally."

"Meaning?"

"When I examined her, she was well past the acute phase. The bleeding had already stopped, cervix was closed, uterine size consistent with someone at least a week into recovery." Hannah's voice dropped. "Emily, she didn't lose that baby because of the attack?"

Emily felt her breath catch. "How certain are you?"

"Very. The miscarriage was already well underway when those men attacked. Probably even foreshadowing before everything." Hannah glanced toward the house, where Elena was helping serve soup to the evacuees. "She knew. She had to have known. This might explain her hyper-anxiety when everything… Quit working."

The implications were excruciatingly clear to Emily. Elena had been walking around for days, maybe weeks, knowing her pregnancy was failing while everyone else planned for a baby that would never come. The ultrasound appointment Matthew had mentioned. The one Elena 'wasn't happy about missing,' suddenly made terrible sense.

"Why wouldn't she tell anyone?"

"Fear. Denial. Or…" Hannah hesitated. "Matthew mentioned their relationship was getting rocky before the pregnancy. Maybe she thought losing the baby would mean losing him too."

Emily thought about Elena's behavior. The manic enthusiasm about baby preparations, the way she constantly touched her belly like she was trying to hold something in place through sheer will. Signs that a trained medical professional should have recognized if she hadn't been so focused on larger community concerns.

"How is she handling it now?"

"That's what worries me. She's not helping anyone, barely speaking to people unless it's to complain about something. But there's also something…" Hannah searched for the right words. "Something bitter about her behavior. Like she blames everyone else for what happened to her."

A crash from inside the house interrupted their conversation. Emily rushed back to find Tom Bradley on the floor, convulsing while his wife screamed for help. His concussion had worsened into seizure activity. Another critical case demanding immediate attention.

"Clear some space!" Emily dropped to her knees beside Tom, turning him on his side as his body jerked uncontrollably. "Hannah, I need diazepam from the emergency kit."

"We used the last of it on Mrs. Chen's anxiety attack this morning," Hannah replied, already moving to steady Tom's head.

Emily's heart sank. No anticonvulsants. No way to stop the seizure except to wait and hope his brain didn't suffer permanent damage. Around them, frightened voices rose as people pressed closer, desperate to understand what was happening to their neighbor.

"Everyone back up! Give him room to breathe!" Emily's voice cut through the panic with practiced authority, but inside, she felt as though her own inadequacy.

The seizure lasted ninety seconds, long enough to cause brain damage, short enough to offer hope. Tom's breathing gradually steadied, but his eyes remained unfocused when Emily checked his pupils with a small flashlight.

"Is he going to be okay?" Tom's wife gripped Emily's arm with desperate strength.

"I don't know," Emily said honestly. "We need to monitor him closely. Any changes, call me immediately."

She helped move Tom to a quieter corner, her mind calculating how long their remaining supplies would last. Pain medication might stretch three more days if she rationed carefully. Antibiotics could handle perhaps two serious infections. Bandages were running low, and they had no blood for transfusions, no equipment for surgery, no way to handle the complex medical emergencies that they already had, let alone anything that a war would bring.

Through the window, Emily saw Elena sitting alone on the back porch, pointedly ignoring the chaos inside. She wasn't helping with patient care, wasn't offering comfort to families, wasn't contributing anything to the community's survival effort. Instead, she sat with her arms crossed, watching Daniel, Matthew and Maddie work together on some kind of water filtration project near the barn. Even from a distance, Emily saw the bitterness radiating from Elena's posture, the way her glare followed every interaction between Matthew and Maddie. Emily knew deep down there was a storm coming from this and turned to gaze inward at the triage that reminded her of images of revolutionary war soldiers, feeling as powerless to help these people now as those that watched them die back then did.

"Emily." Elena appeared at her elbow as if summoned. Her voice carried an edge of hostility rather than concern. "Mrs. Kellerson's daughter is making noise about you not doing enough. Thought you should know people are starting to talk."

Emily studied Elena's face, pale and sharp with barely contained resentment. No trace of grief or sympathy for the dying woman, just a calculated cruelty designed to make Emily doubt herself during an already impossible situation.

"Elena, when did you last actually help with anything? Really help?"

"I'm not a doctor. I'm not useful like precious Maddie with her filters." Elena's voice dripped venom as she glanced toward the window where Matthew and Maddie worked side by side. "Some people get to be the hero. Others just get to watch their lives fall apart."

"Each of us in our own capacity contributes and none are less, Elena. We should talk later. About your recovery, about what you need to process what happened."

Something dangerous flickered in Elena's eyes, a recognition that Emily knew more than she was saying. "Process what, exactly? That my body failed me? That everyone's moved on like my baby never mattered? That Matthew spends more time with his precious Maddie than he ever did with me?"

"About the timing. About when things really started going wrong."

Elena's composed mask cracked, revealing the venom underneath. "Careful, Emily. People might think you're questioning my grief. Wondering if I'm being honest about losing my child." Her smile was razor-sharp. "That would be a terrible thing to suggest, wouldn't it?"

Elena walked away with deliberate indifference, leaving behind the lingering sense of threat masked as wounded innocence. Emily watched her go, recognizing the dangerous edge of someone who'd been caught in a lie and was preparing to lash out rather than face the truth.

Through the window, Elena positioned herself where she could watch Matthew work with Maddie, her expression calculating and cold. She wasn't grieving. She was planning something.

"Doctor Thompson?" A teenage boy Emily didn't recognize appearing beside her. "My mom's asking about her medication. She's diabetic, and we lost everything in the flood."

Another crisis. Another impossible decision. Emily had no insulin to spare, and without it, the woman would slip into diabetic coma within days. She could try to stretch their small emergency supply, but that meant other critical medications would run out faster.

"What's her normal dosage?" Emily asked, already calculating how to divide their limited resources among too many needs.

As she dealt with the medication crisis, Emily's mind kept returning to Elena's hostile behavior. The miscarriage had been inevitable, but the deception about its timing suggested a level of manipulation that went beyond grief. Elena had been using the pregnancy to hold onto a relationship that was already failing, and now she was using resentment and blame to avoid taking responsibility for her lies.

The problem was that bitter people made dangerous choices. Elena was walking around with a secret that could destabilize Matthew's grieving process and a level of hostility that seemed focused on Matthew and Maddie's work without regard for the fact that Daniel was right in the middle of it all. She couldn't see clearly and only resented their friendship that stemmed all the way back to grade school. In a community preparing for siege, that kind of vindictive anger posed its own kind of threat.

"Emily!" Hannah's voice cut through her thoughts. "Mrs. Simon's pulse is getting irregular."

Emily rushed back to the kitchen, where Mrs. Simon's breathing had become even more labored. Her lips were blue, and her pulse felt weak and thready under Emily's fingers. Without advanced cardiac support, they were watching her die by degrees.

"Is there anything else we can try?" Mrs. Simon's daughter asked, tears streaming down her face.

Emily looked at their dwindling supplies, at the forty-two other people who needed medical attention, and the reports of forces moving closer despite the flooding felt overwhelming. Sometimes the kindest thing a doctor could do was acknowledge the limits of what was possible.

"We can make sure she's not in pain," Emily said gently. "We can keep her comfortable and make sure she's not alone."

The daughter nodded, understanding the unspoken message. Death had become a frequent visitor to their community, and they'd all learned to recognize when fighting was futile.

As Emily administered a small dose of morphine. The precious medication that would help Mrs. Simon's final hours, she mentally tallied their remaining supplies. Even if they could stretch everything, even if they rationed carefully and made hard choices about who received treatment, they had maybe a week of medical care left at current consumption rates.

If this Queen of Likes laid siege to the farm, if they cut off what little supply lines the community had forged and forced prolonged defensive action, the community would face a brutal choice. Use their medical supplies to treat combat wounds and let the sick die or maintain humanitarian care and watch defenders bleed out for lack of basic trauma medication.

"Hannah," Emily called quietly. "Can you take over Mrs. Simon's care? I need to talk to my dad."

She found him on the front porch, studying a hand-drawn map that showed suspected invader positions. Radio chatter from other communities painted a picture of coordinated assault forces moving despite the flooding, using the chaos to mask their approach.

"How bad is it?" James asked without looking up from the map.

"Medically? We're running on fumes. If this siege lasts more than a few days, we'll be back to Revolutionary War-era medicine." Emily sat down heavily in one of Sarah's rocking chairs. "Practically? Elena's been hiding the fact that her miscarriage started even before the solar flare. She's emotionally unstable, blaming everyone else for her situation, and she's developing an obsession with Matthew and Maddie's friendship."

James's head snapped up. "Are you certain?"

"Hannah confirmed it. The medical evidence is clear." Emily rubbed her tired eyes. "The question is what we do with that information."

"Matthew has a right to know."

"Matthew has a right to grieve without additional trauma. Elena has a right to privacy about her medical condition. And the community has a right to stability during a crisis." Emily's voice carried the weariness of impossible choices all day. "But Elena's not interested in stability. She's angry, vindictive, and looking for someone to blame. That makes her dangerous. Couple this with the lack of supplies and just not enough time or energy to handle these things… There just isn't time for this."

"There never is anymore." James folded the map, his expression grim. "How long before we're completely out of medical supplies?"

"Best case scenario? Five days if we ration everything and triage cases for comfort measures only that we cannot possibly save. Worst case? Two days if we get hit with combat casualties."

The implications hung between them like a weight. James had been hoping the community could hold out long enough for this wanna be war lord to exhaust themselves or for military intervention to arrive, if it even would. Two to five days wasn't nearly enough time for either possibility.

Emily looked out across the farmyard, where children played between sandbag emplacements and adults worked frantically to prepare defenses. "Every choice we make now comes with a body count."

"I know." James's voice was quiet. "But making no choice guarantees everyone dies."

A radio crackled from inside the house, carrying Beth's voice with an edge of urgency. "James, we've got movement on the southern approach. Advance scouts are probing our outer defenses, despite the flooding."

Emily felt her stomach drop. Their window of preparation was closing faster than anticipated. Within hours, they might be treating gunshot wounds while artillery fire shook the building. The nightmare scenario she'd been dreading was about to become reality.

Elena appeared in the doorway again, but this time her expression held no pretense of concern. "Mrs. Kellerson's family is here. They want to know if she's really dying or if you're just not trying hard enough." Her tone suggested she'd encouraged their doubts. "People are starting to wonder about your competence, Emily."

"Yes," Emily said gently. "If they can get here safely."

Emily studied Elena's face, seeing the calculated cruelty behind the innocent question. Elena wasn't helping the grieving family or offering comfort during their loss. She was stirring up doubt and resentment, undermining Emily's authority during a medical crisis.

"Elena, we should talk soon. About your recovery, about what you need to process what happened to you."

For just a moment, Elena's hostility blazed openly, all pretense abandoned. "I don't need to process anything, Emily. I need people to stop pretending they care about my dead baby while they fawn over precious Maddie and her wonderful innovations." Her voice was pure venom. "But don't worry about me. I'm handling everything perfectly fine."

She walked away before Emily could respond, leaving behind the acrid scent of resentment masked as victimhood. Emily watched her go, recognizing the dangerous nature of blame over healing and she was looking for targets for her rage.

James was studying the radio reports, his face drawn with fatigue and worry. "Beth says there are reports. They say the force bearing down on us is using boats to navigate the flooded areas. They'll be here sooner than we thought."

Emily looked back at the crowded farmhouse, at the injured people depending on her skills and dwindling supplies, at the children who shouldn't have to witness what was coming. She thought about Elena's hostile manipulation, about Mrs. Simon dying in what used to be a kitchen, about the impossible mathematics of triage in a world where every decision could mean life and death.

"Dad," she said quietly, "I don't think we have enough supplies to get through this."

James

The barn's corner where they'd set up Jenkins' radio equipment felt cramped and stuffy, filled with the smell of hay and the electronic buzz of equipment James didn't really understand. Jenkins hunched over the controls, headphones on, turning dials and adjusting things.

"There," Jenkins muttered, fine-tuning something. "Boston frequency."

A woman's voice emerged from the speakers, tired and strained. "…can't get through to the hospital anymore. The whole downtown area is just… God, I don't know how to describe it. Like a war zone, but worse."

James felt his stomach tighten. Boston. Where Maddie and Hannah had barely escaped. He thought about those girls making their way through streets that had apparently gotten much worse since they'd left.

"Multiple groups fighting each other," the voice continued before dissolving back into static. "…bodies in the streets… no police response… stay away from the government buildings…"

Jenkins fiddled with the controls, trying to pull the signal back, but it was gone. He shook his head. "Been like that all morning. Bits and pieces. Sounds like the whole city's gone to hell."

Daniel looked up from where he'd been scribbling notes, and though what good fragmentary reports would do them,

James couldn't say. "Makes our problems look smaller, doesn't it?"

James wasn't sure if that was comforting or terrifying. If Boston was falling apart completely, it meant they truly were on their own. No one was coming to help because everyone else was fighting just to survive.

The radio crackled again, and Jenkins leaned forward eagerly. Jenkins turned the dial one way and then back. Static, then a man's voice: "…tried calling my brother in Portsmouth three times now. Nothing. Either the phones are still down or…" The transmission cut off.

"Damn," Jenkins muttered. "Lost it."

Jenkins tried the frequency he used to contact the nuclear plant. They'd been trying to reach someone at Seabrook since they'd heard of the possibility of a meltdown but got nothing back. Not even static. Just empty air.

"Still nothing?" James asked, though he already knew the answer from Jenkins' expression.

"Dead silence. Could mean their equipment's down. Could mean…" Jenkins trailed off, but they both knew what it could mean. The wind was from the southwest today. If something had gone wrong at the plant, they might never know until people started getting sick.

Sarah appeared in the barn doorway, looking frazzled. "First group from town's here. Maybe fifteen groups. Beth said more are coming."

James stepped outside to see a line of vehicles, carts and horse-drawn wagons making their way up the hill. Old cars, pickup trucks one with duct tape holding the door shut. Water dripped from everything, and most of the vehicles looked like they'd been driven through a lake.

The lead car stopped near the house, and Walt Henley climbed out. James knew Walt from the diner—worked there most mornings before the collapse. Usually had his hair combed neat, but now his clothes were muddy, and he had that shell-shocked look James was getting used to seeing.

"James," Walt called, his voice hoarse. "Town's flooded out. Beth told us to come here."

"Course, you're welcome," James replied, though his mind was already racing. How many people could they actually house? Feed? They'd been stretching their food already.

Kids started climbing out of cars, some crying, others just staring around with big, scared eyes. Parents held them close, looking uncertain about being in a strange place. James saw the hope in their faces mixed with the fear—hope that maybe here they'd finally be safe.

A memory hit him sudden and clear: Ethan's excited voice from what felt like a lifetime ago. *"Grandma! Look what we found! Six whole eggs, and Ryan didn't drop any!"* His grandson's face had been bright with pride over such a simple thing, helping collect eggs from Betty, the black hen who let kids pet her.

That same boy now carried a gun and the emotional trauma of killing someone to protect his family. The change happened so fast James sometimes forgot Ethan was still just a kid. Still a child who should be worried about school, not about which neighbors might be enemies.

His radio crackled. Beth's voice came through. "Thompson farm, this is Martin."

James keyed the handset. "Go ahead, Beth."

"Got word from our scouts. Those raider folks are regrouping down in the valley. Storm messed them up pretty good, but they're not gone. Looks like they're trying to fix their vehicles or find new ones."

"Any idea when they might move?"

"Tomorrow, maybe. Day after at the latest." A pause. "James, there's something else. Heard reports about another group coming up from the coast. Don't know if they're connected, but the timing's suspicious."

Two groups. James closed his eyes briefly. "We'll manage."

"I know you will. Martin out."

James clipped the radio back to his belt, watching Daniel help an old woman out of one of the cars. She was moving slow, probably arthritis made worse by stress and sleeping in cold cars. Reminded him of his own mother.

Sarah came out of the house with armloads of blankets, already figuring out where everyone would sleep. Behind her, Maddie and Hannah carried what looked like first aid supplies. Even Elena was helping, carrying a tray of sandwiches.

Everyone pitched in because that's what you did. That's what separated them from the Queen of Likes and her people—here, folks took care of each other. Nobody got left behind if there was any way to help.

Jenkins' voice carried from the barn's external speaker, loud enough for everyone to hear. "James! Get back in here. Something big happening in Boston."

James hurried back to the radio set up. They found Jenkins hunched over his equipment, face white as a sheet.

"What now?" James asked.

"Government buildings in Boston," Jenkins said, his voice shaky. "Sounds like they've been taken over. Can't get details, but it's bad."

James sank into a nearby chair. "Taken over by who?"

"Don't know. The transmission cut out." Jenkins looked up at them. "But if the state government's gone…"

James felt that cold weight in his stomach again. No state

help. No federal help. Whatever they managed to build here, whatever they could defend, that was it. They were completely on their own.

The radio burst to life with overlapping voices as Jenkins spun through frequencies. Fragments painted a picture he didn't want to see: "…can't reach Portland…" "…roads blocked north of…" "…no one answering in Augusta…"

"James," Sarah's voice called from outside. "We need you out here."

They stepped outside to find chaos. Half the evacuees were getting back in their cars, engines starting up. Kids were crying, adults arguing loud enough to wake the dead.

"What's happening?" James asked.

Sarah looked tired. "Someone had a radio in their car, heard about Boston. Now half of them want to run to Canada, half think we should just give up to whoever's in charge now."

James watched families tearing themselves apart trying to decide between running and staying. Parents holding crying kids while shouting at each other about which choice would get them killed. Old folks sitting in cars, too worn out to care anymore.

"Walt," James called as the diner worker headed for his truck. "Where you planning to go?"

"North. Canada's got to be better than this mess."

"Maybe," James said. "But that's a long way through country full of people like this Queen person. With winter coming. With kids and old folks."

Walt's hands gripped his steering wheel tight. "Might not be safe staying either."

True enough. James couldn't promise anyone they'd be safe—he didn't know himself. But he could offer something: the truth about what they faced and the support of people who'd already proven they could survive the worst.

"Your call," James said. "But if you stay, you're not just visitors. You're family. And family looks out for each other."

Walt stared out his windshield for a long moment. Finally, he turned off the engine. "Come this far, I guess."

One by one, other families made the same choice. Not all—three vehicles headed north, maybe a dozen people total. But most seemed to understand that the farm offered something they wouldn't find on the road: people who cared whether they lived or died.

As things settled down, James went back to the radio. Jenkins was still hunting through frequencies, notebook full of half-heard reports that might mean something or nothing.

"Anything new about our immediate problem?" James asked.

"Those raider folks are definitely still out there," Jenkins confirmed. "Different voices on their radios, so maybe they picked up stragglers from other groups. Could be more of them than before."

"Timeline?"

"Best guess, day after tomorrow. Maybe tomorrow if they decide to move in the dark." Jenkins looked up from his equipment. "James, I caught part of a transmission. Sounds like they're not just planning to raid the place. They want to set up permanent here."

The words hit James like a punch. Not just taking their food and leaving—staying. Turning the farm into a base for more raids. Making slaves of anyone they didn't kill.

Outside, he could hear kids playing despite everything—their voices a reminder of what mattered. Sarah organizing sleeping arrangements like this was just another family reunion. Daniel and Michael talking about where to put lookouts.

Normal sounds of people taking care of each other. The

Queen of Likes and her bunch had forgotten what that meant, choosing to take instead of build. But here, surrounded by folks who'd lost everything except their decency, James felt that stubborn determination that had carried them this far.

They weren't defending just a farm—they were defending the idea that people could choose cooperation over conquest. That communities could survive without becoming monsters.

The radio crackled one more time. A voice James didn't recognize: "Any stations out there, be advised. Large force moving north through the valley. Heading toward Cornish. If anyone's listening, they'll be there by morning."

James checked his watch. Eighteen hours, maybe less. Eighteen hours to turn a farm full of scared refugees into something that could stand against organized killers.

He looked out at the farmyard, watching families settle in for what might be their last peaceful night. Kids who should be thinking about games were learning to tell the difference between friendly and dangerous engine sounds. Parents who should be worried about homework were checking weapons and figuring out how to protect their children.

James continued to look over his farm. His family's farm that was his father's before him and his grandfather's before that and wondered what it would look like tomorrow. He moved toward the house and his wife, who stood looking over the groups of people in their yard and across the driveway in the large tented area within the corral where most of the refugees had been set up either inside or in smaller tents surrounding it.

He gripped Michael and Daniel's shoulders in each hand and said, "Move all vehicles either on their own or by pushing inside the corral. Use them like a barrier. Time to circle the wagons, boys."

Beth Martin walked the perimeter of the Thompson farm as dawn broke gray and uncertain, her boots squelching in mud left by the storm. The smell of wood smoke and cooking beans drifted from the corral, where dozens of cook fires dotted the ground between makeshift shelters. Someone had strung a laundry line between the fence posts, shirts and underwear hanging limp in the humid air. The whole place looked like something out of a history book. A refugee camp that could have existed in any century, any war.

She paused near a group digging a concealed position behind the fallen oak tree. Doug Martinez, who'd hunted these woods for forty years, looked up from the hole he'd been excavating.

"Deep enough?" he asked, sweat already soaking through his shirt despite the early hour.

Beth crouched, examining the angle. From here, anyone in the hole would have clear sight lines to the main road while remaining hidden by the tree's massive root ball. "Another foot, perhaps. You want to be able to stand and shoot without exposing your head."

Doug nodded and went back to digging. His nephew Carlos worked beside him, not speaking. They'd learned that much already. Save your breath for the work.

The transformation happening across the farm filled Beth

with equal parts pride and dread. These were store clerks and mechanics, teachers and farmers. Yesterday they'd been arguing about property lines and whose turn it was to bring coffee to church. Today they dug fighting positions and sharpened stakes for the ditches.

"Chief Martin?"

Beth turned to find Sally Handly approaching with a clipboard—because even at the end of the world, someone needed to track supplies. "What've we got, Sally?"

"Food for maybe five days. This doesn't include what people brought with them. If we're careful and can get them to consolidate, we might get a few more. Medical supplies are better thanks to Hannah and Emily hoarding everything they could grab. Ammunition…" Sally's face tightened. "That's a little more difficult. Some have brought some, and the Thompsons have a sizable amount, but it's scattered across different calibers."

Either way, not enough for a prolonged fight. Not nearly enough.

"We're not trying to win a toe to toe battle," Beth said, loud enough for Doug and Carlos to hear. "Just make it cost more than it's worth."

Movement near the road caught her eye. Three boys approached, Ethan Thompson, Jake Mitchell, and Grayson Hawkins. They emerged from the tree line at a dead run. They'd been out since before dawn, and the way they moved told her they'd found something.

Beth intercepted them near the barn. All three boys were breathing hard, faces flushed with exertion and something else. Fear, maybe. Or excitement. Hard to tell with teenage boys discovering they were good at something dangerous.

"Three vehicles," Ethan gasped out. "Parked about two miles down Route 25. Looks like they're waiting for others."

"How many people?" Beth asked.

Jake stepped forward. "Counted maybe fifteen. But Chief…" He glanced at the other boys. "Some of them don't look right. Saw two women crying. One man tied to a truck bumper."

Beth felt her pulse quicken. Dissent in the ranks, just like the refugees had reported. "Tell me exactly what you saw."

As the boys detailed their observations with guard positions, weapons, and the overall mood of the camp. Beth's mind raced. Fifteen people in an advance group meant probably three times that in the main force. But if some were unwilling participants…

"Good work," she told them. "Get some water, then find your grandpa, Ethan. Tell him I need to speak with him and the others."

The boys ran off, and Beth turned back to survey the preparations. More fighting positions were taking shape. One of the people she didn't recognize was stringing wire between trees at ankle height. She bobbed her head, watching him. Crude but effective in the dark. Teams worked to fell strategic trees and move downed ones from the storm across secondary roads, leaving only the main approach open. Controlling where your enemy could attack was the first rule of defense.

"Chief Martin, what in God's name do you think you're doing?"

Beth closed her eyes briefly before turning. Elena stood behind her, arms crossed, still wearing the same clothes from yesterday. The woman should have been resting after her miscarriage, but here she was, face twisted with indignation.

"Elena, you should be—"

"Don't you tell me what I should be doing." Elena's voice rose, drawing looks from nearby workers. "My boyfriend is out there playing soldier instead of taking care of me, and now you're turning this place into some kind of war zone? There are children here!"

Beth kept her expression neutral, but her cop instincts were screaming. Something in Elena's eyes didn't match her words—a calculating look that vanished as soon as others turned to watch. She was most assuredly performing, to what end Beth could only wait and see.

She glanced around looking for someone from the Thompson family to come alongside her because she'd not spoken but a word or two to Elena since this all began and couldn't understand why she'd address her this way. Either way she responded as kindly as she could to explain things, thinking perhaps she'd not been kept in the loop, having been ill.

"Which is why we're preparing defenses," Beth said calmly. "To protect those children." Her eyebrows raised and head nodded trying to be positive.

"From what? Some made-up threat?" Elena laughed, high and brittle. "You're all paranoid. Creating panic. Matthew said—"

"Matthew's working on the east perimeter," Beth cut in. "If you need him, I can send someone."

Elena's mask slipped for just a second. Pure fury flashing across her features before the grieving girlfriend persona snapped back into place. "I'm just so scared," she said, voice dropping to a whisper that somehow still carried. "After losing the baby, and now all this…"

Several nearby workers made sympathetic noises. Beth watched Elena catalog each response, filing away who might be useful. The woman was good, Beth had to give her that. But twenty years of reading suspects had taught her to spot manipulation, and this… this was exactly what her goal had been.

"Of course you're scared," Beth said, matching Elena's

volume. "Why don't you help with the children? We're setting up a safe area in the storm cellar. They could use someone to keep them calm. Plus, in your weakened condition it would ensure you are not in danger."

Elena's eyes narrowed slightly, she knew she was being handled. But with everyone watching, she couldn't refuse without looking like a bitch. Beth had just effectively removed her from the equation while ensuring everyone knew she would be in hiding during the battle. "If you think that's where I'd be most helpful," she said sweetly.

"I do." Beth smiled, all teeth. "Mrs. Thompson's organizing it. She's by the house."

After Elena flounced off, Beth caught Doug Martinez watching her. "That one's trouble," he said quietly.

"Maybe." Beth turned back to survey the work. "But we've got bigger problems coming."

By mid-morning, the farm resembled something from another era. Teams of diggers worked in shifts, creating interlocking fields of fire while leaving clear retreat paths. The main approach to the farm now requires passing through three potential ambush points. Not enough to stop a determined force, but enough to make them bleed.

Beth found James Thompson in the barn with old man Jenkins and his ham radio setup. Michael, Emily, and Daniel clustered around a hand-drawn map spread across a workbench.

"Boys told you what they saw?" James asked without preamble.

"They did." Beth studied the map. Jenkins had been marking enemy positions as reports came in. "If they're holding unwilling fighters…"

"Could work for us," Daniel said. He'd changed since last year, harder edges showing through his normally easy-going demeanor. "Question is how to exploit it."

"We need to give them a way out," Emily said. "If they're being forced, they just need an opportunity to run."

Michael shook his head. "Run where? The Queen of Likes will hunt them down. Or their families."

"Not if she's too busy with us." James tapped the map. "Hit and run. Make her chase shadows. Every time she sends groups after our people, that's fewer watching the unwilling."

Jenkins adjusted his radio frequency, catching fragments of transmissions. Most were garbage, but occasionally something useful came through. "Got chatter about movement from the coast. Could be more of them, could be something else."

Beth processed this, mind working through possibilities. They couldn't fight on multiple fronts. But if they could turn this force against itself...

"I need paper," she said suddenly. "And someone with good handwriting."

Daniel found both, and Beth began dictating: "To those forced to fight: We offer food, medical care, and protection to any who walk away. No questions asked. Leave your weapons and walk north. You don't have to die for someone else's madness."

"We'll post them along their approach routes," she explained. "Some will tear them down, but others will read them first. Plant the seed of doubt."

"Psychological warfare," Michael murmured. "Might work."

"Everything might work or might fail," James said. "We try it all and see what sticks."

Daniel's head swung side to side. "Leave the weapons for the Queen to retrieve? I don't think this is a good idea."

"Good point," Beth said, "what if we keep lookouts watching and if any do they gather them? Might actually help us put up more of a fight, using their own weapons against them."

"I like it," James said with a small smirk. "Good thinking. I'll set it—"

A commotion outside drew their attention. Beth followed the others out to find a crowd gathering near the corral. At its center, Elena held court, gesturing dramatically as she spoke.

"—telling you, this is insane! We should be negotiating, not preparing for war. If we just talk to them, explain we're not a threat—"

"Like Frank talked before poisoning our water?" someone called out.

Elena whirled toward the voice. "That was different! These are just desperate people. If we show them violence, we'll get violence back. It's simple logic."

Beth began pushing through the crowd, but Elena spotted her coming.

"There she is! Our supposed protector, turning us into killers. Tell me, Chief Martin, how many of us are you willing to sacrifice for your little war?"

The crowd grew quiet, waiting. Beth felt their stares, their fear. These people had trusted her to keep them safe when she had a badge and the law behind her. Now she asked them to trust her with nothing but determination and whatever wisdom she'd gained in six years of keeping the peace.

"I'm not willing to sacrifice anyone," Beth said clearly. "That's why we're preparing. So, when they come—and they will come—we can protect ourselves without losing everything."

"But if we just—"

"They've already killed to get here," Beth interrupted. "Drowned their own people crossing rivers. They're being led by someone who livestreams executions to an imaginary audience. There's no reasoning with that kind of sickness."

She turned to address the wider crowd. "Each of you has a choice. Fight, support those who fight, or shelter with the children. No judgment either way. But if you stay, you follow the plan. We hit them, we fall back. We make them pay for every foot of ground. We don't have to win—we just have to survive until they decide we're not worth it."

"And if they don't decide that?" Elena's voice dripped skepticism.

Beth met her gaze steadily. "Then we keep fighting. Because the alternative is letting them take everything."

The crowd began dispersing, some nodding agreement, others looking troubled. Elena stood her ground a moment longer, that calculating look back in her eyes. Then she smiled, sweet and false, and headed toward the house.

"That one's going to be trouble," James said quietly beside her.

"Already is," Beth replied. "But we've got bigger problems coming."

"Where's Matthew? Maybe he can get her to settle. It's been a battle since they got here, and I just don't know what to do without hurting my son. This is his girlfriend"

"I thought he was working on the platform over there," she said, pointing to the driveway.

The afternoon brought more reports from scouts. The main force was moving slowly, delayed by the storm damage but still coming. More vehicles had been spotted approaching from the south. Identity unknown. And someone had found fresh grave markers along Route 25, hastily dug and unmarked.

Beth stood at the road where they'd established the first ambush point. The crossing created a natural bottleneck where attackers would have to slow down. Doug Martinez was showing a group of volunteers how to move quietly through the underbrush.

"Don't fight their fight," Beth told each group she worked with. "We're not soldiers. We're shadows. Hit them when they don't expect it, then disappear. Make them scared of every tree, every shadow. Make them wonder if attacking us is worth losing more people to an enemy they can't see."

The sun climbed higher, burning off the morning mist. The farm continued its transformation from refuge to battlefield. And somewhere out there, The Queen of Likes was coming with her army of the desperate and insane, while Beth Martin, small-town cop turned guerrilla leader, prepared to meet her with farmers and store clerks who were learning that ordinary people could do extraordinary things when their backs were against the wall.

Near the barn, she found the three boys cleaning their rifles under Ethan's supervision. They handled the weapons with new confidence, earned through necessity rather than years.

"Want to do another scout run before dark," Ethan said. "Check if they've moved."

Beth considered. The boys had proven capable, but they were still children forced into adult roles. "Take the ridge trail. Better cover. And if anything feels wrong—"

"We run," Jake finished. "We know."

She watched them go, these children who'd adapted too quickly to a world gone mad. Behind her, the refugee camp in the corral continued the routines of cooking, washing, tending wounds both physical and emotional. The two worlds existed side by side. The desperate new normalcy of survival and the grim preparations for violence.

"Chief!" Someone called from the radio setup. "Jenkins has something!"

Beth jogged to the barn where Jenkins hunched over his equipment, headphones pressed tight against his ears. He held up a hand for silence, then slowly pulled off the headset.

"Picked up transmissions between their groups," he said. "Lots of confusion. Some units aren't responding to calls. And…" He paused, choosing his words. "Heard at least two mentions of people slipping away during the night. Desertion."

Beth felt a spark of hope. "It's working. The dissent was already there. We just have to give it room to grow."

"There's more," Jenkins continued. "That second group from the south? They're using different call signs. Might not be connected to this one at all."

Another variable in an already complex equation. Beth rubbed her temples. In her patrol car, the biggest decision she'd usually faced was whether to write a ticket or give a warning. Now people's lives hung on her ability to read situations and guess at human nature.

"Double the watch tonight," she decided. "And tell our scouts to identify that southern group if possible. We need to know if we're facing one enemy or two."

As afternoon wore toward evening, Beth made another round of the defenses. The ambush positions were well-concealed. The approaches were channeled. Teams knew their roles. Strike and withdraw, make noise and vanish, always keep moving. It wasn't much, but it was more than nothing.

She found Matthew working with others to reinforce the storm cellar entrance. His face was haggard, grief and exhaustion written in every line. But he worked steadily, methodically, channeling his pain into purpose.

"How's Elena?" Beth asked carefully.

Matthew's jaw tightened. "Resting. Finally." He drove a nail with perhaps more force than necessary. "She's been… difficult."

"Grief makes people act out," Beth offered, though she suspected Elena's behavior had deeper roots.

"Maybe." Another nail, another sharp blow. "Or maybe some people just show their true self when things get hard."

Before Beth could respond, shouts erupted from the corral. They ran toward the sound, finding a cluster of people around two figures near the fence line. Beth pushed through to find a man and woman, both filthy and exhausted, hands raised in surrender.

"Please," the woman gasped. "We saw your signs. We just want out. We can't follow her anymore. She's insane. Completely insane."

Beth studied them quickly, the haunted eyes, the way they flinched at sudden movements, all pointed to abuse. These weren't plants or spies. These were people who'd seen too much.

"Get them water," she ordered. "And food. Emily needs to check them for injuries."

As others rushed to comply, Beth knelt beside the deserters. "How many more want out?"

The man laughed bitterly. "Half of us, maybe more. But she's got the true believers watching everyone. And she…" He shuddered. "She killed Mark yesterday. Shot him for suggesting we find another route. Said he was spreading negative energy."

"Where is she now?" Beth kept her voice calm, professional.

"Maybe five miles back. Setting up for tomorrow. She wants to attack at dawn." The woman grabbed Beth's arm. "She's got at least sixty people. Some are willing, most not. And she's getting worse. Talking to people who aren't there. Making us film everything for her 'audience.'"

Beth processed this quickly. Dawn attack meant they had

perhaps twelve hours. Sixty people, but many unwilling to fight. And a leader descending further into madness.

"Get them inside," she told the others. "Post extra watches. And someone find James—we need to adjust our plans."

As the deserters were led away, Beth noticed Elena watching from the farmhouse porch. The woman's expression was unreadable, but something in her posture suggested satisfaction. Like pieces moving into place on a board only she could see.

Beth turned away, focusing on the immediate threat. Whatever game she was playing would have to wait. They had a battle to prepare for, and dawn would come too soon.

The sun dropped lower, painting the farm in shades of gold and red. Cookfires in the corral sent smoke spiraling into the evening air. Children's voices mixed with the sound of hammering as last-minute preparations continued. And somewhere in the growing darkness, an army of the desperate led by the mad crept closer.

Beth stood at the fence line, watching the tree line, thinking about choices and consequences. Tomorrow, people will die. Some of them might be people she knew, people she'd sworn to protect. But tonight, they prepared as best they could, ordinary people learning that heroes were just folks who kept standing when everything inside them wanted to run.

A hand touched her shoulder. James Thompson stood beside her, looking older than his years but unbowed.

"We'll manage," he said simply.

"Yeah," Beth agreed, though neither of them fully believed it. "We'll manage."

Behind them, the farm settled into watchful readiness. The cooking fires burned lower. Guards took their positions. And in the storm cellar, Elena sat among the children with Marianne, the elderly pharmacist's wife who recognized that calculating look hidden behind expressions of concern, planning something that only she understood.

The first stars appeared overhead, distant and indifferent to human struggles. Beth checked her weapon one more time, then headed to brief the night watch. Dawn would bring violence and chaos, but tonight they could still pretend to be civilized.

Even if they all knew better.

The deserters' intelligence proved valuable as the night deepened. Beth worked with James and the others to adjust their defenses, accounting for the queen's deteriorating mental state and the fractures in her force. More signs were posted. Guard positions were shifted to account for the likely approach routes.

And through it all, Beth held onto one thought: they didn't need to defeat their army. They just needed to help it defeat itself. Every deserter weakened her grip on them. Every hesitation in her ranks strengthened the farm's position. It was still a long shot, but it was better than no shot at all.

As midnight approached, Beth made one final round of the defenses. The farm slept fitfully, guards walking their routes, refugees tossing in makeshift beds.

They waited.

Matthew

Matthew Thompson's hands moved in steady rhythm, tightening bolts on the defensive platform they were constructing in the middle of the driveway. The pre-dawn air hung thick with humidity, another oppressive day building even before the sun rose. He'd been up since three. Elena had shaken him awake to ask if he'd been dreaming about Maddie.

"Were you?" she'd demanded, her face inches from his in the darkness. "You said her name."

He hadn't remembered any dreams, told her so, but she'd spent the next hour listing all the times she'd seen him looking at Maddie, talking to Maddie, laughing at something Maddie said. By the time Elena finally cried herself back to sleep, Matthew knew there'd be no rest for him.

So here he was, channeling his frustration into construction. The platform would give their shooters a protected position overlooking the main approach to the farm, positioned strategically in the driveway to control access. Daniel had designed it, a simple but effective structure that could be built with salvaged lumber and basic tools.

"You're up early."

Matthew startled, nearly dropping his wrench. Daniel stood beside the platform, coffee mug in hand, surveying the progress.

"Couldn't sleep," Matthew said, which was true enough.

Daniel walked around the structure, examining it from all angles. "Good joints. This'll hold. Strategic placement too—anyone coming up the drive will have to deal with this."

They worked in companionable silence for a few minutes, Daniel marking positions for the next support beams while Matthew continued securing the decking. The familiar rhythm of building something useful helped quiet the chaos in Matthew's mind.

"Elena okay?" Daniel asked eventually, his tone carefully neutral.

Matthew's hands stilled on the wrench. "She's… struggling. The miscarriage, everything that's happening. It's a lot."

"Yeah." Daniel took a sip of his coffee. "Jessica had a miscarriage between Ryan and Lily. Hardest thing we'd went through until all this started. Grief does strange things to people."

"Strange," Matthew repeated, thinking of Elena's accusations, her demands, the way she tracked his every movement like a prison guard. "That's one word for it."

Daniel studied him for a moment. "You know, when Jess lost the baby, she pushed me away for a while. Said she needed space to process. I gave it to her, and eventually she came back to me stronger." He paused. "But everyone handles loss differently."

Matthew heard what his brother wasn't saying—that Elena wasn't pushing him away but pulling him closer, tighter, until he could barely breathe. He thought about their relationship before all this, before the pregnancy announcement that had changed everything.

They'd been broken up for more than five weeks when Elena showed up at his door with the test. Weeks of blessed peace after months of escalating arguments about where he went, who he talked to, why he needed to spend so much time with his family. He'd been planning to make the break permanent when she'd held up that little plastic stick with two pink lines.

"I know we've had problems," she'd said, tears streaming down her face. "But this changes everything, doesn't it? You'll do the right thing?"

And he had. Because that's what Thompson men did—they took responsibility, they stood by their obligations. Even when every instinct screamed that something wasn't right.

"Platform's coming along well." Maddie's voice carried across the driveway. She approached from the direction of the house, her father's notebook tucked under one arm. "But I need to steal you both for the catapult. I found something in Dad's notes about torsion springs that could triple our range."

"Catapult?" Daniel perked up. "Now you're talking."

"Dad kept plans from when the historical society built that replica trebuchet for the town festival," Maddie explained. "But he'd made modifications, figured out how to use truck springs for better tension. Said it was 'just for fun' but…" She shrugged. "Turns out his fun projects might save our lives."

Matthew climbed down from the platform, followed by Daniel. They walked to the cleared area beside the barn where the skeleton of their defensive catapult waited. It looked like a rough but functional framework of salvaged lumber and metal parts.

Maddie opened her notebook, showing them detailed diagrams. "See here? If we mount the springs at this angle and adjust the throwing arm length, we can get fifty percent more distance without adding stress to the frame."

"That's brilliant," Daniel said, already moving to examine the current setup. "Matt, help me with this beam."

They worked together for the next hour, implementing

Maddie's modifications. Matthew found himself impressed by how her father's theoretical knowledge translated into practical application. She directed their efforts with quiet confidence, no ego or drama, just focused problem-solving.

The sun crept above the horizon, painting the barn's interior with golden light and Matthew found himself relaxing for the first time in days, lost in the simple satisfaction of building something useful.

"Matthew!" Elena's voice cut through the morning air like a blade. "Matthew, where are you?"

His shoulders tensed immediately. Beside him, Maddie's hands stilled on the spring she was adjusting.

"Over here," he called back, trying to keep his voice level.

Elena appeared around the corner of the barn, still in her nightgown, hair disheveled from sleep. Her eyes found Maddie first, narrowing with an expression Matthew knew too well.

"Of course," she said, voice dripping with false sweetness. "I wake up alone and scared, and you're here with her."

"We're building defensive weapons," Daniel interjected calmly. "Matthew's been helping since before dawn."

Elena's gaze never left Maddie. "I'm sure he has. So helpful. So dedicated." She turned to Matthew. "I need to talk to you. Privately."

Matthew set down his hammer, exhaustion washing over him. "Can it wait? We need to finish this before—"

"No, it can't wait!" Elena's voice rose to a near-shriek. "Nothing I need ever seems important enough to wait, does it? Not when there's work to do, not when *she* needs help with something." Her eyes darted to glare at Maddie then back to Matthew

"Elena—"

"I'm injured and trying to recover, Matthew! I'm grieving

and scared and you're out here playing medieval warfare with another woman!" Tears streamed down her face now, but her eyes remained hard, calculating. "What kind of man does that?"

The manipulation was so transparent Matthew almost laughed. Almost. Instead, he felt the familiar guilt settling over him like a heavy blanket. She was grieving.

No. He couldn't think about that. About the relief he'd felt mixed with the grief when Emily delivered the news. What kind of man felt relief when his girlfriend miscarried?

"I'll be right down," he said quietly.

"Matt, we really need to finish—" Daniel started.

"I said I'll be right there." The words came out harsher than intended.

Matthew set down the wrench he'd been using, each movement feeling like surrender. Elena waited with arms crossed, fury radiating from every line of her body.

"Inside," she hissed. "Now."

He followed her out of the barn, catching a glimpse of Maddie's face—concerned, sympathetic, but also something else.

Elena led him to the small toolshed behind the barn, far enough from the main house for privacy. The moment the door closed, she rounded on him.

"How dare you," she spat. "How dare you humiliate me like that."

"Humiliate you? Elena, I was working—"

"With her. Always with her." Elena's voice dropped to something more dangerous than shouting. "Do you think I'm stupid, Matthew? Do you think I don't see what's happening?"

"Nothing is happening. We're preparing for an attack—"

"Stop lying to me!" She slammed her palm against the shed wall. "I see how you look at her. How you light up when she enters a room. How you suddenly have all this energy for projects when she's involved."

Matthew felt his own anger rising. "Maybe I have energy because I'm doing something useful instead of having the same tired argument for the hundredth time."

"Oh, so now I'm useless?" Elena's tears flowed freely, but her voice remained steady, controlled. "The woman who lost your child is useless?"

"That's not what I said—"

"It's what you meant. I'm just a burden now, aren't I? Now that there's no baby to tie you to me."

The words hung between them, too close to Matthew's own shameful thoughts. He opened his mouth to deny it, but Elena pressed on.

"I know you were relieved," she whispered. "When your sister told us. I saw your face. You were relieved our baby died."

"Elena, please—"

"You wanted to leave me before. The only reason you stayed was the baby. And now..." She laughed, bitter and broken. "Now you can't wait to run to her. Your parents probably love it. They never thought I was good enough for their precious son."

Matthew thought of his parents, how they'd welcomed Elena without reservation, how his mother had immediately started planning for a grandchild. But Elena's version of reality had always been more powerful than truth.

"What do you want from me?" he asked, exhaustion making him honest. "Tell me what you want, and I'll do it."

Elena stepped closer, her hand reaching up to touch his face. For a moment, her expression softened into something almost like the girl he'd fallen for two years ago. The fun, spontaneous girl who'd made him laugh, who'd seemed so different from the serious responsibilities of farm life.

"I want my boyfriend back," she said softly. "The one who chose me. Who put me first." Her hand dropped. "I want you to tell Maddie that Daniel can handle the rest of the defensive work without you. That you need to focus on us, on healing together."

"Elena, we're under attack in less than twenty-four hours—"

"There are dozens of people here who can hammer boards!" Her softness evaporated. "But only one who can help me through this grief. Or am I not worth even that much to you anymore?"

Matthew closed his eyes, feeling the familiar trap closing around him. Every option led to guilt. Every choice was wrong.

"She doesn't need you," Elena continued, pressing her advantage. "She has Daniel, she has your father, she has half the farm hanging on her every word about her precious water filters. But I only have you. And if you can't see that, if you can't choose me when I need you most…"

She let the threat hang unfinished, but Matthew heard it clearly. Choose, or I'll make sure everyone knows what kind of man you really are. The kind who was relieved when his baby died. The kind who abandoned his grieving girlfriend for another woman.

"Fine," he said, the word leaving a taste like bile in his mouth. "I'll tell them I need to stay with you today."

Elena's smile was triumphant. "And you'll tell her to work with someone else from now on. For my sake. For our relationship."

"Elena—"

"It's not too much to ask, Matthew. Not if you really love me. Not if you're really sorry about…" She touched her still-flat stomach. "About everything."

Matthew felt something break inside him. Not dramatically, not all at once, but a quiet fracture that would eventually split wide. But not today. Today he would do what she asked, because the alternative was a scene that would disrupt everyone's preparations, create drama when they needed unity.

"I'll talk to her," he said.

Elena rose on her tiptoes to kiss him, a possessive claiming that felt nothing like affection. "I knew you'd understand. We're going to get through this together, baby. Just you and me."

As she led him back toward the house, her hand gripping his like a shackle, Matthew caught sight of Maddie and Daniel still working on the platform. Maddie glanced in their direction, their eyes meeting for just a moment. She didn't look hurt or surprised. Just sad.

He wanted to call out, to explain, to say something that would make it better. But Elena's grip tightened, and he let himself be pulled away, another piece of his autonomy sacrificed to keep the peace.

Later, he promised himself. Later he'd find a way to explain. Later he'd figure out how to balance Elena's needs with everything else. His brother probably thought he was some kind of loser being led around like this. Anger filled him at the thought and his pace picked up. He just wanted to get out of sight of people.

But as the morning sun climbed higher and the farm bustled with preparations for battle, Matthew Thompson stood at a window watching others work, trapped by his own choices and the woman who claimed to love him while systematically cutting him off from everyone else who might.

And somewhere in the back of his mind, a small voice whispered the truth he wasn't ready to face: This wasn't grief making Elena act this way. This was who she'd always been. The pregnancy had just been another tool, another way to keep him close.

The ultimatum she'd delivered felt less like a crossroads and more like the tightening of chains he'd wrapped around himself the day he'd chosen to "do the right thing."

But that recognition would have to wait. For now, he had a role to play, a grieving girlfriend to comfort, and a growing certainty that he'd made the worst mistake of his life by coming back to her.

The day stretched ahead, full of preparations he wouldn't be part of, connections he wouldn't make, and the suffocating presence of someone who loved not him, but her possession of him.

And tomorrow, if they survived what was coming, he'd have to find the courage to break free.

But today wasn't tomorrow. Today was just another link in the chain, another compromise, another moment of choosing the path of least resistance.

The irony wasn't lost on him. In trying to do the right thing, he'd trapped himself in something deeply wrong. And Elena's ultimatum wasn't a question at all.

It had been a declaration of victory.

Maddie

"—and she says if I keep working with you on projects, it means I don't care about her recovery." Matthew's voice cracked on the last word, his hands fidgeting with a wrench he'd picked up from the workbench without purpose.

Maddie set down her father's notebook, the pages filled with water system diagrams suddenly feeling less important than the pain radiating from her childhood friend. They stood in the barn's equipment area, morning light filtering through gaps in the storm-damaged roof, casting uneven shadows across the tools scattered on the wooden surface.

"Matt, I understand." She kept her voice gentle, matter-of-fact. "Elena's been through something terrible. She needs you right now."

"But it's not just about the baby." Matthew's shoulders sagged as though carrying invisible weight. "She thinks... she thinks there's something between us that isn't appropriate. That I look at you differently than I should."

Heat crept up Maddie's neck, but she forced herself to remain calm. "Do you remember Derek Paulson? Ninth grade?"

Matthew's brow furrowed. "That guy you dated for like three months? The one who played JV football?"

"He was so jealous of our friendship." Maddie picked up a small gear from the workbench, turning it between her fingers.

"Remember when you and I were working on that science project about some dumb bacteria? He threw such a fit that I had to meet you at the library instead of your house. Said it wasn't normal for a girl to spend so much time with another guy, even if they were just friends."

Something shifted in Matthew's expression, a flicker of recognition that made him straighten slightly.

"I broke up with him two weeks later," Maddie continued. "Not because of you specifically, but because I realized that anyone who tried to control who I could be friends with wasn't someone I wanted to be with."

Matthew stared at her, the wrench forgotten in his hands. "I never… I didn't realize…"

"You were always just Matt to me. My friend since third grade who helped me build that terrible volcano for the science fair and didn't laugh when it exploded all over Mrs. Anderson's desk." She managed to smile. "The same Matt who taught me how to throw a proper spiral and listened to me cry when my dad had his first heart attack."

"Maddie." Matthew's voice dropped to barely above a whisper. "I never realized how much you've always calmed my spirit. All these years, whenever everything felt chaotic or overwhelming, talking to you made it… quieter somehow. Clearer." He took a step toward her, emotion raw in his voice. "I should have thanked you for that before now."

He moved as though to embrace her, arms lifting slightly, and for a moment Maddie thought he might ignore Elena's ultimatum and just be her friend. But halfway through the motion, he stopped himself, arms dropping to his sides like he'd hit an invisible barrier.

"I have to go." The words came out strangled. "She's waiting for me, and if I'm gone too long…"

He turned toward the barn door, shoulders rigid with the

effort of walking away. Maddie watched him leave, each step taking him further from the easy friendship they'd shared since childhood. Her chest tightened with an ache that had nothing to do with romantic longing and everything to do with watching someone she cared about disappear into a cage of someone else's making.

The barn felt larger and emptier after he left, filled with half-finished projects and the ghost of conversations they could no longer have. Maddie picked up her father's notebook again, but the diagrams blurred slightly before she blinked the emotion away.

"Maddie?" Daniel's voice carried from the main barn area. She could hear the gentle concern in his tone, the careful way he announced his presence.

She found him emerging from behind a stack of salvaged lumber, metal brackets and gear assemblies gleaming with fresh welds in his arms. He took one look at her face and set the parts down carefully on a nearby workbench.

"I didn't want to interrupt," he said quietly, glancing toward the barn entrance where Matthew had disappeared. "But I caught enough to get the general idea." His expression darkened. "Elena's making him choose between helping his family and keeping her happy."

Maddie nodded, not trusting her voice.

"That's not grief talking," Daniel continued, his tone gentle but firm. "That's control. And I'm sorry you're caught in the middle of it." He paused, watching her carefully. "For what it's worth, you're family to us, Maddie. Whether Elena likes it or not. Matt's just… he's lost right now."

The words hit Maddie harder than she'd expected. Family. After losing her parents, after watching her childhood home flood and her father's store collapse, the Thompson farm had become more than refuge. It had become home. But hearing

Daniel say it out loud, claim her as one of them despite Elena's manipulations, made something tight in her chest finally loosen.

"Thank you," she managed, her voice thick. "That means more than you know."

Daniel studied her for a moment, then gestured to the array of parts spread across a canvas tarp. "Got the new bearing assembly finished this morning. Should handle the wind loads we calculated without seizing up." His tone shifted to something more businesslike, giving her space to compose herself. "Ready to tackle that windmill assembly? I've got the new brackets welded and ready to test."

"More than ready." Maddie moved toward the parts, grateful for the distraction of honest work. "Your metalwork keeps getting better."

"Practice." Daniel picked up a wrench, testing the fit on one of the bolts. "Funny how the end of the world turns everyone into a jack-of-all-trades."

They both laughed. The moment of levity was just what she needed.

They worked together for the next hour, wrestling with the windmill assembly using a combination of pulleys, leverage, and stubborn determination to raise the tower into position. The physical effort felt good, muscles straining against genuine resistance instead of the helpless frustration of watching a friend disappear into someone else's control.

"Hold it steady!" Daniel called from where he worked to secure the base bolts. "If this thing falls over, we'll be picking splinters of the barn wall out of our asses for weeks."

Maddie laughed and said, "Don't make me laugh or that's exactly what will happen."

Maddie braced against the guide rope, feeling the tower's weight try to pull her off balance. "Got it! How's it looking?"

"Like it might actually work." Daniel's voice carried surprise and satisfaction. "Your dad's calculations were spot on. The gear ratios should give us enough torque to pump water even in light wind."

The mention of her father sent a familiar pang through Maddie's chest, but this time it carried more warmth than pain. His knowledge lived on through her hands, through projects that would keep people alive and communities functioning.

"Maddie! Daniel!" Jessica's voice rang across the farmyard. "Come see what you've accomplished!"

They turned to find Jessica approaching with Ryan and Lily in tow, both children bouncing with excitement. Behind them, several other farm residents emerged from various buildings, drawn by the sight of the newly erected windmill.

"Does it work?" Lily asked, her seven-year-old face bright with curiosity. "Will it make electricity like the big ones on the highway?"

"Better," Daniel said, ruffling his daughter's hair. "This one makes water. Clean water from the well, pumped up to the storage tank without anyone having to work the hand pump."

"That's actually more useful than electricity right now," Jessica added, admiration clear in her voice. "How long before it's operational?"

"Few more hours to connect the pump mechanism," Maddie replied, studying the tower's alignment. "Maybe tomorrow morning for full testing."

"Look at that!" Old Man Jenkins appeared at the edge of the gathering crowd, pointing at the windmill with obvious approval. "Haven't seen one of those working since I was a boy. My grandfather had one on his farm in Nebraska. Pumped water for forty head of cattle through droughts that killed off half the crops."

"This is a beautiful thing," Walt Henley said, shaking his

head in wonder. Walt had arrived with the latest group of evacuees, looking hollow-eyed and defeated. Now his face showed something approaching hope. "To think we can build something useful from scraps and old knowledge."

Maddie felt warmth spread through her chest, a sharp contrast to the ache Matthew's departure had left behind. This was what her father had tried to teach her all those years in the store. That knowledge applied with care and precision could improve people's lives. If they knew what parts could create something better from the wreckage of what came before.

"Hey Maddie!" A familiar voice called from across the farmyard. Hannah approached with quick steps, medical bag slung over her shoulder and a young woman trailing behind her. "We finished the morning medical rounds early. Thought we might help with whatever project has everyone gathering."

The young woman beside Hannah looked to be maybe sixteen, with dark hair pulled back in a practical ponytail and clothes that had seen hard use. Her eyes darted nervously between the faces in the crowd, but when they settled on Maddie, something shifted in her expression.

"This is Zoe," Hannah said, gesturing to her companion. "She is one of the people who arrived with me and Jake. Zoe, this is Maddie Foster. The one I told you about who builds all kinds of things."

"The engineer," Zoe said, a note of awe in her voice. "Hannah said you figured out how to make clean water from almost nothing."

Maddie felt her cheeks flush. "I'm not an engineer. I just read my father's notes and try not to blow anything up."

"Don't let her modesty fool you," Daniel interjected. "This woman has single-handedly solved more infrastructure problems in the past month than most people tackle in a lifetime."

Zoe studied the windmill with obvious fascination. "Where did you learn to build something like this?"

"My dad kept notebooks," Maddie explained. "Designs, calculations, theories he never got to test. I'm just trying to bring his ideas to life."

"That's amazing." Zoe's eyes shone with genuine admiration. "To take someone else's dreams and make them real. That takes a special kind of intelligence."

Hannah smiled at the exchange. "Zoe has some experience with mechanical systems. Thought she might be able to help with the water projects."

"What kind of experience?" Maddie asked, always eager to find another pair of skilled hands.

"My dad was a mechanic before…" Zoe's voice faltered slightly. "Before everything changed. He taught me about engines, pumps, hydraulic systems. Well, actually made me pass him all the wrenches and things. Basic stuff, but I understand how things work together."

"Basic is perfect," Daniel said warmly. "Most of what we're doing here is basic principles applied creatively. Maddie's father may have been the theorist, but we're all learning to be practical engineers."

"Could you show me the water filtration systems?" Zoe asked Maddie. "Hannah mentioned you've got several different designs running."

"Of course." Maddie felt her enthusiasm building. "We've got ceramic filters, sand and gravel beds, even a solar disinfection setup. Different solutions for different problems."

As they walked toward the water treatment area behind the barn, Hannah fell into step beside Maddie. "She's had a rough time," Hannah said quietly. "Lost most of her family, spent weeks with a group that…" She paused, choosing her words carefully. "Let's just say they had some dangerous leadership."

"What kind of dangerous?" Maddie asked, remembering her conversation with Mrs. Henderson about the Queen of Likes.

"Violent. Unpredictable. Led by a person completely lost. Out of touch with reality." Hannah's voice dropped further. "Zoe managed to escape, but she's still processing what she witnessed."

"She seems to be holding up well."

"She's resilient. Reminds me of you, actually; channeling trauma into useful work instead of letting it paralyze her."

They reached the water treatment area, where three different filtration systems operated in parallel. The ceramic filter setup that Maddie had salvaged from the hardware store, a multi-stage sand and gravel system built from salvaged materials, and the newest addition was a solar disinfection array using clear plastic bottles arranged on a south-facing platform.

"This is incredible," Zoe breathed, moving from system to system with obvious understanding. "You've got mechanical filtration, biological processing, and UV sterilization. It's like a miniature water treatment plant."

"Each system handles different contaminants," Maddie explained, warming to her subject. "The ceramic filters catch bacteria and sediment, the sand beds handle larger particles and some chemical filtering, and the solar setup deals with viral contamination."

Zoe crouched beside the sand filter, examining the layered media. "Activated charcoal layer for chemical absorption?"

"Exactly. Crushed charcoal from wood fires, layered between fine and coarse sand." Maddie felt a surge of excitement at finding someone who immediately grasped the engineering principles. "My dad's notes showed how different particle sizes create optimal flow rates while maximizing contact time."

"Your father was brilliant," Zoe said, straightening up. "This setup could support fifty people easily, maybe more with some modifications."

"Actually," Hannah interjected, "that gives me an idea. What if we could scale this up? Create systems for the other communities in the area?"

Maddie's pulse quickened. "We'd need more materials, more people who understand the maintenance requirements…"

"But it's possible?" Zoe asked.

"More than possible." Maddie pulled out her father's notebook, flipping to a section filled with calculations and diagrams. "Dad designed modular systems specifically for community-scale deployment. I just never had the resources or manpower to attempt them."

"What if we did now?" Hannah's voice carried growing excitement. "Between the three of us, plus Daniel's metalworking skills, plus whatever materials we can salvage from the flooded areas… I'm sure once things settle down some of the kids and others would help find them."

"We could create a network," Zoe finished, her eyes lighting up. "Connected communities with reliable water supplies, trade, and skill sharing. Make the whole region more stable."

Maddie felt something shift within her, the ache from Matthew's departure transforming into a different kind of energy. This was bigger than personal relationships or individual survival. This was about building something that could last, serving the practical needs of people trying to rebuild their lives.

"There's more," she said, flipping through the notebook pages. "Water pumping, basic electrical generation, even some food preservation techniques. Dad was working on integrated systems—communities that could be largely self-sufficient with just a few key low-tech gadgets."

"Like settlements in a strategy game," Zoe said with a grin. "Build the water source, add the power generation, unlock the advanced buildings."

Hannah laughed. "I love that you're comparing post-apocalyptic survival to video games."

"Hey, those games taught resource management and systems thinking," Zoe replied defensively. "Turns out they were more educational than anyone realized." Her chest puffed up proudly.

"She's not wrong," Maddie said, surprised by her own laughter. "Half of what I'm doing is resource allocation and optimization puzzles."

They spent the next hour going through the notebook together, with Zoe asking increasingly sophisticated questions about flow rates, filtration media, and maintenance cycles. Her time spent helping her dad complemented Maddie's theoretical knowledge perfectly, while Hannah's medical training provided crucial insight into health and safety requirements.

"We could start with three pilot sites," Maddie said finally, sketching rough locations on a piece of scrap paper. "The main settlement here, the group at the old school, and maybe one of the smaller communities down where the feed store is. Those are all buildings that can house people."

"Test the designs, work out the problems, then expand from there," Zoe agreed. "Build expertise along with infrastructure."

"It would give people hope," Hannah added quietly. "Something to work toward beyond just day-to-day survival."

A shout from the farmyard interrupted their planning. "Maddie! Hannah! You need to see this!"

They hurried back to find a crowd gathered around the windmill. Daniel stood beside the tower, a broad grin splitting his face.

"Water!" he called out, pointing to a steady stream flowing from the pump outlet into a collection barrel. "She's working!"

Cheers erupted from the assembled crowd. Children ran toward the flowing water, adults clapped and laughed, and even the most battle-hardened refugees allowed themselves smiles of genuine joy.

"First automated water pumping we've had since the grid went down," someone called out.

"Better than automated," Jessica corrected, moving to stand beside her husband. "This runs on wind. No fuel, no complex maintenance. Just good engineering and natural power."

Maddie felt tears prick her eyes as she watched people fill containers with fresh, clean water pumped by her father's design. Children splashed their hands in the stream, adults tasted it and nodded approval, and elderly refugees looked at the windmill with expressions approaching reverence.

"Your dad would be proud," Hannah said softly beside her.

"He would be," Maddie agreed, her voice thick with emotion. "He always said the best technology was the kind that worked so well people stopped thinking about it. It just became part of how they lived."

"Like this," Zoe said, gesturing to the celebration around them. "In five years, kids will grow up thinking this is just how water works. They won't remember what it was like when every drop had to be hand-pumped or carried from the river."

"That's the goal," Maddie said. "Make survival so reliable it stops feeling like survival and starts feeling like living."

As the celebration continued around them, Maddie caught sight of Matthew watching from the farmhouse porch. Even at a distance, she saw the longing in his posture, the way he leaned toward the crowd like he wanted to join them but couldn't quite bring himself to approach.

"He's struggling," Hannah said, following Maddie's gaze.

"Yeah." Maddie turned back to the windmill, to the flowing water and laughing children and the future spreading out before them like a map of possibilities. "But that's his choice to make."

The words hurt to say, but they were true. She could build water systems and power networks, could turn her father's dreams into working reality, could help communities thrive instead of merely surviving. But she couldn't save Matthew from the cage he'd chosen to enter.

James and Beth approached congratulating them on the water but reminding everyone they had other work to do. "Water won't do us much good if we're dead." Beth called out.

"Great job on the water," James said, gripping Daniel on the shoulder. "Your mother will be forever grateful but how about that catapult?"

Maddie and Daniel led James to the completed replica of a good old-fashioned trebuchet and watched as he looked it over with eyebrows raised and a wide grin.

"Does it work?"

"Sure does," Daniel said, proudly wrapping his arm around Maddie's shoulder. "Gonna be a show for sure when they meet up with this badass medieval monstrosity."

They laughed, walking back toward the barn to check on positioning with Old Man Jenkins. Maddie between Daniel and James… Like family.

She looked over her shoulder to see Matt still watching from the porch Elena standing behind him with that smug look Maddie was fast growing annoyed with.

Grace

The morning light filtered through the canopy of leaves overhead, casting dappled shadows across Grace's makeshift camp. She held her dead iPhone at the perfect angle, the black screen, now with spidering cracks across the face, reflecting her carefully arranged smile that was beginning to take on a grotesque twist in the fractured image as she addressed her imaginary audience.

"Good morning, beautiful humans! Your girl Grace is back with another exclusive survival update!" Her voice carried that practiced enthusiasm she'd perfected through thousands of streams, bright and engaging despite the mud streaked across her cheeks. "Last night's content was absolutely insane. Mother Nature really tried to test our resilience, but we're still here, still thriving, still bringing you that authentic apocalypse lifestyle content!"

Behind her, the force of her followers, now diminished to forty-two, sat scattered around the flooded campsite in various states of exhaustion and misery. Most avoided looking at her directly, having learned that eye contact during her "broadcasts" often led to being pulled into whatever performance she was creating. A few watched with the hollow fascination of people observing a car accident in slow motion.

Rebecca Mitchell, in one of the rare moments allowed out of her cage, crouched near the burned remains of their cooking fire, methodically sorting through wet supplies with movements that spoke of careful practice, ensuring she didn't draw the queen's attention. Her clothes hung loose on her diminished frame, and her once-neat hair fell in tangles around her face. To any observer, she appeared broken and defeated. Exactly what Grace needed to see.

"And speaking of thriving," Grace continued, panning her phone across the camp, "let's check in with our community members! Rebecca, honey, wave to our amazing followers!"

Rebecca raised her hand in a small, tired gesture that Grace interpreted as enthusiastic participation. What Grace couldn't see was that Rebecca was cataloging the positions of her inner circle, noting who carried weapons and who seemed most worn down by the endless performance.

"Isn't she just glowing with that survivor energy?" Grace gushed. "This is what real community building looks like, people. When you strip away all the fake societal constructs and get down to authentic human connection. Ain't that right miss Becca?"

Rebecca smiled weakly and nodded but saving her from Grace's further attention, a branch cracked somewhere in the woods beyond their camp. Grace's smile flickered for just a moment, her eyes darting toward the sound with something approaching genuine fear. But she recovered instantly, tilting her phone to catch better light.

"Ooh, mystery audio! Very atmospheric. The production value out here is just incredible." She giggled, the sound holding an edge that made several followers exchange worried glances. "Nature really knows how to set the mood for compelling content."

The crack came again, closer this time, followed by voices. Grace's followers tensed, hands moving toward weapons, but she waved them off with practiced authority.

"Don't worry, everyone! I'm sure it's just more community members looking to join our amazing survival network. Remember, we're building something beautiful here!"

Two figures emerged from the trees, moving with the careful swagger of men who'd survived by taking what they wanted. Sean Burke led the way, his younger brother Tommy following close behind. Both carried assault rifles slung across their backs and bore the kind of scars that came from fighting in close quarters.

Grace's eyes lit up with genuine excitement as she took in their appearance—the tactical gear, the confident postures, the dangerous edge that would translate perfectly to her imaginary audience.

"Oh my God, everyone!" She spun to face her phone, practically vibrating with enthusiasm. "We are about to have some amazing guest content! Look at these absolute units! This is going to be such an incredible collaboration!"

Sean's eyes narrowed as he studied the camp, taking in the armed followers, the defensive positions, and Grace herself with her dead phone held like a sacred object. "You the Queen of Likes we heard about?"

"That's Queen Grace to you, gorgeous," she replied with a brilliant smile, already positioning herself for the best camera angle. "And you are about to become very famous! Tell our followers your names—this is going live to thousands of people!"

Tommy Burke shifted uncomfortably, glancing at his brother. They'd heard stories about the crazy bitch leading this group but seeing her in person was something else entirely. She was talking to a phone that obviously didn't work, treating their arrival like some kind of social media event.

"Sean Burke," Sean said finally, playing along out of curiosity. "This is my brother Tommy. We heard you might be interested in some local intelligence.”

"Burke brothers!" Grace clapped her hands together. "I love it! Very authentic tough-guy aesthetic. Our audience is going to eat this up!" She turned to address her phone again. "Remember to smash that subscribe button if you're loving this crossover content! The engagement on this stream is going to be absolutely insane!" she giggled and paused to fix something with the phone.

She glanced at Rebecca, her discarded content provider and smiled at how she watched the interaction with carefully hidden interest. New arrivals meant new information, possibly new opportunities. She returned to her task and continued sorting supplies, but Grace was sure she listened to every word. Rebecca would never miss out on the quality content.

"Intelligence?" Grace's eyes sparkled with possibility. "Like, exclusive behind-the-scenes information? Industry secrets? Oh, this is perfect! We're definitely doing a whole investigative series!" Her hands rose and she shimmied her torso accentuating the jiggle of her breasts before them.

Sean and Tommy exchanged a look. They'd come here to trade information about Cornish's defenses for supplies and maybe recruits. Instead, they'd found a woman who seemed to think she was filming a reality show.

"We know about the town you're planning to hit," Sean said, pulling out a hand-drawn map. "Cornish. Had family there before all this started. Know the layout, defensive positions, weak points."

Grace practically bounced with excitement and again both Sean and Tommy's eyes shifted to her chest. She grinned and continued, "Exclusive insider information! This is exactly the kind of premium content our followers deserve!" She held up her phone, angling it to capture both the Burke brothers and their map. "Make sure you're getting this, everyone. This is how real journalism works in the new world!"

She moved closer to Sean, drawn by his confidence and the way his tactical vest emphasized his broad shoulders. "You know, you've got amazing on-camera presence. Very authentic alpha energy. Have you ever considered content creation as a career path?" She cooed, moving closer to brush up on him.

Sean found himself oddly flattered by her attention, even knowing she was insane. There was something magnetic about her complete confidence, the way she commanded attention even while talking to a dead phone.

"Can't say I have," he replied, allowing a small smile.

"Oh, you're a natural!" Grace beamed, reaching out to adjust his vest like a stylist preparing a model. "The camera loves that strong, silent type. Very authentic survival male energy."

Frank Wilson pushed through the crowd of followers; his face flushed with anger and frustration. He'd been trying to assert his authority over this group since he arrived, only to watch Grace's madness overshadow every practical decision. Now she was fawning over these newcomers like they were celebrities instead of potential threats.

"Grace, we need to talk about their intel," Frank interrupted, his voice sharp with authority. "I know Cornish better than anyone. These boys are giving you outdated information. They haven't even been there since they killed the old pharmacist."

She spun around and glared at him but immediately returned to Sean and Tommy. "Ooh, you two are bad boys, now aren't you?"

"Their info is not—"

Grace put her hand up in front of him and her smile faltered slightly, a flash of irritation crossing her features before the performer's mask snapped back into place. "Frank, sweetie, we're in the middle of filming premium content here. Can't you see our guest experts are sharing valuable insights?"

"Guest experts?" Frank's voice rose. "Grace, these are the Burke brothers. They robbed the pharmacy in Cornish and killed George Miller in cold blood. Tommy there shot an old man for his medication stash."

The camp fell silent except for the sound of wind in the trees and the distant call of crows. Grace's followers watched nervously as Frank challenged her narrative during what she clearly considered a live broadcast.

Grace's jaw tightened almost imperceptibly. In her mind, Frank wasn't just questioning the Burke brothers' credentials— he was actively sabotaging her show, creating negative energy that would tank her engagement metrics, undermining her authority in front of her audience.

"Frank," she said sweetly with that dangerous undertone her followers had learned to fear, "you're bringing some really toxic energy to our content right now. Our followers don't want to hear about past drama. They want authentic, forward-looking survival content."

"Authentic?" Frank stepped closer, his own anger overriding caution. "You want authentic? These boys' information is old. The Thompson farm isn't some undefended homestead anymore. By now they've got organized defenses, trained fighters, probably thirty or forty people armed and ready."

Sean's face darkened. "You calling us liars, old man?"

"I'm calling you uninformed," Frank shot back. "And dangerous. Grace, if you attack that farm based on their intel, you're going to get half our people killed."

Grace's phone hand began to shake slightly, the first crack in her performance. Frank was creating chaos in her narrative, making her look weak and indecisive in front of her new guest stars and her imaginary audience. The algorithm hated conflict that didn't fit the brand.

"Cut!" she snapped, lowering her phone with sharp, jerky movements. "Frank, what the hell are you doing? You're completely ruining the flow here!"

But Frank, emboldened by his local knowledge and frustrated by her madness, pressed on. "I'm trying to keep us alive! These boys led a robbery that got an innocent man killed, and now they're feeding you false information that's going to get more people killed!"

Tommy Burke's hand moved to his sidearm. "Watch your mouth, grandpa."

"Or what?" Frank turned to face him directly. "You'll shoot another old man? That your solution to everything?"

Grace watched the confrontation escalate, her mind racing through possibilities, but something else was happening. She glanced around and instead of seeing shiny content everything was dark and gray. She saw the mud, saw the dirt of people's faces but only for a flash before the veil returned. Frank was creating negative content, undermining her guest collaboration, making her look like she couldn't control her own community. But the Burke brothers represented exciting new energy for her show, fresh faces with authentic survival credentials.

The choice was obvious.

"You know what?" Grace raised her phone again, her smile returning with renewed intensity. "This is actually perfect! Real, unscripted drama! Our followers love authenticity, and Frank here is giving us some amazing behind-the-scenes content about community management challenges!"

She moved between Frank and the Burke brothers, positioning herself as the mediator in her own show. "Sometimes in content creation, you have to make tough decisions about your team. Not everyone understands the vision."

Frank stared at her, finally recognizing the complete disconnection from reality in her eyes. "Grace, for God's sake, listen to yourself. You're talking about people's lives like they're social media metrics."

"Because that's what leadership is!" Grace's voice rose, her performance becoming more manic. "Making hard choices for the good of your community! Building engagement through authentic experiences!"

She spun to face her followers, many of whom were backing away as they sensed the approaching storm.

"Here's what's going to happen," Grace announced with the authority of someone revealing a plot twist to her audience. "Frank has been bringing negative energy to our community. Creating drama, undermining morale, questioning our beautiful collaborations."

Rebecca continued her sorting, but Grace noted how her attention sharpened. She'd been watching Grace's psychological patterns, and like the others, learning to read the signs of escalation. This was different, more focused, more dangerous and Grace grinned.

"Rebecca, honey," Grace called out sweetly, "would you bring Frank's belongings here? I think it's time for some community restructuring."

Rebecca looked up with carefully crafted confusion. "His belongings?"

"Everything. Clothes, supplies, weapons. All of it." Grace's smile never wavered, but her eyes held that flat, empty quality that preceded violence. "Frank's going to experience some authentic consequences for his negative energy."

Frank backed away as several followers moved to comply with Grace's orders. "Grace, what are you doing?"

"Creating premium content!" she replied brightly. "You see, our followers love accountability moments. When someone consistently brings toxicity to the community, sometimes you have to demonstrate real consequences."

Rebecca approached with Frank's pack and rifle, her movements careful and deliberate. As she handed them to Grace, their eyes met briefly. Rebecca's expression held just the right amount of nervous compliance, but Grace was too focused on her performance to notice the calculating intelligence beneath.

"Strip," Grace ordered Frank, her voice suddenly cold.

"What?"

"You heard me. Everything off. Rebecca's been our shining example of community integration, but you?" She gestured to the Burke brothers. "You've been nothing but problems. So, you can take her place in our accountability program."

Frank looked around the camp at faces turned away in shame, fear, or helpless sympathy. A few followers started to protest, but Grace's inner circle moved their hands to weapons.

"Grace, please," Frank said quietly. "I was trying to help. The information about the farm—"

"Is negative content that our audience doesn't want to hear!" Grace's mask slipped completely for a moment, revealing something wild and hungry underneath. "You're tanking our engagement metrics! Do you understand what that means for our growth potential?"

She regained her composure with visible effort, the smile returning like a switch being flipped. "But don't worry, everyone! This is all part of building a stronger community. Sometimes you have to prune the negative influences to help the positive ones flourish!"

Frank's hands shook as he began removing his clothes, the morning air cold against his skin. Around the camp, followers found reasons to look away, checking weapons, organizing supplies, anything to avoid witnessing what their leader had become.

"Rebecca, would you prepare our accountability space?" Grace asked sweetly, gesturing toward the makeshift cage they'd constructed from salvaged chain link. "I think Frank will benefit from some quiet reflection time."

Rebecca nodded, moving toward the cage with the submissive efficiency Grace expected.

"This is insane," Frank whispered as Rebecca unlocked the cage door.

Grace clapped her hands together as Frank was secured in the cage, naked and shivering. "Perfect! Now that's what I call community accountability! Our followers are going to love this authentic demonstration of leadership!"

She turned to the Burke brothers, her enthusiasm fully restored. "Now, where were we? Oh yes, your amazing intelligence about our target! Tell us everything—our audience is dying to hear expert analysis!"

Sean found himself oddly impressed by Grace's ruthless efficiency. She'd eliminated a challenge to her authority while demonstrating her power to potential new allies. The woman was clearly insane, but she was also clearly in charge.

"Like I was saying," he began, unfolding his map again, "Cornish is mostly farmland. Scattered houses, one main road through town. The Thompson place sits on high ground about two miles out—big farmhouse, some outbuildings, maybe twenty people total when I was there last."

Grace filmed eagerly, holding her phone to capture every detail. "This is exactly the kind of strategic content our followers need! Continue!"

Tommy joined in, warming to the attention. "Most of the defenders are going to be farmers and townspeople. Probably some hunting rifles, maybe a few handguns. Nothing organized."

Frank's voice carried from the cage, hoarse with anger and humiliation. "You're going to get them all killed, Grace. The farm isn't defenseless anymore."

Grace's smile tightened, but she didn't look toward the cage. "Rebecca, would you ask our accountability participant to keep quiet during our strategic planning session? This is premium subscriber content."

Rebecca approached the cage, making a show of following orders while actually checking on Frank's condition.

"Outstanding intelligence gathering!" Grace announced, returning her attention to the Burke brothers. "This is exactly why collaborations are so important for authentic content creation. Fresh perspectives, expert insights, real strategic value!"

She moved closer to Sean, drawn by his confidence and the way he commanded his brother's respect. "You know, I'm thinking we should do a whole series together. 'Strategic Planning with the Burke Brothers'—very authentic military consulting energy."

Sean found himself responding to her attention despite knowing she was completely divorced from reality. There was something magnetic about her complete confidence, the way she made everything sound like the most important thing in the world.

"Could be interesting," he replied, allowing her to adjust his vest again.

"Oh, it's going to be incredible!" Grace practically glowed with excitement. "The engagement numbers alone—our followers love expert guest content!"

Frank's voice rose from the cage again, desperate now. "Grace, listen to me! James Thompson is former military. His son-in-law served in Afghanistan. This isn't the soft target these boys think it is!"

Grace spun toward the cage, her performance finally cracking under the pressure of continued contradictions to her narrative. "ENOUGH!"

The word exploded from her with shocking violence, causing everyone in the camp to freeze. Her followers had seen her angry before, but this was different, more focused, more dangerous.

"I am so tired," she said, her voice dropping to a whisper that somehow carried more menace than shouting, "of negative energy disrupting our content creation process."

She walked slowly toward the cage; her phone still held like she was broadcasting live. "You know what, everyone? I think it's time for some exclusive premium content. The kind of authentic community management demonstration that really shows what effective leadership looks like."

"Grace," Rebecca said carefully, "maybe we should focus on planning our next moves instead of—"

"Rebecca, sweetie," Grace interrupted without looking away from Frank, "this is exactly what our followers want to see. Real consequences for real problems. Authentic accountability in action."

She raised her phone, angling it to capture both herself and the cage. "Today we're going to demonstrate what happens when someone consistently undermines community morale and strategic planning. This is advanced leadership content, so make sure you're subscribed for notifications!"

Frank pressed himself against the far side of the cage, suddenly understanding that his situation had moved beyond humiliation into genuine danger. Around the camp, followers began backing away as Grace's inner circle moved into position.

"You see," Grace continued in her bright performer's voice,

"building a successful community requires hard choices. Sometimes you have to remove toxic influences for the good of the whole group. It's just like content moderation, but in real life!"

She pulled her sidearm, the metal gleaming in the morning light. Frank's eyes widened as he realized she wasn't just performing anymore—she was creating what she considered premium content, and he was the featured guest.

"Grace, no," Rebecca said, taking a step forward. "This isn't—"

"Necessary," Grace finished for her. "I know it seems harsh, but our followers understand that real leadership requires real action. This is exactly the kind of authentic content that builds serious engagement!"

The Burke brothers watched with fascination and growing unease. They'd seen plenty of violence, but Grace's performance made it feel like they were watching a movie rather than witnessing real events.

"Wait," Sean said suddenly, something in Grace's manic energy making him nervous. "Maybe we should talk about this. He's got intel about the area, right? Might be worth keeping him around for information."

Grace turned to him, her smile brightening. "Oh, that's such a thoughtful perspective! Very strategic thinking! But you see, the problem with keeping negative influences around is that they contaminate the whole community dynamic."

She gestured to her followers, many of whom were now openly staring at the ground or backing toward the tree line. "Look how his toxic energy is affecting our whole group! Everyone's so uncomfortable, the mood is completely ruined. That's what negativity does—it destroys authentic community engagement."

Frank found his voice. "Grace, please. I have information

about other communities, supply caches, safe routes. I'm valuable alive."

"Alive, yes," Grace agreed cheerfully, "but not here. You've proven you can't integrate with our community values. So we're going to give you a beautiful send-off! Very cinematic, very authentic. Our followers are going to be talking about this content for weeks!"

"Grace," Rebecca said carefully, "what if we did something even more engaging? Like a trial format? Let the community decide? That would be incredible interactive content."

Grace paused, considering this. "Ooh, that's actually brilliant! Community participation, real democracy in action! Very authentic grassroots engagement!"

She turned back to her phone, excitement building up again. "Change of plans, everyone! We're going to do live community voting! Interactive content at its finest!"

Frank sagged with relief, but Rebecca caught his eye and shook her head slightly. Grace's attention span for "interactive content" was measured in minutes. This was just delaying the inevitable unless they could find another solution.

"Sean, Tommy," Grace called out, her voice bright with new inspiration, "you're going to be our expert witnesses! Tell our community about the strategic value of negative influences versus positive team building!"

The Burke brothers exchanged glances, realizing they'd somehow become participants in Grace's insane performance rather than outside observers.

"Well," Sean said slowly, "in our experience, discipline is important for group cohesion..." he said slowly while bobbing his head as though trying to convince them.

"Exactly!" Grace clapped her hands. "Expert testimony! This is going to be amazing content!"

But even as she spoke, her eyes kept drifting back to Frank in the cage, carrying violent hunger building beneath her performer's enthusiasm. The trial format was just another layer of entertainment before the inevitable conclusion.

Grace's madness had finally escalated beyond what the group could tolerate, but the woman still commanded enough fear and firepower to maintain control.

For now.

The morning sun climbed higher, burning off the mist that clung to the flooded landscape, while Grace continued her performance for an audience that existed only in her fractured mind. But Rebecca Mitchell, the broken woman who was learning to be something else entirely, watched and waited and planned.

The Queen of Likes had finally gone too far.

Ethan

The barn loft reeked of dust and mouse droppings, mixed with the green scent of hay that had been drying since before the world ended. Ethan, Grayson and Jake, in their secret hideout spying on the adults as they liked to do, peered through knotholes and watched the entry. Teen boys pretending to be spies now found themselves in real and adult situations. Below, morning shadows stretched across the farmyard where they saw adults moving with the purposeful urgency of people preparing for war.

"Anything new?" Grayson whispered, shifting on the hay bale beside him. The old straw crackled under his weight, releasing that sweet, dusty smell that reminded Ethan of summers when the biggest worry had been whether they'd get to the swimming hole before it got too crowded.

"Dad's talking to that Doug Martinez guy about positions," Ethan murmured back. "Looks serious."

Jake crawled over from his position near the ladder. "They're setting up another checkpoint down by the old stone wall. Saw them carrying sandbags."

The three boys had claimed the loft as their unofficial headquarters, stringing up a tarp between the rafters to create a hidden space where they could watch, plan, and process the increasingly adult responsibilities thrust upon them. Red threads still circled their wrists, though the fabric had faded and frayed from wear.

Ethan shifted his weight, and something poked into his ribs. The handle of the knife his grandfather had given him. The blade stayed sharp, kept clean, ready for use he hoped would never come. The weight of it had become familiar, a constant reminder that childhood had ended the moment he'd pulled that trigger in the garden.

"Movement by the house," Grayson whispered, pointing through his own spy hole. "Elena's coming out with Zoe."

Through the weathered boards, Ethan could see Elena making her way across the yard. Zoe walked beside her, the teenager who'd escaped and quickly proven herself helpful around the farm. They headed toward the small shed behind the main house, probably looking for privacy to talk.

"Think we should listen?" Jake asked, his voice carrying that edge of mischief that had gotten them in trouble countless times before the collapse.

"Elena's been through enough," Ethan replied, but even as he said it, his curiosity prickled. Something about Elena's behavior had been bothering him for days—the way she yelled at Uncle Matt and watched him and Maddie when she thought no one was looking, the calculating expressions that flashed across her face when she thought herself unobserved, all annoyed him. Uncle Matt used to be the fun one till she came along.

"They're going into the toolshed," Grayson reported. "The one with the broken window."

The shed sat maybe two feet from the barn, close enough that voices might carry if the wind was right. Ethan felt the moral weight of the decision—eavesdropping was wrong, an invasion of privacy. But in a world where information could mean the difference between life and death, where Frank had already proven that enemies can hide among friends, maybe wrong was a luxury they couldn't afford.

"Just for a minute," he decided. "If it's private stuff, we leave them alone."

They crept to the edge of the loft and down the ladder into the last paddock, where a loose board provided a direct sight line to the shed and clear sound between the broken window and where they listened. The morning air carried the smell of cooking bacon from the main house, mixed with the sharper scents of wood fires and diesel fuel. Through the shed's broken window, they saw Elena settling onto the workbench while Zoe perched on a wooden crate.

"…so tired of pretending," Elena's voice drifted across the space between buildings, carried by a breeze that also brought the distant sound of hammering. "Everyone treating me like some kind of tyrant for asking Matt to stand by me right now."

Zoe's response was too quiet to hear, but Elena's laugh carried clearly bitter and sharp-edged.

"Oh, poor Elena," she continued, her voice taking on a mocking tone. "Lost her baby, needs everyone to tiptoe around her feelings. If they only knew."

Ethan felt his stomach clench. The boys exchanged worried glances, each recognizing that they'd stumbled onto something that felt dangerous.

"Knew what?" Zoe asked, her voice just loud enough to catch.

Elena was quiet for a long moment, and when she spoke again, her words carried a confession that would shatter lives.

"The baby wasn't Matthew's." She let out a loud, annoyed sigh.

The simple statement hit Ethan with a pain in his stomach like he might vomit. Beside him, Jake's sharp intake of breath was audible, and Grayson's face went pale as the implications sank in.

"When Matthew and I were having problems, and we were having serious problems truth be told. Before all this chaos started; I was sleeping with his best friend Jason. Jason Brennan, from town." Elena's voice held no shame, only a kind of cold satisfaction. "Matthew was talking about the break being permanent. Said he needed space, needed to figure things out. I didn't get pregnant on purpose, but when the test came back positive, I knew it wasn't his but thought it might… You know, help things."

"You used the pregnancy to get him back?" Zoe asked. Shock in her tone that was hard for her to hide.

"Jason was fun, but he was going nowhere. Dead-end job, lived with his parents, spending his weekends getting drunk at Murphy's. Matthew had the farm, the family money, the future." Elena shrugged, a gesture they saw through the broken window. "When I found out I was pregnant, the choice was obvious. I told Matthew it was his, that I didn't know about it before we broke up. It had only been six weeks. Could have easily been his. If I hadn't had my friend in the middle of it anyone could assume it."

Ethan's hands clenched into fists, his nails digging into his palms. His uncle Matt, his role model, the man who'd taught him to drive the tractor and showed him the best fishing spots, had been manipulated, lied to, trapped.

"But you lost the baby," Zoe said carefully.

"I knew there were problems," Elena replied with chilling matter-of-factness. "The last ultrasound before everything went dark showed major developmental issues. The doctor said I caught something from Jason and the sack was weakened but there were chromal something issues. He gave me antibiotics."

"Did you tell him about what you caught?"

"I couldn't do that, he would know," Elena said with a gasp.

"I don't understand he needs antibiotics too," Zoe said. She was growing impatient with Elena, and it came through in her tone.

"Nahh, I just said I was sick and waited till the medicine was gone." She giggled at her own smarts, tapping her head with her index finger to note how smart she was.

"You could have just said there were problems and moved on. He came back, right?"

"But Matthew was being so attentive, so caring after I told him about the pregnancy. His whole family was excited about it. Why would I ruin that by telling them it was doomed?"

"But didn't Emily notice issues when she checked you? I overheard them talking about it. She heard a heartbeat when you got here."

"Yeah, but I'd been to the doctor the day before and he said the rupture had begun and gave me some pills and stuff. He said it could take a week or so."

Jake's face went white with fury. Ethan saw him struggling to remain silent, his whole body tense with the effort of not charging down to the shed to confront Elena directly.

"So, you've been lying this whole time?" Zoe's voice held a note of horror.

"I've been managing a difficult situation," Elena corrected. "Matthew was already pulling away from me and we were on a break before I told him about the pregnancy. When I actually lost the baby during all that chaos with the attack, I could have told him the truth then. But his guilt about not protecting me better, his family's support, the way everyone rallied around the 'tragic girlfriend who lost her baby'—why would I give that up?"

"But now that people know you lost it…"

"Now I get to be the grieving mother who needs Matthew's

devotion to heal." Elena's smile was visible through the window, cold and calculating. "And if that starts to wear thin, well, there are other options. Did you see how Matthew looked at Maddie during their little windmill project? All I have to do is make enough noise about their 'inappropriate' friendship, and his guilt will keep him right where I want him."

Ethan felt sick. This woman—this person his uncle cared about—was systematically destroying Matthew's life, manipulating his decency and sense of responsibility to serve her own ends.

"What about Jason?" Zoe asked.

"What about him?" Elena laughed again. "For all I know, he's dead in some ditch. Half the town scattered when things got bad. Besides, he served his purpose."

"His purpose?"

"He was fun for a romp. What was I supposed to do? Tell Matt his best friend had been hitting on me the whole time."

The boys sat in stunned silence, processing the full scope of Elena's manipulation. She hadn't just lied about the pregnancy. She'd been seeing his best friend.

"You don't feel bad about any of this?" Zoe's voice carried disbelief.

"Feel bad about securing my future? About making sure I wasn't left alone when the world fell apart?" Elena stood up, brushing dust from her clothes. "Zoe, honey, you're young. You still think fairness matters. But survival means taking what you need, when you need it. Matthew's a good man; decent, responsible, loyal. Exactly the kind of man a woman needs when civilization collapses."

"But you don't love him."

"What is love? Matt's kinda hot and he takes care of me. I get lots of attention and once things settle down I could probably have my pick if he ends up wanting a break again." Elena moved toward the shed door. "What I need is security, protection, a place in a family that can survive what's coming. Matthew provides all of that. Whether I love him or not is irrelevant."

They watched Elena leave the shed, heading back toward the main house with the casual air. As though she'd just discussed the weather rather than destroying a man's life. Zoe remained behind, sitting on her crate with her head in her hands.

The boys hurried back up to the loft long after Elena disappeared, each processing what they'd heard. The morning sounds continued around them but felt less important at the moment. Adults preparing defenses, children playing between the sandbag walls, the normal rhythm of a community under threat. But everything felt different now, tainted by the knowledge of Elena's calculated cruelty.

"We have to tell someone," Grayson whispered finally.

"Tell them what?" Jake's voice was tight with anger. "That we were spying on private conversations?"

"That Uncle Matthew is being manipulated by a psychopath," Ethan replied, his own voice shaking. "That everything he's been feeling guilty about is based on lies."

"But we can't prove any of it," Jake pointed out. "It's her word against ours. And we weren't supposed to be listening."

Ethan stared out through the knothole, watching his uncle emerge from the house and taking a wide arc to avoid Maddie on his way to help with the defensive preparations. Matthew's shoulders slumped, as though he carried grief and guilt upon them. His movements careful and deliberate like a man afraid of making another mistake. Meanwhile, Elena watched him from the porch, her expression satisfied.

"He deserves to know," Ethan said quietly.

"Maybe," Grayson agreed. "But deserving and surviving aren't the same thing anymore. If we tell him now, while we're preparing for an attack, it could destroy his focus. Get him killed."

The terrible logic of their new world settled over them like a blanket. In the before times, this kind of revelation would have demanded immediate action—confrontation, explanation, the messy business of sorting out truth and consequences. But with enemies approaching and the community's survival hanging in the balance, even truth became a tactical consideration.

"After," Jake said finally. "After we deal with this Queen person and her army. Then we figure out how to tell your uncle Matthew what we heard."

Ethan nodded reluctantly, filing the knowledge away like ammunition to be used when the time was right. They'd learned to carry burdens beyond their years, and this was just another weight to add to the load.

A distant crack echoed across the farmyard, startling them. A gunshot, far enough away to be someone else's problem but close enough to remind them that danger lurked beyond their defensive perimeter.

"Scout patrol I bet," Grayson said. "Your dad said they'd be pushing closer today."

"Want to go take a look?" Ethan asked, grateful for the distraction from Elena's revelation.

They gathered their equipment—binoculars, notebooks, the small two-way radio that connected them to the main command post. Their movement through the loft had become routine, each boy knowing exactly where to step to avoid the creaky boards that might give away their position.

They emerged into the main barn where the smell of motor oil mixed with hay dust were more of a comfort than anything. Daniel looked up from the workbench at the far end where he was assembling ammunition.

"Heading out again?" he asked, his voice carrying both

pride and worry.

"Just a quick look around the perimeter," Ethan replied. "Check if those shots meant anything."

Daniel nodded, understanding the need for current intelligence. "Radio check every thirty minutes. And boys..." He paused, making eye contact with each of them. "No heroes. If you see anything that looks like trouble, you call it in and get back here. Clear?"

"Clear," they chorused, though Ethan caught the look that passed between Jake and Grayson. They'd all learned that sometimes 'no heroes were easier said than done.

The farm's defensive perimeter had grown since those men attacked in the garden, extending beyond the original property lines to include strategic high ground and clear sight lines. The boys moved through it with practiced efficiency, using cover and concealment techniques that had become second nature.

The forest beyond the farm smelled of pine needles and damp earth, with undertones of decay from vegetation killed by the unusual weather patterns. They followed game trails that had become their preferred routes, paths that offered good visibility while keeping them hidden from casual observation.

"There," Jake whispered, pointing through a gap in the trees.

Two figures moved through the woods maybe two hundred yards away, picking their way carefully through the underbrush. They wore mismatched military gear and carried weapons with the casual competence of people accustomed to violence. Scouts from The Queen's force, probing the farm's defenses.

Ethan raised his binoculars, studying their equipment and movement patterns. The men looked tired, hungry, operating with the desperate efficiency of people who knew their survival depended on finding easier targets than the Thompson farm was proving to be.

"They're mapping approaches," Grayson said quietly. "Look how they're checking sight lines from that ridge."

The scouts moved with purpose, one covering while the other advanced, communicating through hand signals. Professional enough to be dangerous, but not so professional that they'd spotted three teenagers watching them from concealment.

"We should report this," Jake whispered, reaching for the radio.

But as he keyed the handset, one of the scouts stopped, head tilted in a listening posture. The radio's static had carried farther than expected in the still morning air.

"Shit," Ethan breathed, watching the scouts change direction, moving toward their position with predatory focus.

"Move," Jake hissed, shoving the radio back into his pack.

They retreated deeper into the woods, using techniques learned through cat-and-mouse games with patrols and scouting parties. But these men were good, experienced enough to track them despite their precautions.

"Split up," Ethan decided quickly. "Meet at the fallen oak. If anyone gets cornered, make noise—draw them away from the farm."

They scattered, each taking a different route through the familiar woods. Ethan could hear the scouts behind them, their movements growing more confident as they closed the distance. His heart hammered against his ribs, pumping adrenaline that made every sense hyperacute.

A branch snapped to his left—too close. Ethan dropped behind a moss-covered log, pressing himself against the damp earth that smelled of mushrooms and decay. Through the undergrowth, he saw one of the scouts moving carefully between the trees, weapon at the ready.

The man's face was scarred, probably from some post-collapse conflict, and his eyes held the flat alertness of a predator. He moved past Ethan's hiding spot, then stopped, something catching his attention.

Jake's scream cut through the forest.

Ethan's blood turned to ice as he recognized the sound—not pain, but fear. Jake was in trouble, and the sound was coming from the direction of the fallen oak where they'd planned to meet.

The scarred scout spun toward the noise, abandoning his careful search in favor of speed. Ethan followed, staying low, using every piece of cover the forest offered. Jake's voice echoed again, angry now rather than afraid.

"Let go of me!"

Ethan reached the clearing where the massive oak had fallen during a storm years before. Jake struggled in the grip of the second scout, a younger man with nervous eyes and twitchy movements. The man held Jake like a shield, one arm around his throat, the other pressing a pistol to his head.

"I know you're out there!" the scout called out. "Come out now, or your friend gets a bullet!"

The scarred man emerged from the trees, weapon raised, scanning for targets. "Just kids," he said dismissively. "Probably playing soldier."

"Kids with radios," the younger man replied. "They've been watching us, reporting our positions. That's why the farm's been so ready for us."

Ethan's mind raced through options. Jake was in immediate danger, the scouts had valuable intelligence about their surveillance network, and any shot would bring the entire farm's defense force running. Possibly into an ambush.

But Jake was his brother in all the ways that mattered, and

brothers didn't abandon each other.

"Two of us left," the scarred scout said, moving into position. "Call out, or we start cutting pieces off this one until you do."

The casual cruelty in his voice decided it. These weren't soldiers following orders or desperate people making hard choices. These were predators who'd found prey, and they would torture Jake for the entertainment value alone.

Ethan moved with all the stealth he could find, circling around to get behind the scarred scout. His grandfather's knife felt heavy in his hand, the blade that had stayed sharp through finally about to serve its purpose.

The man's attention focused forward, searching for movement from Jake's hidden friends. Ethan stepped carefully, avoiding twigs and dry leaves, closing the distance one silent foot at a time.

Five feet. Three feet. Close enough to smell the man's unwashed clothes and the oil from his weapon.

Ethan struck without hesitation, driving the blade up under the man's ribs, angling toward the heart. The scout stiffened, weapon falling from nerveless fingers, and turned to look at his killer with surprise rather than anger.

"Just a kid," he whispered, blood foaming at his lips.

"Not anymore," Ethan replied, and meant it.

The younger scout spun toward the sound, his grip on Jake loosening with shock. "Tommy? Tommy, what—"

Jake broke free, throwing himself sideways as Grayson erupted from concealment on the opposite side of the clearing. The scout tried to track multiple targets, his nervousness becoming panic as he realized his partner was down and he was surrounded.

"Drop the weapon!" Grayson shouted, though his voice

cracked with the strain.

"Stay back!" The scout's pistol wavered between targets. "I'll kill all of you little bastards!"

Jake rolled behind the fallen oak's massive trunk, coming up with a rock in his hand. Without hesitation, he hurled it at the scout's head, striking the man in the temple with a solid crack that dropped him like a stone.

Silence settled over the clearing, broken only by their ragged breathing and the distant sounds of the forest. Two men lay dead or unconscious, killed by teenagers who'd learned that survival meant crossing lines they'd never imagined approaching.

"Holy shit," Grayson breathed, staring at the bodies. "We actually…"

"Yeah," Jake said quietly, rubbing his throat where bruises were already forming. "We did."

Ethan cleaned his grandfather's blade on the dead scout's shirt, the blood coming away easier than expected. The man who'd called him 'just a kid' stared at nothing, his scarred face peaceful in death.

"Are you okay?" he asked Jake, noting the way his friend's hands shook.

"I will be," Jake replied, though his voice carried a hollowness that hadn't been there an hour before. "He was going to torture me. Make me scream to draw you guys out."

"But he didn't," Grayson pointed out, kneeling to check the unconscious scout's pulse. "We stopped him."

"We killed him," Ethan corrected. "Let's not pretend it was something else."

They stood around the bodies, three boys who'd crossed the line between childhood and something harder, more necessary. The red threads around their wrists caught the filtered sunlight, symbols of brotherhood that now also represented the shared violence.

"The radio," Jake said suddenly, remembering their mission. "We need to report what we found."

Ethan keyed the handset, speaking in the calm, professional tone they'd practiced with each other. "Command, this is Scout Team One. We ran into some scouts out on the north ridge."

His grandfather's voice crackled back: "Ethan? Ethan, are you boys alright?"

"Yeah, Grandpa but they jumped us and we had to… Well, we need some help out here. Can someone come?"

"What happened? Are you in danger?"

"Not anymore, but— Just come?"

After the communications ended the three of them stood staring at the two men. "We should search them," Grayson suggested, "Look for maps, radio frequencies, anything that might help."

They went through the scouts' equipment, finding ammunition, rations, and a hand-drawn map showing the farm's defensive positions. The intelligence was valuable, but it also confirmed what they'd feared. There were scouts that had been watching them for days, learning their patterns and weaknesses.

"Look at this," Jake said, holding up a piece of paper covered in cramped handwriting. "It's like a report. 'Thompson farm heavily defended, multiple fighting positions, estimated thirty to forty combatants.'"

"At least they're taking us seriously," Ethan said with a bit of a smile.

"Maybe too seriously," Grayson said, his voice pitched high with worry. "If they think we're that strong, they might bring more people. Or try different tactics."

They walked back toward the farm in silence, each

processing what they'd experienced. The forest around them looked the same—green leaves filtering sunlight, the smell of pine and earth, the rustle of small animals in the underbrush. But they'd changed, crossed a threshold that left them fundamentally different than the boys who'd climbed into the loft that morning.

"We can't tell them about Elena," Grayson said suddenly. "Not now. Not after this."

Ethan nodded, understanding. They'd gained valuable intelligence and neutralized an immediate threat, but they'd also learned that carrying the understanding and consequence of that necessary violence was heavier than any of them could have imagined. Adding the burden of Elena's revelation to Matthew's current stress could break him when the family needed him most.

"After the battle," he agreed. "When we've got time to deal with the consequences."

Jake said nothing, walking slightly apart from his friends. He'd killed to protect them, accepted the psychological burden of ending a life to preserve the lives he valued. The red thread around his wrist had become something more than a symbol of brotherhood, it was a reminder of the prices they were all willing to pay.

They emerged from the forest to find the farm in controlled chaos. Their radio report had triggered defensive preparations, adults taking positions and children being moved to secure areas. Daniel and two other men stopped on their way to meet them in the woods.

"You boys okay?"

"Yeah," Ethan said, "you'll find them out by the fallen oak."

"Are they secure?"

Jake looked up from the ground where he'd been kicking at

a dirt clod. "They're dead," he said matter of factly.

"Did you?" Daniel didn't finish.

"They attacked us," Grayson replied. "We defended ourselves."

"None of you were hurt?"

"We're good. We gathered some information from them. We were taking it to Grandpa."

"Good work," Daniel said, gripping Ethan's shoulder. "Your mother wants to see you. All of you get on back to the farm

In the distance, smoke rose from the direction of Cornish proper. The attack was moving closer, and the real battle was still to come.

The intelligence from Ethan's reconnaissance lay spread across the kitchen table like pieces of a deadly puzzle. James Thompson studied the hand-drawn maps and intercepted radio frequencies while the farmhouse buzzed with controlled urgency around him. Smoke from Cornish proper still rose in the distance, a dark smudge against the afternoon sky that reminded everyone how close the danger had crept.

"thirty or forty people, maybe more, but a third unwilling," Beth Martin said, tracing her finger along the enemy's suspected approach route. "That's actionable if we can find a way to exploit it."

Daniel looked up from where he was cleaning weapons. "The boys did good work. Real good intelligence gathering."

"They did," James agreed, though the cost of that professionalism weighed heavy on his mind. He'd watched Ethan deliver his briefing with the detached efficiency of a seasoned soldier, Jake still pale from his first kill, Grayson supporting his friends through trauma that should never touch children their age.

"Radio frequencies are our biggest advantage," Old Man Jenkins added from his position by the ham radio setup. "If I can tap into their communications, we might get advance warning on their tactics."

Sarah emerged from the storm cellar where she'd been

organizing emergency supplies, her face drawn with exhaustion. "Medical station's ready. Emily's got the dining room set up for triage, and we've moved all non-combatants to the cellar."

"What about Elena?" James asked, noting Matthew's absence from the planning session.

"With the others," Sarah replied carefully. "She's... uh, struggling with everything that's happened."

James nodded, filing away another concern for later. Elena's behavior had grown increasingly erratic since her arrival and subsequent issues, and Matthew seemed torn between supporting her and contributing to the community's defense. Something was off to James with the two of them but he couldn't quite place it. He understood her needy nature with everything that was happening but there was more to it.

"Perimeter's as ready as we can make it," Michael reported. Startling James when he entered through the back door with mud caked to his boots. "Doug Martinez has the east approach covered, and we've got overlapping fields of fire from here to the main road."

Beth spread her own map beside the intercepted intelligence. "If they come straight up Route 25, they'll hit our first checkpoint here." She tapped a position near the flooded bridge. "Fallen trees will force them to dismount and approach on foot through the kill zone."

"And if they try to flank?" Daniel asked.

"Terrain works against them," Michael replied, his head swaying side to side. "Flooding's made the low ground impassable, and the high ground puts them in the open. Either way, they'll have to come at us where we're strongest."

The radio crackled, Jenkins adjusting frequencies to clear it up. "Getting chatter from their forward elements. Sounds like they're setting up about two miles out, waiting for the main force."

At this point, every decision rippled outward, affecting lives he'd sworn to protect. The farm had become more than a refuge. It was the heart of a community that refused to surrender to chaos.

"Timeline?" he asked.

"Best guess, they'll move at first light," Beth replied. "Attack with the sun at their backs, try to overwhelm us before we can coordinate a proper defense."

A distant rumble drew everyone's attention to the windows. James felt his hand move instinctively to his sidearm as the sound grew louder, the distinctive growl of diesel engines approaching fast.

"Vehicles," Michael said, moving to the window. "Multiple contacts, coming up the main road."

The farmyard erupted into controlled chaos as defenders took positions, weapons trained on the approaching convoy. Through the glass, James saw three vehicles climbing the hill—a box truck and a blue Ford pickup pulling a large flatbed trailer loaded with what looked like supplies.

"Wait," Beth called out, lowering her rifle. "That's Pete's truck. I'd recognize that piece of junk anywhere."

Sure enough, Pete Morrison climbed down from the cab of the lead vehicle, his weathered face split by a grin that looked out of place in their grim circumstances. Behind him, Mike Grover and his son Tommy emerged from behind both men moving with the easy confidence of people bringing good news.

"How the hell?" Daniel breathed, staring at the functional vehicles. "We haven't been able to get anything running."

Pete approached the porch, his grin widening as he took in their defensive preparations. "Found parts in a metal shed out behind the Moss place. Walls thick enough to shield the electronics from that electromagnetic pulse. Took some work, but we got 'em running."

James felt a surge of hope mixed with cautious relief. Functional vehicles meant mobility, supply runs, the possibility of evacuating wounded or non-combatants if the battle went badly.

"What's the cargo?" he asked, gesturing toward the loaded trailer.

"Everything," Mike Grover replied, his voice carrying satisfaction. "Feed store was a total loss from the flooding, but we emptied it before the water got too high. Tommy here had the idea to hit every one of the stores in the plaza for anything left."

Tommy Grover, barely eighteen but carrying himself with new confidence, started listing their haul. "Medical supplies from the veterinary clinic and whatever we could scavenge from the pharmacy, ammunition from Paulson's gun shop, enough canned goods to feed fifty people for a month. Even got some solar panels and batteries from that new-age couple's place near the lake."

Sarah's face lit up for the first time in days. "Medical supplies? Real medical supplies?"

"Antibiotics, surgical equipment, enough pain medication to stock a small hospital," Pete confirmed. "That veterinary clinic was a goldmine. Turns out animal medicine works just fine for humans when push comes to shove."

Emily appeared from the house, medical bag in hand, drawn by the commotion. When she saw the supplies being unloaded, her expression transformed from weary resignation to something approaching joy.

"Pete Morrison, you beautiful bastard," she breathed, hurrying toward the trailer. "Do you have any idea what this means?"

"Means we can patch up anyone who needs patching," Pete replied, but his attention had shifted to Beth, who stood in the gathering crowd.

The change in Beth was immediate and dramatic. Her professional composure cracked, revealing something raw and vulnerable underneath. Without warning, she launched herself at Pete, arms wrapping around his neck as she kissed him with desperate intensity.

The farmyard fell silent except for the idle rumble of diesel engines and the distant sound of children playing near the storm cellar. Pete's arms encircled Beth's waist, lifting her off the ground as the kiss deepened, two people who'd been dancing around their feelings finally surrendering to the moment.

"Well," Daniel said quietly, a grin tugging at his lips. "That's one way to say thank you."

"About damn time," Sarah added. Her tone held the satisfaction of having been watching their tentative courtship for months.

When they finally broke apart, Beth's cheeks blazed red, but her smile held no regret. "I've been wanting to do that since before the world ended."

"Should've done it sooner," Pete replied, his weathered hands gentle as they framed her face. "Might not have waited so long to come courting with supplies."

The moment of levity felt precious in their grim circumstances, a reminder that hope and human connection could survive even the darkest times. The community absorbed this small victory, shoulders straightened, and smiles appeared on faces that had carried too much weight for too long.

"Alright, enough romance," James said with mock sternness. "Let's get this gear distributed and stowed away before our uninvited guests arrive for dinner. Let's tuck these vehicles out behind the house. Keep 'em ready to roll out the other side of the driveway in case we need to evacuate in a hurry."

The next hour transformed the farm's defensive capabilities. Medical supplies bolstered Emily's makeshift hospital, ammunition was distributed to fighting positions, and the solar panels offered the possibility of limited electrical power for the first time since the electromagnetic pulse.

But it was the vehicles that changed everything. Functional transportation meant the community wasn't trapped, weren't sitting ducks waiting for slaughter. If the battle went badly, they could evacuate civilians, relocate supplies, maintain the community's survival even if they lost the farm.

"Pete," James said as they finished unloading the last of the medical equipment, "I can't tell you what this means. You've given us more than supplies. You've given us options."

"Just returning the favor," Pete replied, wiping grease from his hands. "Your family took me in when I had nowhere else to go when I first came here. Time I started paying that debt."

Beth approached, her earlier embarrassment replaced by professional focus. "Can you get the other vehicles running? The ones that have been sitting since the pulse?"

"Some of them, maybe," Pete replied thoughtfully. "Depends on how much shielding they had, how sophisticated their electronics were what parts can be interchangeable. Give me a few days and the right parts, I might be able to jury-rig something."

"We might not have a few days," Michael pointed out, glancing toward the smoke still rising from Cornish.

Jenkins looked up from his radio equipment, headphones pressed against his ears. "Enemy chatter's picking up. Sounds like they're coordinating for a dawn assault. Multiple approach routes, diversionary tactics."

The brief moment of celebration faded as reality reasserted itself. They had better supplies, functional vehicles, and a defensible position, but their forces still outnumbered them and carried the momentum of desperate violence.

"Positions," James ordered, slipping back into command mode. "Everyone knows their assignments. Final equipment checks, then get some rest if you can. Tomorrow's going to test everything we've built here."

As the adults dispersed to their various preparations, James found himself standing alone in the farmyard, watching the sun sink toward the western horizon.

A hand touched his shoulder. Sarah stood beside him, her expression carrying the same mix of hope and dread that filled his own chest.

"Think it'll be enough?" she asked quietly.

"It has to be," James replied, though the words carried more determination than confidence.

Matthew

The first gunshot cracked across the dawn air like the world breaking in half. Matthew Thompson dove behind the defensive barrier they'd constructed in the driveway, his heart hammering against his ribs as dirt exploded where his head had been a second before. Scattered rifle fire erupted from the tree line. Probing shots. Probably from advance scouts testing their defenses and searching for weak points.

"Matthew!" Elena's voice rose above the sporadic gunfire, shrill with panic. "Matthew, where are you?"

He spotted her fifty yards away, standing in the open farmyard like a target painted in bright colors. She spun in circles, arms waving frantically, making herself visible to every shooter in the woods.

"Get down!" he roared, breaking cover to sprint toward her. A bullet whined past his ear, close enough to feel the displaced air. His boots pounded against hard-packed earth as he ran, expecting the crack of another shot with each step.

Elena saw him coming and ran toward him instead of seeking cover, her face twisted with relief and something else that made his stomach clench, preparing for her next verbal assault.

"I knew you'd come for me," she gasped, throwing her arms around his neck just as he tackled her behind a stone retaining wall. "I knew you wouldn't abandon me like everyone else."

Matthew pressed himself against the mortared stones, hearing the occasional impact of bullets whizzing off the stones, testing their cover. Chips of granite scattered as the wall absorbed random shots from the probing force.

"What the hell are you doing out here?" He had to raise his voice over the intermittent gunfire. "You're supposed to be in the storm cellar with the others!"

"I couldn't find you!" Elena's fingernails dug into his shoulders, her grip desperate and possessive. "Everyone was running and shouting orders, and I didn't know where you were. I was scared they'd hurt you!"

A single shot rang out from somewhere near the barn, one of their own defenders returning fire. Matthew felt the familiar weight of responsibility settled on his chest. Elena, creating chaos during critical moments, pulling him away from where the community needed him most was getting to be problematic.

"You have to get to the cellar," he said firmly, trying to untangle her arms from around his neck. "It's not safe here."

"I'm not leaving you." Her voice carried that dangerous edge he'd learned to recognize, the tone that preceded an outburst and emotional blackmail. "Not when there are people trying to kill us. We stay together."

Another scattered volley from the woods made them both duck lower. Matthew saw Daniel and Michael coordinating defensive positions near the house, their movements professional and purposeful. His family needed every able body preparing for what was coming, but Elena's presence turned him from defender into babysitter.

"Elena, listen to me—"

"No!" She pulled back to look at him, tears streaming down her face. "I won't be shoved aside like I don't matter. Like losing our baby means I'm disposable now. You're all I have left, Matthew. If something happens to you…"

The familiar guilt settled over him like a lead blanket. She was grieving, traumatized, clinging to the only stability she had left in a world gone mad. But then he thought about yesterday— how she'd demanded he stop working with Maddie on essential defensive preparations, how her jealousy had forced him to abandon critical community work when lives depended on their readiness.

"Uncle Matt!" Ethan's voice cut through the scattered gunfire, urgent and strained. "Uncle Matt, we need to talk to you!"

Matthew turned to see his nephew approaching in a low crouch, Jake and Grayson flanking him. All three boys carried weapons and moved with grim competence that belonged on adult faces.

"Get back to the cellar!" Matthew shouted. "All of you!"

"We can't!" Jake replied, sliding into cover beside them. "There's something you need to know. About Elena. About everything."

Elena's grip on Matthew's arm tightened, her fingernails drawing blood through his shirt sleeve. "I don't want to hear anything from them. They're just children playing at being soldiers."

"They're not playing," Matthew said quietly, seeing the weight in Ethan's eyes, the hollow look that came from crossing lines that couldn't be uncrossed. "What is it?"

Ethan glanced at Elena, then back at Matthew. His young face carried a burden he couldn't contain, the kind of knowledge that aged people before their time. "We overheard something. Yesterday morning. In the toolshed."

"Whatever they think they heard—" Elena began, but Grayson cut her off.

"We heard you talking to Zoe about the baby," he said, his voice dripping with disdain but steady despite the chaos around them. "About Jason Brennan," he said raising an eyebrow and pursing his lips.

"Whatever are you talking about?" Elena spat before spinning Matthew back toward her.

"What? What about Jason?" Matthew asked glancing from the boys to Elena.

"Nothing my love. Just jokes about how funny he was and fun to be around."

"Bullshit," Ethan shouted. "Quit lying."

"I don't know what you're talking about, that was all it was about."

"Really?" Ethan sneered at her. "About how you knew the baby wasn't Uncle Matthew's."

Ethan's accusation slammed into his mind. The scattered gunfire faded to background noise as his world narrowed to Elena's face, watching emotions flicker across her features—surprise, anger, and then something cold and calculating.

"I don't know what you think you heard," she said carefully, "but children often misunderstand adult conversations. Especially when they're eavesdropping on private moments."

"We understood perfectly," Jake said, his voice carrying an edge that made him sound older than his years. "You said you were sleeping with Jason when you and Uncle Matthew were broken up. You said the baby was his, not Matthew's. You said you used the baby to get Matthew back because he had money and a future."

"You said, Jason was fun, but Matthew was more stable," Grayson added.

Elena's mask cracked, revealing something ugly

underneath. She turned on the boys with sudden viciousness, her voice dropping to a hiss. "You little bastards. You've been spying on me, haven't you? Sneaking around, listening to private conversations like the pathetic little children you are."

"Elena—" Matthew started, but she wasn't finished.

"Don't you dare take their word over mine!" she snarled at the boys. "You think you know everything, but you're just kids playing dress-up with guns. You don't understand what adults have to do to survive, what sacrifices we make to keep communities like this together."

Jake's face flushed with anger. "We understand plenty. We understand you've been lying to Uncle Matthew for months, making him feel guilty for things that weren't his fault."

"Shut up!" Elena's voice rose to a shriek. "Just shut up, you interfering little brats! This is between Matthew and me, not some children who think they're soldiers!"

Matthew felt something crack inside his chest, a sound like ice breaking on a frozen pond. The guilt he'd carried for weeks. Guilt for not protecting Elena better, for feeling a small measure of relief when she lost the baby because of how hard it would be in this mess, for resenting the time her demands had stolen from essential community work, all of it was built on lies.

"Matthew," Elena said quickly, spinning back to him with desperation replacing her rage, "you can't believe them. They're just trying to cause trouble. After everything we've been through together, after losing our child—"

"It wasn't our child though, was it?" The words came out flat, emotionless. "It was Jason's. Deep down I think I knew that all a long but wouldn't accept it."

Elena's mask slipped completely, revealing the calculating manipulator underneath. Then she forced tears to her eyes, her voice breaking with practiced precision. "How can you say that? How can you believe them over me? I'm grieving, Matthew. I'm traumatized and scared, and you're choosing to believe three little boys who were spying on a private conversation."

A rifle shot cracked from the tree line, the bullet striking stone somewhere to their left. But the physical danger felt distant compared to the emotional devastation unfolding in his chest.

"The timing," he said slowly, pieces falling into place. "Emily said the miscarriage had already started before the attack and she wasn't sure she could stop it. But you knew. You knew the baby was dying, and you knew it wasn't mine, and you let me think…"

"I was protecting you!" Elena's voice rose above the scattered gunfire. "I was protecting us! What good would it have done to tell you the truth? The baby was gone either way!"

"But I suffered," Matthew said, feeling anger building like pressure in a boiler. "I blamed myself for not keeping you safe. I felt guilty for every moment I spent working with Maddie on defenses that might save lives. You made me choose between community survival and your jealousy, and it was all based on lies."

Elena's tears dried instantly, replaced by cold fury. "So what if it was Jason's? So what if I didn't tell you every detail? I chose you, Matthew. When I found out I was pregnant, I chose you over him. That should count for something."

"You chose my bank account. My family's money is what you chose." Matthew corrected, standing up despite the ongoing scattered fire. "You chose how I would work myself to death to give the child stability. You never chose me."

"I loved you!" Elena scrambled to her feet, following him as he moved toward his assigned position. "I still love you! Doesn't that matter more than who the father was?"

Matthew turned to face her, seeing her clearly for the first time since she'd walked back into his life with that pregnancy test. The beautiful girl he'd fallen for was still there, but underneath lay something calculating and hollow, a void that fed on other people's guilt and kindness.

"You don't love me," he said with calm certainty. "You love what I represent. You love having someone to control, someone who'll sacrifice community needs to keep you comfortable. But that's not love, Elena. That's possession."

Her face contorted with rage, all pretense of grief abandoning her. "Fine! You want the truth? Jason was better in bed than you ever were. He was fun and exciting, and you were boring and predictable. But he was going nowhere, and you had prospects. So yes, I used the pregnancy to get you back. So what? At least I chose stability over stupidity!"

She turned her venom back on the boys, who were still crouching nearby. "And you three little shits think you've accomplished something? You think breaking up a relationship makes you heroes? You're just pathetic children who can't mind their own business!"

The final piece of Matthew's guilt cracked and fell away. Elena stood before him revealed—not a grieving mother or traumatized victim, but a manipulator who'd used his decency as a weapon against him and his family for months.

"We're done," he said simply.

"No!" Elena lunged forward, grabbing his arm with desperate strength. "We're not done! I need you, Matthew! Without you, I have nothing!"

"Then you should have thought of that before you built our entire relationship on lies."

Matthew jerked his arm from her grip and pulled free. He looked at her with something like pity mixed with disgust and started toward his defensive position. Elena stumbled backward, her heel catching on loose stone, and she fell hard against the retaining wall.

"I'm bleeding!" she screamed, holding up her hand to show scraped knuckles. "I'm hurt, and you're just standing there! What kind of man abandons an injured woman during a battle?"

But Matthew recognized the performance, the way she escalated minor injuries into major dramas when she needed sympathy. The scrapes were real but superficial, nowhere near serious enough to justify her theatrical response. All of it came to him with alarming clarity. She used the attack to cover the miscarriage and then continued to use that to keep him in her grasps with guilt.

"You're fine," he said, shouldering his rifle. "Get to the storm cellar. That's an order, not a request."

"I won't!" Elena's voice rose above the sporadic gunfire, drawing attention from defenders who should have been focused on the approaching threat. "I won't be thrown away like garbage! If you abandon me now, everyone will know what kind of man you really are!"

"Let them know," Matthew replied, walking away from her toward his assigned position. "Let them know I finally stopped letting you sabotage this community's survival."

Elena's scream of rage followed him across the farmyard, but Matthew felt lighter with each step. The constant drain within him surrounding that false responsibility lifted from his mind, replaced by the clear purpose of defending his real family, the community. The people who'd loved him without conditions or manipulation.

He reached Daniel at the ammunition distribution point, his brother's face showing relief mixed with concern.

"Thought Elena might keep you tied up," Daniel said carefully.

"She tried," Matthew replied, checking his weapon with steady hands. "But I'm done being tied up. Where do you need me?"

"East perimeter," Daniel pointed toward a cluster of defenders. "Scouts are probing that approach. Could use someone who knows how to shoot."

Matthew nodded, starting toward his position. Behind him, Elena continued her performance, screaming about abandonment and betrayal to anyone who would listen. But her voice was just noise now, no different from the scattered gunfire that punctuated the morning air.

He'd taken perhaps ten steps when the sniper's bullet found him.

The impact spun him around, hot metal tearing through his shoulder and dropping him to his knees. Blood soaked through his shirt, spreading in a dark stain that looked black in the morning light. Pain exploded through his body, sharp and immediate, followed by the creeping numbness. Oddly, he wasn't frightened or anything. Finally released from the grip of Elena's grasp he was as peace.

"Matthew!" Daniel's voice, filled with panic.

"Sniper!" someone shouted. "East tree line!"

Matthew tried to stand, tried to reach for his rifle, but his left arm wouldn't respond. When he tried to move the pain shot down his arm and across his chest. He was bleeding heavily onto the farmyard soil.

Through the haze of pain and shock, Matthew saw Elena watching him from behind the stone wall. Her expression wasn't concern or fear, but something that looked almost like satisfaction; as if his injury somehow validated her claims about his cruelty.

The scattered gunfire continued around them, defenders returning fire toward the sniper's position, voices shouting coordinates and medical requests. But Matthew's world had narrowed to the spreading warmth of his own blood and the strange peace that came with finally understanding the truth.

He'd broken free from Elena's web just in time to bleed out in the dirt.

The irony might have been funny if consciousness wasn't slipping away like water through his fingers.

The farmhouse dining room reeked of antiseptic and blood, transforming what had once been Sarah Thompson's pride into a battlefield hospital. Emily carefully cleaned the entry and exit wounds on Matthew's left shoulder, her hands steady despite the chaos that erupted and subsided in the past two hours. The mahogany table where they'd shared Sunday dinners now supported three injured defenders, while wounded attackers lay restrained on makeshift stretchers near the windows.

"Hold still, Matt," Emily murmured, her voice sharp but kind. "C'mon little brother sit still or I'll give you one of those noogies you're so fond of."

She tried to make light if things, to calm him but when he laughed, it made him wince in pain. "Clean through and through. Broke your collarbone, but missed the major vessels," she told him before getting back to work on it.

Matthew grimaced as she irrigated the wounds. Blood loss

had left him pale and shaky, but his eyes remained alert. "How bad?"

"You'll live," Emily replied, applying fresh gauze to both wounds. "Collarbone will heal in six to eight weeks. You'll be in a sling for a while, but no permanent damage."

The morning's violence had been swift and brutal. The advance scouts had established sniper positions in the tree line, keeping the farm's defenders trapped behind cover while the main force prepared for assault. Matthew had been caught in the open after his confrontation with Elena, an easy target for the hidden marksman. Then Michael led a counterattack that broke their momentum, capturing two wounded raiders and buying them precious time.

"There." Emily secured the bandages, checking the sling she'd fashioned from torn bed sheets. "Keep the arm immobilized for now. The bone will knit, but it needs time and rest."

Hannah appeared at her elbow with fresh bandages, her face drawn with exhaustion. They'd been treating wounded for over an hour, working in the tense silence that came after violence. The captured raiders had been sedated and restrained, but their presence filled the room with unspoken questions.

"Mrs. Henderson's anxiety attack has stabilized," Hannah reported quietly. "Used the last of the diazepam, though. And Tom Bradley's concussion symptoms are worsening."

Emily nodded grimly, mentally calculating their dwindling supplies. Every medication used now was one less available for the main battle still to come. She moved to check on Tom, noting his unequal pupils and disoriented responses.

"How many fingers?" she asked, holding up her hand.

"Four," Tom replied, though she'd shown him three. His wife gripped his other hand, knuckles white with tension.

"It's getting worse," Hannah said quietly.

"I know." Emily pressed her lips together. Without proper equipment—CT scans, neurosurgical intervention—Tom was living on borrowed time. "Keep monitoring him. Any change in consciousness, call me immediately."

A groan from across the room drew their attention to one of the captured raiders. The man stirred on his stretcher, fresh bandages covering a gunshot wound to his thigh. His eyes opened slowly, unfocused with pain medication.

"Easy," Emily said, moving to his side. "You're safe. We've treated your wound."

The raider blinked several times, trying to focus. He was young, maybe twenty-five, with the hollow look. It was painfully obvious; he'd seen too much violence. His tactical vest was removed, revealing a thin frame showing prolonged inadequate nutrition.

"Where..." he croaked, voice raw.

"Thompson farm," Emily replied matter-of-factly. "You were shot during the attack. We've stabilized you."

Fear flickered across the young man's features. "You're gonna kill me."

"We're doctors," Hannah said firmly, checking his IV line. "We don't kill patients."

The raider's laugh held no humor. "She does. She kills everyone who disappoints her. Makes us watch while she films it." His voice dropped to a whisper. "Makes us help."

Emily exchanged glances with Hannah. The psychological profile emerging from the captured raiders painted a picture of coercion rather than voluntary participation.

"Who makes you?" Emily asked gently.

"The Queen." The words came out like a curse. "Queen of Likes. That's what she calls herself. Crazy bitch talks to a dead phone all day, thinks she's broadcasting to millions of people."

Hannah's hand stilled on the IV tubing. Something in her expression shifted, a recognition that made Emily's pulse quicken.

"This Queen," Hannah said carefully, "what does she look like?"

The raider's eyes darted nervously. "Blonde hair. Pretty, I guess, under all that crazy. Always filming everything, talking about engagement and followers and content." He shuddered. "She made us execute Mark yesterday for questioning her orders. Called it 'accountability content' for her imaginary audience."

"Blonde," Hannah repeated, her voice barely above a whisper. "How old?"

"Young. Twenty maybe, possibly even younger. Outta Portland, I think. But it says stuff about Boston, so who knows. Talks about it sometimes when she's…" The raider paused, searching for words. "When she's having episodes. Screams about her friends betraying her, about losing her platform."

The color drained from Hannah's face. Emily watched her expression cycle through disbelief, horror, and dawning recognition.

"Hannah?" Emily prompted. "What is it?"

"It can't be," Hannah breathed, sinking into a nearby chair. "She drowned. We saw her go under."

The raider continued, oblivious to Hannah's distress. "Started calling herself the Queen after she took out Sherman. Said she was building a community, creating content. But it's just… it's just murder and madness. She filmed people dying, talks to that dead phone like it's still working. There's this group of sick dudes that are playing into this and using her crazy. They're the enforcers but she's out of her mind. I mean bat-shit crazy."

"What's her real name?" Hannah's voice cracked with

emotion.

"Grace something. I think. Why? You know her?"

Hannah's sob was answer enough. Emily moved quickly to her side filled with concern as she watched her crumble.

"She was our friend," Hannah whispered. "Our best friend. From college. We thought she was dead."

The raider's expression shifted to something approaching sympathy. "Wish she was. Would've been kinder than what she became. The things I've seen her do…" He closed his eyes. "She's not your friend anymore. Whatever she was before, she's something else now."

Emily helped Hannah to her feet, guiding her away from the wounded. "Hannah, talk to me. What happened to this Grace?"

"She had a breakdown," Hannah said, tears streaming down her face. "During our escape from Boston. Complete psychotic break. She'd been off her antipsychotics for days, maybe weeks. Paranoid delusions, thought we were trying to sabotage her social media career."

"And she drowned?"

"She jumped off a dock in Portsmouth. To escape some men who were…" Hannah's voice broke. "She was playing out some fantasy for these guys. They were not playing though; they got her to strip down to her undies and… Emily they were gonna rape her. We tried to intercede, but she jumped into the river. The current took her under. We watched her go down and never come back up."

Emily processed this information with clinical detachment, even as her heart ached for Hannah's pain. "But she survived."

"Apparently." Hannah wiped her eyes with shaking hands. "And became this monster. This Queen of Likes who murders people for content that doesn't exist."

Their friend; someone Hannah and Maddie had loved and tried to save, became the very threat now bearing down on their community. The tragedy was almost too large to comprehend.

"Does Maddie know?" Emily asked gently.

"She has to be told." Hannah straightened through her grief. "She's probably still working on that rock throwing thing with Daniel. Someone needs to—"

"I'll send for her," Emily interrupted. "But Hannah, you need to understand, this changes nothing about what we have to do. If this Grace really is leading that force, if she's as unstable as you're describing—"

"She has to be stopped," Hannah finished, her voice hollow. "I know. I just… I never imagined it would come to this."

Emily moved to the window, looking out at the farmyard where people continued their defensive preparations. Somewhere beyond the tree line, their former friend was planning an assault that would likely leave most of them dead. The cosmic cruelty of it felt overwhelming.

"Jake!" she called to Hannah's younger brother, who was helping distribute ammunition near the barn. "Can you find Maddie? Tell her we need her in the house asap!"

The boy nodded and ran off, leaving Emily to contemplate the impossible situation they faced. The Queen of Likes was this Grace girl. A college student and social media influencer. Someone that Hannah and Maddie had risked their lives to save. That was when Daniel found them and he said it was a shit show and they had to hightail it outta there. Now she commanded an army of coerced followers, filming executions for an audience that existed only in her fractured mind.

"She used to make these silly videos," Hannah said quietly, staring out the window. "Dancing, lip-syncing, outfit changes. Thousands of followers who loved her bubbly personality. She was so proud of her platform, her engagement rates."

"What happened to her medications?"

"Lost in the chaos after the pulse. We tried to help her, tried to get her to take what little she had left. But she thought we were poisoning her, trying to destroy her career. Maybe if we'd done something different…"

"You can't blame yourself," Emily said firmly. "Untreated psychosis, especially with someone who already had social media obsessions and delusions; the breakdown was probably inevitable."

Through the window, they saw Maddie approaching the house, her expression curious rather than concerned. Emily dreaded what they were about to put her through.

"Let me tell her," Hannah said, composing herself. "She should hear it from me."

Maddie entered through the kitchen door, wiping grease from her hands with a shop rag. "Jake said you needed me urgently. Is someone badly hurt?" She glanced at Matthew, dipping her head with a smile.

Emily stood Hannah struggled for words, watched the moment when Maddie registered her friend's tear-stained face and saw this was no chit chat.

"Hannah? What's wrong?"

"Maddie, sit down. Please." Hannah guided her to a chair, then knelt beside her. "It's about Grace."

"Grace?" Maddie's brow furrowed and she glanced up at Emily then over to where Matthew sat listening. "What about Grace? She's…" The words died as understanding dawned. "No. Hannah, no."

"She's alive," Hannah said gently. "And she's… Maddie, she's the Queen of Likes. She's the one leading the force that's been attacking communities. She's the one coming for us."

Maddie's face cycled through the same emotions Emily had

witnessed in Hannah—disbelief, horror, and finally a kind of numb acceptance.

"The girl who used to cry at ASPCA commercials?" Maddie whispered. "Who organized charity drives and worried about her followers' mental health? That's not Grace Hannah, you know her. This must be someone else."

"That girl died in Portsmouth harbor," Hannah replied. "What survived… it's not her anymore. The raider described someone completely disconnected from reality, living in a world of imaginary broadcasts and manufactured content."

"She's filming murders," Emily added quietly. "Executing her own followers for 'negative engagement.' Whatever Grace was before, what's coming for us is something else entirely."

Maddie sat in stunned silence, processing the revelation. Emily saw her working through the implications, their community protection considerations warring with personal grief.

"Can she be reasoned with?" Maddie asked finally. "If we could talk to her, remind her who she used to be—"

"The raider says she barely acknowledges reality," Hannah interrupted. "She talks to a dead phone, treats violence like content creation. Maddie, she's too far gone."

"What if we captured her? Could you treat her?" Her eyes pleaded with Emily as they shot back and forth.

"I don't know," Emily said with a sigh. She shook her head and continued, "Maybe if we had a place to contain her and some heavy anti-psychotics. But from the sounds of what she was already on, she was two steps away from a facility as it was."

The thought of it settled over them like a shroud. Their college friend, someone they'd loved and lost and mourned, had become the primary threat to everyone they now cared about. The personal had become tactical, grief had become strategic necessity and Emily didn't have the words to help them through this.

"We have to stop her," Maddie said finally, her voice steady despite the tears tracking down her cheeks. "Whatever she's become, we can't let her hurt these people."

Emily nodded, recognizing the moment when sentiment gave way to survival. "The family needs to know. James, Beth, everyone involved in the defense. They should understand what they're facing."

"A social media influencer having a psychotic break," Hannah said bitterly. "Leading an army of terrified followers who it seems don't want to play this game of madness, against people trying to build something decent."

Through the window, Emily saw storm clouds gathering on the horizon—both literal and metaphorical. The real assault was still coming, led by their friend but who was now something unrecognizable.

The raider groaned softly from his stretcher, drawing their attention back to the wounded. Emily returned to her patients, checking vitals and adjusting medications while her mind raced through this new information and question what they faced.

"Emily," Hannah said quietly, "there's something else. Grace was always… dramatic. Even before the breakdown. She craved attention, validation, being the center of everything."

"Meaning?"

"If she really thinks she's broadcasting, if she believes she has an audience watching—she'll want this battle to be spectacular. She won't just want to win. She'll want it to be… compelling content."

Emily felt ice form in her chest. A mentally unstable leader seeking dramatic content rather than tactical victory was far more dangerous than simple violence. Grace wouldn't just try to defeat them—she'd try to create a show.

"We need to warn the others," Emily said, moving toward the door. "They need to understand they're not just fighting an army. They're fighting someone who wants to turn their deaths into entertainment."

Grace held her dead iPhone at the perfect angle, capturing the cringeworthy sight of Frank stumbling behind her truck like a broken puppet. Wrists tied and attached to the bumper while the rope around his ankles kept him moving at just the right pace for optimal footage. And the blood streaking his naked body added authentic visual drama that her followers would absolutely love.

"This is what real accountability looks like, everyone!" she called through the truck's rear window, her voice bright with enthusiasm. "When someone consistently brings negative energy to your community, sometimes you have to get creative with your management techniques!"

Frank's pathetic attempts to keep up with the truck's crawling pace made for what she thought was viral content. Grace panned her phone to capture his stumbling gait. The way he flinched every time loose gravel bit into his bare feet was excellent. The morning light caught the mud and blood that painted his skin in artistic streaks that would photograph beautifully and truly take the aesthetic to the next level.

"See how much more positive our group dynamic is without toxic influences disrupting the flow?" Grace continued her narration, watching Frank through the cracked rear window. "This is advanced community building, people. Not everyone understands the vision but remember." She practically sang, her voice taking on a high pitch. "That's what separates successful platforms from the wannabes."

Her convoy had been moving since dawn, thirty-eight loyal followers picking their way through the storm-damaged landscape toward their target. Some people had abandoned the community during the night. All of them, weak-minded individuals who couldn't handle authentic content creation. But Grace filmed their approach to Cornish like the epic journey it was. It provided engaging commentary for the millions of subscribers hanging on her every word.

"Look at this incredible location scouting, everyone!" Grace's excitement built as the devastated town came into view. "Natural disaster aesthetic, authentic post-apocalyptic vibes, perfect lighting for the kind of liberation content we're going to create today! Use hashtag apocalypse aesthetic for twenty percent off new merch."

The truck stopped, and Grace climbed down with feet landing in a mucky puddle. She ignored it completely and moved toward the rear of the truck, immediately positioning herself for what she deemed the best camera angle. Frank collapsed behind them like a discarded mannequin, but that was fine, his exhaustion added authenticity to the shot.

Grace turned her phone toward him, capturing his kneeling form against the backdrop of ruined buildings. "Let's check in with our special guest! Frank, tell our amazing followers what you've learned about community engagement and positive energy!"

Frank raised his head, and Grace acted like she was zooming in on his face. The defeat in his eyes would translate beautifully to her audience. She felt it was authentic, emotional content that you simply couldn't fake.

But then he opened his mouth and ruined everything.

"Grace," he croaked, "there's nobody watching. There's no audience. You're talking to a dead phone."

Her reminder hit Grace like static interference, disrupting the crystal-clear reception she'd been maintaining with her platform. A strange ringing filled her ears, and the world tilted sideways for a moment. The phone in her hands felt suddenly heavy, wrong, like holding a piece of dead metal instead of her lifeline to millions of devoted fans.

She looked around at her followers, expecting them to laugh at Frank's obvious attempt to sabotage her ratings, but instead she saw something that made her stomach clench. The air wavered like a heat shimmer, and for a split second the faces around her transformed.

They were staring at her. All of them. Not looking at Frank, scanning for threats, or maintaining proper security protocols. They were watching her with expressions that didn't match her reality at all.

Where Grace saw loyal community members supporting her content creation, their faces showed something else entirely. Terror. Revulsion. The kind of hollow-eyed exhaustion that came from witnessing atrocities they couldn't prevent.

"Cut!" Grace snapped, lowering her phone with sharp jerky movements. The crack across its black screen caught the morning light, reflecting her own face back at her—wild-eyed, makeup streaked with sweat and dirt, mouth twisted into something that barely resembled a smile. For one horrible instant, she saw herself as they saw her.

The vision shattered like glass.

Jonas and Sean hurried to her side. They rarely communicated with her. Only worshipped from afar. She glanced at each of them and they whispered in each ear.

Jonas first in the left. "Grace, Frank is trying to tear down your platform."

Then Sean on the right. "The other influencers, Grace. They're watching."

Grace spun around and they melted back into the throng of loyal followers. "Frank, what the hell are you doing? You're completely destroying the narrative flow! Can't you see we're creating premium content here?"

But the interference was getting worse. Grace blinked hard, trying to clear her vision, and for just a moment the world looked different. Dirty. Gray. Wrong. The sweet metallic taste of blood coated her tongue, and she could smell Frank's terror-sweat mixing with the stench of unwashed bodies and human waste.

Her loyal followers became hollow-eyed prisoners. Her successful platform became a broken phone. Her beautiful community became something she didn't want to examine too closely.

The effort of rebuilding her reality made her head pound. Grace pressed her free hand against her temple, feeling the pulse of blood vessels working overtime to maintain the fantasy. Static buzzed behind her eyes like a broken television searching for a signal that would never come.

"Mom?" The word escaped in a small squeak before Grace could stop it. She spun around, searching the empty air beside her. "Mom, where did you go? The signal's getting weak. I can't see you anymore."

Her mother had been there just moments ago, standing proud and beaming as Grace demonstrated her leadership skills. But now there was nothing but empty space and the sound of wind through broken buildings carrying the smell of decay and abandonment.

"The reviews are coming in," Grace whispered, reading feedback that scrolled across her vision like ghostly subtitles. "Oh no. Oh no… no, no, no…the engagement numbers are terrible. Someone's been sabotaging my platform."

She turned back to Frank with sudden clarity, seeing him clearly for the first time. Not a community member struggling with personal growth, but a saboteur deliberately tanking her metrics. The pieces fell into place with horrible precision.

"It's you." Grace's voice dropped to something more dangerous than screaming. "You're the one posting negative reviews. You're working for my competitors, trying to destroy everything I've built."

"Grace, please—" Frank began, but Grace cut him off with a dismissive gesture of her hand.

"No more negative content!" Her voice rose to levels that made several followers step backward. "I am so tired of people trying to destroy my platform! This is premium subscriber content, and you're killing my engagement rates with your toxic energy!"

Grace gestured to her most reliable community managers, Jonas and Sean, the ones who understood her vision well enough to facilitate her content creation process. "Get the rope. Real rope this time. We're going to create some authentic accountability content that will really drive engagement through the roof!"

She began pacing around Frank's kneeling form, phone held high to capture every angle. Each step required tremendous concentration to maintain the illusion. The weight of the dead device made her arm ache, but she couldn't acknowledge that pain without admitting the truth she couldn't face.

"You see, followers, this is what happens when you allow negative influences to contaminate your content creation process. Poor engagement metrics, subscriber loss, algorithm suppression. It all traces back to people who don't understand the vision!"

Frank tried to say something, but Grace was too focused on her shot composition to listen. The town hall would provide perfect staging for what she had planned. Great visual elements, authentic emotional stakes, the kind of dramatic content that separated real influencers from amateur wannabes.

"This is going to be absolutely incredible footage!" Grace announced, walking backward while filming Frank's journey toward the building and up the steps. "Natural lighting, authentic setting, real consequences for negative energy! Our platform analytics are going to go through the roof!"

Her community managers worked with professional efficiency, positioning Frank on the front steps while Grace provided running commentary about camera angles and audience engagement. The rope flew out of the upper story window, the noose end landing on the stoop behind him. She stood smiling, they'd done this before, and understood the technical requirements for quality content creation.

"Any last words for our followers, Frank?" Grace held her phone close to his face, capturing his expression in beautiful high definition. "Want to apologize for trying to sabotage our amazing community building efforts?"

Frank's voice came out as a barely audible whisper. "You're bat shit crazy." Then he looked up at the group standing around watching as they prepared to hang him. "Can't you all see? Can't you see what is happening here?" He pleaded but each of them just looked at the ground. He looked into her eyes with a venom that was incredible, and grace smiled lifting the phone to capture it. Then Frank hissed. "Your mother abandoned you because she's ashamed of what you've become."

Grace's entire world tilted sideways. Gripping something deep and raw in the place where her parents' voices used to provide constant encouragement and validation. She looked around desperately, searching for their familiar faces in the crowd of followers.

The static behind her eyes exploded into white noise. For a moment that lasted forever, Grace saw everything with perfect clarity. The terrified faces of her prisoners. The broken phone in her hands. Frank's naked, beaten figure standing on his tip toes with the rope tightening. The blood under her fingernails. The smell of death that followed her everywhere.

The truth crashed over her like ice water, and she gasped, stumbling backward as reality tried to reassert itself.

Nothing. Just empty air and the growing certainty that something was very, very wrong with her platform.

But the camera was still rolling. It had to be. The alternative was unthinkable.

Grace's mind worked frantically to patch the cracks in her delusion, layering new fantasies over the crumbling foundation of her sanity. The effort left her dizzy and nauseous, but content creators had to maintain professionalism even during technical difficulties.

Grace's smile returned, brighter and more terrible than before. "Pull the rope."

Frank's feet left the ground with a soft scraping sound that would add great audio texture to the final edit. Grace filmed every moment, providing enthusiastic commentary about community accountability and authentic consequences while Frank's performance of writhing three feet off the ground reached its natural conclusion.

Each second of the execution required enormous effort to maintain her fantasy. The phone felt like it weighed a hundred pounds. Her arm trembled with the strain of holding it steady while her mind fought to process Frank's death as content creation rather than murder.

When his body stopped moving, Grace lowered her phone with a satisfied air of a surety that she'd created premium content. The black screen reflected nothing but her own haggard face, but she saw millions of hearts floating across it like digital snowflakes.

"That's what I call authentic! This is going to go viral and skyrocket me to real fame. I'm going to be the top influencer across the whole net." She walked back toward the truck with a star struck half smile, murmuring to herself. "Real consequences for real problems! This is the kind of decisive leadership that builds successful communities!"

But when Grace looked around at her followers, expecting congratulations and positive feedback, she found something else entirely. Their faces showed horror instead of appreciation, fear instead of admiration. Even her most reliable community managers looked uncomfortable, as if they couldn't appreciate the artistry of what they'd just witnessed. All but Jonas and Sean. They were loyal but not usually seen. She tilted her head and looked at them smiling at Frank's swaying body and thought how curious they were.

The disconnect between what she saw around her and what she needed to see made her head throb. Grace pressed her palm against her forehead, trying to force her brain to maintain her grip on the fantasy that kept her functional.

"What's wrong with everyone?" Grace's voice carried genuine confusion. "This was amazing content! Look at the composition, the lighting, the authentic emotional stakes! Why isn't anyone celebrating our engagement success?"

The silence stretched until it became oppressive. Grace raised her phone again, scanning the faces of her community for signs of enthusiasm or proper platform engagement.

"Fine," she said finally, her voice dropping to something that made the silence seem friendly by comparison. "If you can't appreciate authentic content creation, maybe we need to discuss your commitment to this platform."

She pointed her phone at random faces in the crowd, watching them flinch away from her attention like her lens carried some kind of infection. "Who else has been bringing negative energy to our community? Who else thinks they know better than their content creator?"

No one moved. She called out, "Who's onboard with the platform?"

Three hands shot up immediately—followers desperate to demonstrate their loyalty. Grace's smile returned as she fed on their fear, drawing strength from their terror like a solar panel absorbing sunlight.

"Excellent! Audience participation! This is exactly the kind of interactive content that drives serious engagement metrics!" She selected a young woman near the back of the group. "You! Tell our followers why Frank's accountability moment was necessary for successful community building!"

The woman's voice shook as she recited the expected response about negative energy and authentic engagement. Grace filmed her with approval, but her attention kept drifting to the empty spaces around her where her parents' voices should have been providing encouragement.

"Dad?" she whispered, turning her phone toward a patch of empty air. "Are you getting this footage? Look at how well I'm managing community dynamics! The engagement numbers are going to be incredible once the algorithm picks this up! Do you see? I told you influencer was an occupation."

Grace then started having a full conversation with the empty space, her voice alternating between desperate hope and defensive anger as she responded to criticism only she could hear. Her followers watched in growing alarm as their leader discussed platform analytics with invisible parents while Frank's body swayed gently in the background and none of that was helping.

The effort of maintaining multiple simultaneous delusions made her hands shake. Grace gripped the phone tighter, knuckles white with strain, as she argued with hallucinations that felt more real than the living people surrounding her.

"I know the metrics look bad right now, but that's because of saboteurs like Frank!" Grace explained to her unseen audience. "People who don't understand the vision, who try to tank my engagement rates! But look at this content! Look at how authentic and dramatic it is!"

The conversation continued for several minutes, Grace's responses growing more agitated as she argued with hallucinations about subscriber counts and algorithm suppression. Her followers' expressions showed how much they realized what they were witnessing was something beyond simple instability, this was complete disconnection from any shared reality.

Grace was aware of her history but in this moment couldn't distinguish what was real from what was hallucinations.

"They don't understand what I'm building!" Grace suddenly screamed at the empty air. "None of them appreciate my content creation! But I'll show them! I'll create footage so amazing, so compelling, that nobody will be able to ignore my platform!"

She spun back toward her followers, eyes blazing with renewed purpose. "Change of plans, everyone! We're going to create the most incredible liberation content anyone has ever seen! The kind of authentic, emotional, dramatic footage that goes viral across every platform!"

Grace pointed toward the smoke rising from the direction of the Thompson farm. "That community sitting up there on top of the hill thinks they can ignore us, thinks they can avoid being part of our amazing content! But we're going to give them engagement they'll never forget!"

She caught the Burke brother's looks as they exchanged worried glances. They'd expected a simple raid on a lightly defended farm, not such an epic role in the liberation.

"Grace," Sean said carefully, "maybe we should stick to the original plan. Quick assault, secure supplies, extract efficiently."

"Quick assault?" Grace's laugh held no humor. "That's not content! That's not authentic engagement! Our followers deserve better than basic raid footage!"

She began pacing again, phone held high as she narrated her vision for the attack. "We're going to film everything! Every moment of liberation! The emotional drama, the beautiful chaos of community transformation! Content so real and gripping that it will redefine how people think about survival and cooperation!"

Even her most reliable community managers looked uncertain now, finally recognizing that Grace's need for dramatic content. She smiled at them weakly before a commotion on the far side of their camp interrupted her planning session.

A figure approached from the direction they'd been moving. Walking with the desperate determination of someone who had nothing left to lose. As the person drew closer, Grace could see it was a young woman, mud-caked and hollow-eyed, carrying herself like a refugee from some terrible disaster.

Grace's entire demeanor transformed. Fresh content possibilities bloomed in her mind as she recognized the dramatic potential of an unexpected arrival. New perspectives, authentic emotional stakes, the kind of spontaneous development that made for truly spectacular platform engagement.

"Stop right there!" Grace called out, raising her phone to capture the approaching figure. "This is incredible! Everyone, we're getting some amazing spontaneous content! A real, live refugee approaching our community!"

The woman staggered into their camp, her clothes torn and filthy, her face marked by what Grace thought might be genuine trauma. She collapsed in the gravel, gasping with exhaustion that would translate beautifully to Grace's audience.

Grace moved closer, filming the woman's distress with professional enthusiasm. "Tell us your story! Our followers need to hear about whatever brought you to our amazing community! This is exactly the kind of authentic human drama that drives serious engagement!"

The woman looked up at Grace with calculating eyes that didn't quite match her performance of helplessness. "Are you the Queen?"

Grace's excitement spiked. This refugee understood her platform, recognized her content creation expertise. "That's right! I'm Grace, the Queen of Likes! And you've just found the most successful survival community in the region!"

"My name is Elena," the woman said, her voice breaking with what sounded like authentic grief. "I escaped from a community that betrayed me after I lost everything. They turned on me when I needed them most, chose to protect the people who caused my suffering."

Grace's eyes lit up with predatory interest. Personal betrayal, authentic emotional trauma, insider intelligence about their target community. This was exactly the kind of premium content that would drive her platform metrics through the roof.

"Tell me everything," Grace said, kneeling beside Elena while continuing to film. "Our followers need to hear about the toxic community dynamics you escaped from. The false consciousness about loyalty and cooperation that we're going to help them overcome."

Elena's story poured out in carefully crafted fragments. Abandonment after personal loss, rejection by people she'd trusted, the cold cruelty of a community that protected its favorites while discarding its most vulnerable members. With each detail, Grace's excitement built as she recognized the narrative possibilities.

"This is perfect!" Grace announced to her followers. "Real insider intelligence combined with authentic emotional stakes! Elena here is going to help us create the most amazing community transformation content anyone has ever filmed!"

She helped Elena to her feet, supporting her like a sister while her phone captured every moment of their bonding. "Together, we're going to show that community what happens when they abandon their most vulnerable members. We're going to show you something so emotionally powerful that it will revolutionize how people think about survival and loyalty!"

Elena's smile was sharp and hungry as she looked toward the Thompson farm. "I want to watch their faces when they realize what's coming for them. I want them to understand that discarding people has consequences."

"Exactly!" Grace clapped her hands together, nearly dropping her phone in her enthusiasm. "Consequence of betrayal! This is going to be absolutely incredible content!" she squealed with excitement.

The two women stood together at the edge of the devastated town. Behind them, Frank's body swayed gently on the front steps of the town hall, while Grace's followers watched their leader embrace someone who understood her vision of turning human suffering into entertainment.

Rebecca

Rebecca Mitchell crouched beside the smoldering remains of their morning cookfire, methodically sorting through wet supplies while Frank's body swayed like a grim pendulum. Her hands moved with efficiency, but her mind raced through calculations that bore no relation to inventory management. Grace finally crossed the line from unstable leadership into complete madness, and Rebecca was running out of time to save what remained of her soul.

The execution became a turning point. Not because Frank was innocent. Far from it, he was a collaborator, an opportunist who profited from Grace's instability while it served his purposes. But Grace killed him for contradicting her fantasy, murdered him for the entertainment of an audience that existed only in her fractured mind. Grace turned human death into content creation, forcing her followers to watch, participate, and become complicit in her descent into monstrosity; otherwise, they risked the same fate. She'd killed the others who challenged or failed her, but this was the first time she tortured and strung them up like this. She was devolving, and what she was changing into was terrifying.

"Rebecca, honey!" Grace's voice carried across the camp, melodic and bright with artificial enthusiasm. "Come help me interview our amazing new community member! This is going to be a testament of what genuine news is. An expose'!"

Rebecca looked up to see Grace filming the newcomer—Elena, she called herself. A young woman who appeared out of nowhere with a story of betrayal and abandonment that seemed tailored to feed Grace's persecution fantasies. But Rebecca saw more. And Elena's performance felt calculated rather than Grace's constant reference to any authentic.

"Coming," Rebecca called back, with just the right note of eager compliance. She spent time perfecting that tone, learning to sound grateful for Grace's attention, and playing up to her to gain confidence and get out of the damn cage. All while hiding the growing rebellion that burned within her like acid. She hadn't forgotten that this woman is who was responsible for the murder of her husband and possibly the loss of her children. She played the game and bided her time but, never would she be anything but vengeance that would exact payment for these atrocities.

Rebecca approached the two women, noting how Elena positioned herself to be filmed from her best angle, how her tears started and stopped with suspicious precision. This wasn't a broken refugee seeking sanctuary. This was someone with an agenda, someone who recognized Grace's madness and planned to use it.

"Tell Rebecca about the toxic community dynamics you escaped from," Grace instructed, holding her dead phone between them like a microphone. "She's one of our most successful integration stories! Perfect example of how authentic community building can transform people!"

Elena looked at Rebecca with calculating eyes, taking in her hollow cheeks and carefully controlled posture. "They threw me away after I lost my baby," Elena said, her voice breaking on cue. "The man I loved chose to protect the woman who stole him from me instead of supporting me through my grief."

Rebecca nodded sympathetically while her mind processed

the implications. Elena's story contained all the elements Grace craved—betrayal, emotional trauma, clear villains to target for what she called 'accountability content.' But the details felt rehearsed, performed rather than lived.

"That's terrible," Rebecca said with practiced compassion. "But you're safe now. Safe… here with us. Grace builds real communities where people support each other through difficult times. Isn't that right, Grace?"

The words tasted like poison, but Rebecca learned to swallow her revulsion and play up to Grace's insecurities. To survive, Rebecca had to play her role perfectly, maintaining the facade of a broken woman saved by Grace's wisdom and leadership. She wanted to leave, just slip away in the night, but she couldn't. These people… They all needed rescue.

Grace beamed at Rebecca's response, clearly pleased with her performance. "See? This is what authentic community integration looks like! Rebecca showed how proper leadership and positive engagement transform toxic dynamics!"

Elena smiled, but Rebecca caught the flash of something cold and hungry in her expression. This woman wasn't seeking refuge—she was seeking revenge. And Grace, in her madness, would be more than happy to provide it.

"Where exactly did you escape from?" Rebecca asked carefully, though she suspected she already knew the answer.

"A farm north of here," Elena replied. "The Thompson place. They call themselves a community, but they're just a family cult that protects their favorites while discarding anyone who becomes inconvenient."

Rebecca's blood turned to ice water in her veins. The Thompson farm. The name hit her hard, bringing back the memory of when Hannah made it home from Boston. Daniel and his family had helped Hannah and her friend Maddie; they brought her home before continuing on to their own family farm in Cornish. Daniel told them if they ever needed help, to come find them there. Good people, he said. People who helped instead of hurt.

Rebecca made the decision to send word ahead. She had to warn them and tell them about the breach. Rebecca had lost sight of Hannah and Jake during the chaos of Grace's raid on their community. Since then, she prayed every night her children remembered Daniel's offer, that they found their way to the Thompson farm where decent people would protect them instead of exploiting them. She wasn't about to let Grace kill her children.

The very place Grace was now planning to destroy for content.

"The Thompson farm," Grace repeated, her eyes lighting up with predatory interest. "That's perfect! Elena, you're going to be our insider guide for the most amazing liberation content anyone has ever filmed!"

Rebecca fought to keep her expression neutral while her world collapsed around her. All this time, she clung to the hope that Hannah and Jake would be alive somewhere, and safe. The Thompson farm was a beacon in her darkest moments, proof that not everyone surrendered to madness.

And now Grace planned to turn it into her next performance venue.

"Tell me everything about their defenses," Grace continued, filming Elena's response with professional enthusiasm. "Our followers need your take on the target. We need intelligence about the toxic dynamics we're going to transform!"

Elena launched into a detailed description of the farm's layout, defensive positions, and key personnel. She spoke with the bitter precision of someone who memorized every slight, every moment of rejection, cataloging grievances to be settled with interest.

"The woman who stole my boyfriend is named Maddie," Elena said, her voice dripping venom. "She thinks she's so special with her water filters and engineering projects. But she's just a manipulative bitch who destroys other women's relationships for sport."

Rebecca winced when she heard Maddie's name but regained her composure quickly.

Grace's excitement spiked visibly. Personal drama, romantic conflict, clear antagonists for her liberation narrative. Elena was providing exactly the kind of content framework that Grace's fractured mind craved.

"This is incredible!" Grace announced to her assembled followers. "Real insider intelligence combined with authentic personal stakes! We're going to create transformation content that will revolutionize how people think about community loyalty and romantic betrayal!"

Rebecca watched the planning session with growing horror, realizing that Grace's attack on the Thompson farm wouldn't be a simple raid for supplies. The attack would be a performance designed to settle Elena's personal grievances and satisfy Grace's need for dramatic content. The revenge fantasies of two mentally unstable women would cause the destruction of decent people who had built something worthwhile.

Including, quite possibly, her own children.

"Rebecca!" Grace called out suddenly. "Come help Elena get cleaned up and fed! We want her looking perfect for tomorrow's content creation!"

Rebecca nodded obediently, guiding Elena toward the supply cache where they kept salvaged clothing and medical supplies. As they walked, she studied the newcomer more carefully, noting the calculated way Elena presented her vulnerability, the strategic tears that appeared whenever Grace's attention focused on her.

"You're not really a refugee, are you?" Rebecca said quietly once they were out of Grace's earshot.

Elena's mask slipped for just a moment, revealing something sharp and predatory underneath. "I'm a woman who's been wronged by people who thought they could discard me without consequences. Grace is going to help me even the score."

"Grace is insane," Rebecca replied, her voice flat with exhaustion. "She talks to dead phones and kills people for imaginary audience ratings. If you think you can control her madness, you're making a fatal mistake."

"I don't need to control her," Elena said with cold satisfaction. "I just need to point her in the right direction and let her destroy the people who hurt me. She'll get her content, and I'll get my revenge. Everyone wins."

"Except the innocent people who'll die for entertainment."

Elena shrugged, the gesture carrying no trace of remorse. "Nobody's innocent. The Thompson family chose to protect Maddie over me. They made their choice, and now they'll live with the consequences."

Rebecca felt something crack inside her chest, a sound like ice breaking under pressure. Elena wasn't just using Grace's madness. She was feeding it, providing it with targets and justification. Two unstable women enabling each other's worst impulses while decent people prepared to pay the price.

Including Hannah and Jake, if they were still alive, if they found sanctuary at the Thompson farm as Rebecca hoped and prayed for months.

"The children there," Rebecca said carefully. "Surely some of them are innocent."

"Children adapt," Elena replied dismissively. "They'll

learn to appreciate authentic community dynamics once Grace shows them what real leadership looks like." She paused and her lip curled with irritation. "Except those boys. Those little bastards ruined everything."

The casual cruelty of the statement struck Rebecca in its detached callousness. Elena wasn't just seeking revenge against specific individuals. She was willing to traumatize children, destroy families, tear apart an entire community to satisfy her personal grievances. She saw all she needed to and decided to play into her profound narcissism rather than risk her telling Grace about the comments of her instability.

Rebecca helped Elena clean the mud and blood from her clothes, playing the role of the helpful community member while her mind raced through possibilities. Grace's force was down to thirty-eight followers after the latest round of desertions. Maybe a dozen were true believers who would follow Grace into hell for the promise of being part of something special. The rest were coerced participants, people trapped by circumstance and fear who would jump at any chance to escape.

"There," Rebecca said, stepping back to examine Elena's improved appearance. She grasped a small section of hair pulling it forward and gently brushing a leaf from the end. "You have such luxurious hair. Absolutely beautiful. Grace will be pleased with how you look for tomorrow's filming."

Elena studied her reflection in a broken mirror, adjusting her hair and expression until she looked like the perfect victim-turned-insider. "You're very good at this," she said. "Playing the loyal follower while thinking whatever thoughts you're trying to hide."

"I've learned to survive. I think we all know Grace isn't all there. I feel sad for the poor, broken girl. I only try to take care of her like the mother she lost in all this."

"We all develop survival skills," Elena agreed. "The

question is whether you're smart enough to recognize which side is going to win."

Rebecca met Elena's gaze in the cracked mirror, seeing the calculation behind her performance. She saw that she wasn't fooling her but wasn't going to give in to her manipulations. "I know exactly which side I'm on," she said and went back to brushing out her hair. She knew deep down this woman was calculating every move, every expression, but what she couldn't possibly calculate was Grace. That would be her fatal mistake.

The answer seemed to satisfy Elena, though Rebecca suspected they meant very different things by it. Elena returned to Grace's side, launching into more detailed descriptions of the Thompson farm's layout and personnel, while Rebecca resumed her tasks and held the broken phone at whatever angle Grace required.

But her mind was elsewhere, racing through the intelligence she was also gathering by careful observation. Grace's inner circle was smaller now, reduced to maybe six hardcore enforcers who profited from her madness. Her followers were increasingly desperate, held in line more by fear than loyalty. And Grace herself was spiraling deeper into delusion with each passing day, her grip on reality so tenuous that contradicting her fantasy became a death sentence.

All of which meant opportunities for someone patient enough to wait for the right moment.

When they were done with the segment, Rebecca made her way through the camp, checking on supplies and casualties with the efficiency Grace expected from her most reliable community member. How the hell she went from caged animal to valued member still amazed her. Grace's attentions and delusions shifted so quickly, things forgotten or replaced by delusion, all she had to do was play the game. Grace thought she was keeping tabs on things, but she was really cataloging resources, identifying potential allies, mapping the psychological terrain for the rebellion she was finally ready to attempt.

Tommy Burke sat apart from the main group, cleaning his rifle with the hollow focus of someone trying not to think too hard about what he'd witnessed. His brother Sean talked quietly with three other followers near their vehicle, their voices carrying the nervous energy of people reconsidering their life's choices.

"Terrible thing about Frank," Rebecca said quietly, settling beside Tommy with a bowl of soup she salvaged from their dwindling supplies.

Tommy looked up, his young face marked by exhaustion and something approaching shell shock. "He didn't deserve that. I mean, yeah, he was an asshole, but Grace just… she killed him for disagreeing with her."

"She's been getting worse," Rebecca said, keeping her voice carefully neutral. "The stress of leadership, the responsibility for so many people's welfare. It changes people."

"Changes them into what?" Tommy's voice cracked slightly. "She talks to people who aren't there, films everything like it's some kind of show with a dead phone! The damn thing is not just dead but smashed… And now this Elena woman shows up with her revenge fantasy…"

Rebecca ladled soup into Tommy's bowl, noting how his hands shook slightly as he accepted it. "You joined up for supplies and protection, didn't you? Not to be part of whatever this has become."

"We all did," Tommy replied. "Sean and me, we thought Grace was building something real. A community that could survive what's coming. We messed up in the first days, you know. Messed up bad robbing the pharmacy and the old man got shot. It was an accident but nothing we could do, so we ran. We only wanted to find someplace safe. But this…" He gestured toward where Grace was filming Elena's continued performance. "This isn't survival. This is just madness with weapons."

"Sometimes good people get trapped in bad situations and mistakes are made," Rebecca said carefully. "The question is what they do when they recognize the truth."

Tommy met her gaze, understanding passing between them like an electric current. "What can anyone do? She's got the true believers, the weapons, the momentum. Anyone who opposes her ends up like Frank."

"Not if enough people oppose her at the same time."

The words hung in the air between them, carrying implications that could get them both killed if overheard by the wrong ears. But Rebecca reached the point where the risk of action outweighed the certainty of complicity.

"How many others feel like you do?" she asked quietly.

Tommy glanced around the camp, his gaze settling on specific faces. "Most of us, I think. But being unhappy and being willing to do something about it are different things."

"What if they knew they weren't alone? What if they understood that other people were willing to act?"

"Then maybe," Tommy said slowly. "But it would have to be coordinated. All at once. Grace's core people are still loyal, and they're not going to hesitate to kill anyone who threatens her."

Rebecca nodded, filing away the information. A coordinated revolt was possible, but it would require careful planning and precise timing. More importantly, it would require people to believe that resistance was possible, that Grace's power wasn't absolute.

"The Thompson farm," she said, changing the subject carefully. "Elena mentioned they have children there."

"Yeah," Tommy's expression darkened. "Grace is planning something special for tomorrow. Says it's going to be her biggest content creation event yet."

Rebecca's chest tightened with familiar anguish. Hannah and Jake, if they made it to the Thompson farm, would be among those Grace planned to traumatize for her imaginary audience.

"Sometimes," Rebecca said quietly, "protecting children becomes more important than protecting yourself."

Tommy looked at her sharply, recognizing the steel beneath her careful words. "What are you thinking?"

"I'm thinking that tomorrow might be the last chance any of us have to remember who we used to be."

Before Tommy could respond, Grace's voice cut across the camp with renewed enthusiasm. "Everyone! Gather around for a special planning session! Elena's going to share insider intelligence about our target community, and we're going to coordinate the most amazing liberation content anyone has ever filmed!"

Rebecca and Tommy joined the reluctant crowd assembling around Grace and Elena. The newcomer cleaned up well, presenting herself as the perfect victim seeking righteous vengeance against the people who wronged her. Grace filmed everything with manic energy, providing commentary about authentic emotional stakes and narrative frameworks.

"This is what real content creation looks like!" Grace announced, panning her phone across the assembled faces. "Personal drama combined with community transformation! Tomorrow's footage is going to revolutionize how people think about survival and loyalty!"

Elena launched into another recitation of her grievances, painting the Thompson farm as a den of favoritism and cruelty that desperately needed Grace's particular brand of liberation. She spoke with the bitter precision of someone who nursed her resentments until they grew into something monstrous.

As the planning session continued, Rebecca caught the eyes of other followers, noting which ones looked uncomfortable with Grace's escalating rhetoric, which ones seemed horrified by Elena's casual descriptions of the children they planned to terrorize. A network of potential allies was taking shape, held together by shared revulsion at what their leaders were planning.

The session broke up near midnight, followers dispersing to their sleeping areas with the hollow efficiency of people trying not to think too hard about tomorrow's plans. Rebecca made her final rounds, checking weapons and supplies while keeping careful track of who was where, which vehicles held the most ammunition, where Grace's core supporters would be sleeping.

She found herself near the camp's perimeter, where a small group of followers sat around the dying embers of a cook fire. They looked up as she approached, their faces marked by the same exhaustion and moral uncertainty she saw all evening.

"Terrible thing about Frank," one of them said quietly.

"It's going to get worse," Rebecca replied, settling beside them with the weary authority of someone who saw Grace's madness evolve. "Tomorrow, she's planning to attack a community with children. Real children, not combatants. And Elena's going to help her turn it into entertainment."

The group exchanged glances, recognizing the moment when passive resistance must become something more active or lose all meaning.

"What can we do?" another follower asked. "Grace's people will kill anyone who opposes her."

"Not if we act together," Rebecca said, with quiet conviction. "Not if we choose the right moment, when Grace is focused on her performance instead of watching for threats from within."

She looked around the circle, meeting each person's gaze. "Tomorrow, when Grace attacks that farm, she's going to be filming everything for her imaginary audience. Her attention will be on creating content, not maintaining security. That's when people who remember what decency looks like have to choose whether they're going to remain complicit or take action."

The silence stretched until one of the younger followers spoke up. "What kind of action?"

Rebecca smiled, and for the first time in she couldn't remember how long, it felt genuine. "The kind that gives those children a chance to grow up in a world that values their lives more than someone else's entertainment."

Maddie

The walk-out basement beneath the Thompson farmhouse carried an odor of damp concrete and old preserves, a sharp contrast to the chaos erupting above their heads. Maddie Foster arranged clean bandages on a makeshift supply table while Hannah Mitchell sorted through medical equipment they'd salvaged from the flooded town. Gunfire cracked sporadically outside, each shot making both women flinch despite their efforts to maintain calm.

"Hand me those antiseptic bottles," Hannah said, her voice steady but tight with controlled tension. "Emily wants everything organized by urgency level."

Maddie passed the brown glass bottles, noting how Hannah's hands trembled slightly as she arranged them. The basement windows were covered with thick boards, blocking most natural light and creating an atmosphere of bunker-like isolation, while battery-powered lanterns cast dancing shadows across the concrete walls.

"At least we're safer down here," Maddie offered, trying to inject optimism into the oppressive atmosphere.

A distant explosion shook dust from the ceiling beams. Both women froze, listening to the muffled shouts and running footsteps that filtered down through the floorboards above.

"That didn't sound like our weapons," Hannah whispered.

Heavy footsteps thundered down the basement stairs. Michael appeared in the doorway, his face grim. Behind him, two men carried a third between them—wounded, pale, but conscious.

"Medical attention," Michael said curtly, helping lower the injured man onto one of their prepared cots. "Prisoner. Took a bullet in the shoulder during their assault on the east perimeter."

Hannah moved immediately to examine the wound. The prisoner was young, maybe twenty-five, with hollow eyes but something approaching relief on his face.

"I got caught on purpose," he said quietly as Hannah began cleaning his wound. "Had to get this to you." He reached into his shirt pocket with his good arm, producing a crumpled piece of paper. "From someone inside our group. Said lives depended on it."

Hannah's hands stilled on the bandages. She stared at the paper, her face cycling through disbelief and dawning recognition.

"Hannah?" Maddie prompted. "What is it?"

"The handwriting," Hannah whispered, her voice breaking. "It looks like my mother's handwriting."

She unfolded the note with trembling fingers, reading the hastily scrawled words aloud. "Bitter woman—says Maddie took her man. Knows all positions—revenge. Feeding Queen intel—wants Maddie hurt."

Maddie listened to the words and like physical blows almost hurt. Matthew appeared at the bottom of the stairs, his left arm in a sling, and stopped short when he saw her expression.

"What's wrong?" he asked.

Maddie handed him the note without speaking. She watched his face as he read, seeing the moment when understanding registered. His jaw tightened.

"Elena," he said flatly. "Has to be."

"She's been feeding them our defensive positions," Michael said, reading over his brother's shoulder. "Everything they need to know."

The prisoner nodded grimly. "This girl, see? She come walking into camp all muddy and crying. She's been giving the Queen all the details of this place. The layout of your buildings, weapon placements, personal information about your people. She's a sly one, that girl. Playing up to the queen like she was some kind of fiddle."

"Where is Elena now?" Hannah demanded. "Someone needs to go check if it's her."

"Nobody knows," Michael replied. "She left the storm cellar hours ago."

Footsteps clattered down the stairs. Ryan Thompson, Daniel's seven-year-old son, appeared with tears streaming down his face. Behind him, Lily clutched her brother's hand while Grayson Hawkins supported elderly Marianne Miller, whose face bore fresh scratches and bruises.

"Ryan, what happened?" Michael demanded, moving toward the children.

"The mean lady hurt Mrs. Miller," Ryan sobbed. "She was saying terrible things about Maddie and Uncle Matthew in the storm cellar. When Mrs. Miller told her to stop, she grabbed her and started shaking her."

Lily stepped forward, her small face fierce. "We all jumped on her! Me and Ryan and Sophie and the other kids. We pulled her hair and scratched her face until she let go of Mrs. Miller."

"She was screaming at us," Another one of the children added, his voice tight with anger. "Calling us names, saying we'd chosen the wrong side. Then she slapped Ryan and ran upstairs."

Marianne Miller straightened despite her injuries. "That woman was never grieving. She was just mean. Mean straight through to her core."

Matthew stared at the elderly woman's bruises, his expression cycling through guilt and rage. "She hurt you because of me. Because I believed her lies."

"She hurt me because she's evil," Marianne corrected firmly.

The prisoner spoke up again. "There's more you need to know. The woman who wrote that note—Rebecca Mitchell—she's organizing resistance inside our group. Most of us don't want this fight. We're being forced. You don't understand," his breath hitched, "they'll kill anyone who tries to leave."

Hannah's breath caught. "She's alive. My mother's alive."

"That's your mom? She's trying to end this from the inside," the prisoner continued. "Save as many people as possible on both sides. Please, you've got to help us."

Another explosion shook the building, closer this time. Dust rained from the ceiling.

"We need to warn the others," Michael said, moving toward the stairs. "James needs to know about this intelligence leak."

"And about the resistance," Hannah added, gripping the note. "If my mother's organizing people inside their group—"

Jake Mitchell appeared at the top of the stairs. "Hannah! Grandpa James needs everyone upstairs. They caught more prisoners, and one of them is asking specifically for you. Says he has another message from Mom."

Hannah looked at Maddie, torn between staying and racing upstairs for news of her mother.

"Go," Maddie said firmly. "This is about your family."

As Hannah hurried up the stairs with Jake, Maddie

absorbed the devastating revelation. Elena's jealousy hadn't been simple emotional instability. It was a calculated revenge that endangered everyone.

"If this is about me," Maddie said suddenly, "if Elena wants revenge against me specifically, maybe I should—"

"No." Matthew's voice cut through her words like a blade. "Whatever you're thinking, no."

"But if it might save the children—"

"Maddie." Matthew stepped forward, his good hand catching her arm and spinning her toward him. For a moment they stood close enough that she could see the flecks of gold in his brown eyes, could feel the warmth radiating from his body despite the basement's chill. "Elena doesn't want justice. She wants to watch you suffer, and then she wants you dead. There's no negotiating with that kind of hatred."

"But... I don't understand why. I never—"

"You didn't have to. This isn't about you Maddie. You're just the excuse. I'm so sorry," Matthew said.

The moment stretched between them, heavy with unspoken understanding. The shared revelation of everything they'd both lost and found. Then another explosion rocked the building, and the spell broke.

"Elena's not getting any more of our family," Matthew said quietly, releasing her arm. "Not the children. Not you. Not anyone."

Maddie nodded, seeing past his injury to the decent man who'd been manipulated and used by someone incapable of genuine emotion. Around them, the battle raged on, but in the basement of the Thompson farmhouse, the real enemy had finally been revealed.

The prisoner struggled to sit up despite his wound. "Your people should know—Rebecca's message wasn't just about the intelligence leak. She's planning something for when the real assault begins. If enough of us refuse to fight at the crucial moment…"

"A mutiny," Michael said, understanding immediately.

"A chance," the prisoner corrected. "Maybe the only one we'll get to end this without everyone dying."

"Watch the fighters," the man said, "You'll know who your enemy is truly. None of us are actually shooting at anyone. Please, just watch them you'll see."

Outside, the sound of gunfire intensified, and somewhere in the distance, voices shouted coordinates and tactical updates. The battle for the Thompson farm was escalating, but now they knew they weren't just fighting Grace's army—they were fighting to give Rebecca Mitchell and her hidden allies time to save both sides from the madness of their leaders.

"I'll take care of it," Michael said, and raced up the stairs.

Ethan

The kitchen table became a war council, Rebecca's crumpled note spread flat between coffee-stained maps and scattered ammunition. James Thompson leaned over the handwriting that promised hope and delivered desperation in equal measure, while Beth Martin traced likely approach routes with her finger. The smell of gunpowder drifted through the boarded windows, mixing with the metallic taste of fear that filled everyone's mouth.

"She's risking everything to get us this intelligence," Hannah said, her voice thick with pride and terror. "But how do we let her know we received it? How do we coordinate with people we can't reach?"

"Radio frequencies are compromised," Beth replied, shaking her head. "Grace's people monitor everything. One wrong transmission and Rebecca's cover is blown."

Emily paced beside the window, her medical bag slung over her shoulder as she prepared for the casualties that would come. "We need a way to signal that won't endanger her or those in the resistance."

"What about a runner?" Daniel suggested. "Someone who could get close enough to pass a word without being caught."

"Through enemy lines?" Michael's voice, that of a father

who'd already lost too much. "That's a suicide mission."

Ethan Thompson stepped forward from where he'd been standing with Jake and Grayson near the doorway. His grandfather's knife felt familiar at his belt, no longer foreign metal but part of him now. The red thread around his wrist caught the lantern light as he moved.

"We could do it," he said quietly.

The adult conversation stopped. James looked up from the note, his weathered face cycling through understanding and immediate rejection.

"Ethan, no," Emily said sharply. "Absolutely not."

"We know those woods better than anyone," Grayson added, stepping up beside his friend. "We've been moving through them since everything fell apart. We can get close without being seen."

Jake nodded, though his voice trembled slightly. "We're small, quiet. Adults would never make it through their perimeter."

"You are children," Michael said firmly, but something in his tone suggested he was trying to convince himself as much as them.

"We're survivors," Ethan replied, meeting his father's gaze. "And Jake's mom is out there organizing people who want to end this. She needs to know we got her message."

Beth studied the three boys, taking in their steady postures, the way they'd naturally formed a unit without conscious thought. "What exactly are you proposing?"

"It doesn't matter. I won't allow it," Emily said, tears forming in her eyes.

"We can at least hear them out," Beth replied.

Michael pulled Emily close saying, "They might have some ideas. They do wander those woods daily."

Emily nodded.

"Circle around through the east woods," Ethan explained, pointing at the map. "Come up behind their lines where they won't expect scouts. Find someone from Rebecca's resistance, pass the message, get back."

"Message received," Jake said simply. "That's all she needs to know. That her plan is working."

Hannah knelt beside Jake, her eyes bright with unshed tears. "That's our mother out there. If something happened to you while trying to reach her…"

"Nothing will happen," Grayson said with quiet confidence. "We've done this before."

"Not like this," James said, his voice heavy with authority and love. "Not behind enemy lines during active combat."

Ethan looked at his grandfather, seeing the fear beneath the leadership mask. "Grandpa, someone has to try. Jake's mom is risking her life to save everyone. We can get word to her."

The room fell silent except for the distant crack of sporadic gunfire. Sarah Thompson emerged from the cellar stairs, her face drawn with exhaustion from tending the wounded.

"What's happening?" she asked, immediately sensing the tension.

"The boys want to volunteer for a reconnaissance mission," James explained, his tone suggesting the matter was closed.

"It's not reconnaissance," Jake corrected, his voice stronger now. "It's communication. Mom needs to know we're working together."

Sarah looked between her husband and grandson, reading the stubborn determination in Ethan's face that she'd seen countless times in James. "How dangerous?"

"Very," Beth replied honestly. "But if Rebecca's organizing a mutiny from inside their ranks, coordination could save lives on both sides."

Another explosion shook the house, closer than before. Plaster dust drifted from the ceiling as everyone instinctively ducked.

"They're probing the north perimeter," Daniel reported, rushing in from outside. "Testing our responses, learning our patterns."

"Elena's intelligence," Matthew said grimly, following his brother. "She's giving them everything they need."

The gravity of their situation settled over the room like a shroud. Grace's forces knew their defenses, their strengths, their weaknesses. Rebecca's resistance might be their only hope of avoiding a massacre.

"One hour," James said finally, his voice carrying the pain of necessary choices. "You have one hour to get in, make contact, and get back."

"Dad," Emily protested. "They're just kids."

"They're right," he continued, ignoring his daughter's objection. "Someone has to try, and they're our best chance. As much as I hate the thought, they've been sneaking through those woods all this time. What else are we supposed to do?"

Emily whimpered

"I'll go," Michael said.

"Okay, well, do you know the deer trail over to the big maple? You can slip down into the shady gully before you'll be in open sight. You'll haveta shrink dad to get through the two tree-gap to make the blueberries. They're the shorties so you'll haveta belly crawl," Ethan said squirreling his finger across the map.

Michael looked at James and shrugged his shoulders.

"Okay, are you sure you can do this without being seen?"

"Yes, Grampa. We do it all the time."

James looked at Emily then back to Ethan. "Your dad is going to be at the tree line. If you run into anything at all you fire a shot and we'll come running."

"Yessir," Ethan said, standing taller."

"But you follow orders absolutely. No heroics, no deviations. Message delivery only."

Ethan nodded solemnly, feeling proud that they'd gained his grandfather's trust. "Message received. That's all. In and out without a trace."

"And if you can't make contact safely, you abort, come back and report," Beth added. "No unnecessary risks."

"We understand," Grayson replied for all of them.

Sarah moved to embrace Ethan, her arms tight around his shoulders. "Do as grampa says and come back," she whispered against his hair. "All of you come back."

Twenty minutes later, the three boys moved through the east woods like shadows given form. Ethan led, reading the terrain with instincts honed by necessity. Behind him, Grayson watched their flanks while Jake covered their rear. They moved in practiced silence, communicating through hand signals and shared understanding.

The forest felt different in wartime. Every broken branch might hide an enemy. Every bird call could mask human movement. The boys stayed low, using game trails and natural cover to mask their approach.

"Movement ahead," Ethan whispered suddenly.

Three figures crashed through the underbrush fifty yards ahead, moving away from Grace's camp with the desperate haste of people who'd finally chosen flight over fight. A man and two women, probably fleeing during the chaos of preparation.

"What do we do?" Grayson asked.

"They could warn Grace's people about us," Jake pointed out.

Ethan studied the fleeing refugees, weighing options. "We stop them."

The boys moved to intercept, using the refugees' noise to mask their own approach. The figures were focused on escape, not security, making them easy targets.

"Stop," Ethan called out when they were close enough. "Hands up."

The refugees spun around, terror replacing relief on their faces. They saw three boys with weapons and steady eyes, and their hands shot skyward.

"Please," one of the women gasped. "We're leaving. We don't want any part of this."

"Neither do we," Grayson replied. "But you're going to wait right here until we're done."

They used rope from their packs to secure the refugees to separate trees, gags fashioned from torn cloth. Ethan knelt in front of each prisoner, his voice calm and matter-of-fact.

"If you make any noise, we'll come back and kill you. If you try to escape, we'll track you down and kill you. Stay quiet, stay still, and we'll collect you on our way back and you might even get dinner."

The refugees' eyes went wide, but they nodded frantically.

"Good," Ethan said, rising. "We'll be back."

The boys resumed their journey toward Grace's camp, leaving the bound refugees behind for now. They continued through the woods until they reached their observation position.

"There," Ethan whispered, pointing through the trees.

Grace's camp spread across the intersection where the road split toward the Thompson place, vehicles arranged in rough defensive positions around damaged buildings. Smoke rose from cooking fires, and figures moved between the trucks with the tired look of people who'd been fighting too long.

Jake gripped Ethan's shoulder, his whole body trembling. "I can see her."

Following his gaze, Ethan spotted a woman kneeling beside a truck, her dark hair visible even at distance. Rebecca Mitchell, organizing supplies.

"Mom," Jake breathed, the word barely audible.

The single syllable carried all his grief, hope, and desperate love. Jake rose slightly, every muscle in his body oriented toward the woman who'd given him life and lost him to chaos.

Grayson reacted instantly, tackling Jake to the forest floor and pressing him deep into the fallen leaves. Jake struggled silently, his need to reach his mother overwhelming rational thought.

"Jake, stop," Grayson whispered urgently. "You'll get us all killed."

But Jake couldn't stop. His mother was fifty yards away, alive, breathing, real. His body fought against Grayson's restraint with desperate strength.

Grayson held up his wrist, the faded red thread stark against his dark skin. He pressed it against Jake's wrist, thread touching thread, their brotherhood made physical.

"Brothers," Grayson whispered. "You're not alone. We're here."

Jake's struggles slowed as he focused on the matching threads, on the promise they represented. His breathing gradually steadied, though tears streamed down his dirt-smudged cheeks.

"I know," Jake whispered back, his voice breaking. "I know, but she's right there."

"And we're going to help her," Ethan promised quietly.

"But only if we're smart about it."

The sound of footsteps crashing through underbrush froze all three boys. Someone was approaching their position, moving with the careless noise of a person who felt safe in friendly territory.

A man emerged from behind a cluster of trees thirty yards away, rifle slung over his shoulder, clearly seeking privacy for natural necessities. He was young, maybe early twenties, with the hollow-eyed look that marked everyone in Grace's camp.

Ethan made a decision that would have terrified him when the world first fell apart. Now it felt natural, necessary. He rose from concealment and moved through the trees like smoke, placing himself behind the distracted man.

"Don't move," Ethan whispered, pressing his grandfather's knife against the man's neck. "Don't make a sound."

The man froze, hands slowly rising in surrender. Grayson appeared twenty feet away, rifle trained on the prisoner with steady hands.

"Are you team Grace," Ethan asked quietly, "or team Rebecca?"

The man's shoulders sagged with relief. "Please don't shoot. Most of us are team Rebecca. We're trying to end this."

"Message received," Ethan said simply. "Tell her message received."

The man nodded frantically. "I'll tell her. Rebecca will know what that means?"

"Yes. And tell her we're ready," Jake added, his voice thick with emotion. "Whatever she's planning, we're ready."

Ethan withdrew the knife and melted back into the trees. Within seconds, the three boys vanished, leaving the man alone with his relief and Rebecca's message.

They moved swiftly through the woods toward where

they'd left the refugees. Jake's breathing hitched with suppressed emotion, but his feet never faltered. Grayson stayed close to his left shoulder while Ethan navigated their route.

"She looked strong," Jake whispered with a hitch in his voice as they retraced their steps. "Tired, but strong."

"She's organizing resistance," Grayson replied.

"She's going to end this," Ethan added with quiet conviction. "Then you'll see her and you guys will be a family."

Jake stopped suddenly, pressing his back against a large oak. His shoulders shook as emotion finally overwhelmed him. Grayson moved immediately to his side while Ethan kept watch.

"I wanted to run to her," Jake whispered. "Just run down there and—"

"I know," Grayson said simply.

"She's so close I could have called out to her."

"But you didn't," Ethan pointed out. "You stayed smart."

"Because of you," Jake said, looking at Grayson. "The threads. I felt them and remembered I wasn't alone."

They stayed quiet for a moment, listening to the forest around them. Birds called from the canopy above, and somewhere in the distance, a truck engine rumbled to life.

When Jake's breathing steadied, they continued to where they'd left the refugees. The three figures were exactly where they'd left them, bound and waiting.

Ethan approached the nearest woman, kneeling beside her. "We're going to take you with us," he said quietly. "You'll walk in front of us through the woods. Once we reach our camp and you speak to my grandfather, you'll be safe. But until then, you stay tied."

The woman nodded frantically, understanding she had no choice but trusting these boys more than Grace's camp behind them.

One by one, the boys freed the refugees from the trees but left their hands bound, leading them single file toward home. The refugees walked ahead of them, understanding their captivity was temporary but absolute.

"Keep moving," Grayson said quietly when one of them stumbled. "Not far now."

The journey took longer with three bound prisoners, but they moved steadily through the woods. The refugees followed the boys' directions without complaint, recognizing that compliance meant survival.

The farmhouse came into view through the trees, warm light spilling from windows despite the boarded frames.

"We did it," Jake said quietly.

Grace

Grace stood tall atop the battered Humvee, sweat plastering her matted hair to her skull and cracked phone held high like a sacred relic. The device's spider-webbed screen caught fragments of harsh sunlight, reflecting her wild eyes in the shattered kaleidoscope pieces. She could feel it; waves of digital energy vibrating through the sweltering air, comments pouring in like rushing water, hearts floating like confetti in a parade of validation.

"We're back, my beautiful revolutionaries!" she crooned into the dead screen, voice vibrant despite the crushing heat that made the very air shimmer. Electric on her tongue, each syllable charged with the power of connection. "Against all odds, despite traitors and cowards, we are marching forward to take what is rightfully ours. This, my loves, is the redemption arc you've been waiting for."

The sun beat down on her skull like applause, each ray a tiny notification of approval. She tilted her face skyward, letting the heat bake away the grime and blood that coated her cheeks, feeling reborn in the furnace of her own making. The brutal light blazed overhead, and in its merciless glare, she saw the faces of her followers—millions of them, stretching to the horizon, their eyes bright with adoration.

"Ten million tuned in," murmured a voice just behind her ear, breath hot against her neck. "Biggest numbers ever."

She twisted slightly, just enough to glimpse Frank, limping alongside the convoy, naked, battered, but still smug in his tone. His flesh hung in strips where the rope had torn it, and his feet left bloody prints on the scorched asphalt. The heat made his wounds weep, pus and blood mixed with sweat. He winked, a red gash across his swollen face grinning wider than his mouth. "They're watching your every move, Grace. Don't screw it up."

Her smile sharpened into something that could cut glass. "Don't worry, Frankie. I never screw up the finale."

The heat shimmered around her like applause, and in the rising thermals, she imagined the clamor of comment notifications—the sweet digital symphony that fed her soul. She held the phone aloft as if it were a scepter, her throne built from rusted steel and baked humanity. Every moment closer felt like the world clicking back into place, like puzzle pieces finding their proper configuration.

Below her, the convoy trudged through the stagnant pools left by the recent flooding, their boots squelching in mud that had been baked into a crusty shell on top but remained soupy underneath. The stench was overwhelming—rotting vegetation, dead things, human waste, and something sweet and putrid that made even the hardened survivors gag. They were drenched in sweat, hungry, and hollow-eyed, but Grace saw only a glorious battalion of loyal followers. Their suffering was beautiful— authentic, raw, the kind of material that drove engagement through the roof.

Rebecca lingered near the back, head bowed, her silence irritating. The woman moved like a broken marionette, strings tangled, movements jerky and uncertain. Sweat soaked through her torn clothes, and flies buzzed around the festering cuts on her arms. She was better when she smiled for the camera, more useful when she'd repeated Grace's slogans with proper enthusiasm. Now she was dead weight, dragging down the energy of the entire production.

"Engagement is down," Frank whispered, appearing at her other side like smoke given form. His voice carried the wet sound of damaged vocal cords, and the heat had turned his wounds into seeping sores. "It's Rebecca, dragging your numbers. She's a vibe killer."

"I know," Grace said sweetly, brushing sweat-soaked hair from her eyes. The strands felt like wet rope, thick and tangled. "We'll fix that."

Grace tilted the phone toward her feet. Filming for aesthetic, her feet as she hopped down from the Humvee, her boots splashing into the fetid puddles with satisfying drama. She stalked the convoy like a general inspecting her troops, each step deliberate, theatrical. Overly acted out for the live stream. The water was warm, almost body temperature, and it squished unpleasantly through the holes in her boots. The smell rose with each step. Decay and death baking in the merciless sun.

She pressed her cracked phone screen into faces, demanding smiles, making demands for energy, for positivity. The device felt heavier than it should, weighed down by the millions of eyes watching through its dead lens. Those who faltered earned slaps or curses, others gave hollow cheer, their voices like broken speakers crackling with static. She saw none of that, only graphs ticking upward, follower counts swelling in her head like a beautiful fever.

"Come on, people!" she barked, spinning in a circle, arms spread wide. "This is exclusive content! Your families, your friends, your communities, they're all watching! Don't let them down with this pathetic energy!"

A young man near the front of the convoy raised his fist weakly, his voice cracking from dehydration. "For the Queen!"

"That's better!" Grace clapped her hands, the sound sharp in the oppressive heat. "Feel that? That's authenticity! That's what builds and creates an influencer!"

She paused over a pair of brothers, huddled together in whatever shade they could find. Their lips were cracked and bleeding, their bodies emaciated, ribs visible through sweat-soaked shirts. But they managed a weak cheer when she pointed the camera at them, their eyes reflecting her madness like broken mirrors.

Grace rewarded them with a cracked grin. "That's the spirit," she whispered, leaning close enough to smell their fear-sweat mixed with the stench of unwashed bodies. "Your engagement is safe."

The older brother's voice cracked like dried leather. "We won't let you down, Queen."

"I know you won't," Grace purred, patting his sunken cheek. "Because disappointed audiences don't subscribe. They don't share. They don't make legends."

From the makeshift prisoner cage tied to one of the trucks, Elena shrieked, her hands bound but her tongue loose. The cage was crude—chain link and metal posts, more animal pen than human containment. The metal was scorching hot from the sun, and Elena's fingers were blistered where she'd tried to grip the links. Her expensive clothes were soaked with sweat and filth, clinging to her shivering frame despite the heat.

"Please, Grace, please! I supported you! Maddie's the real saboteur! She wants your audience and your power. She's poisoning everyone against you. I've seen it! I swear!"

Grace approached like a prowling wolf, her grin sharp enough to cut glass. Each step was measured, calculated for maximum dramatic effect. The stench around the cage was worse the closer Grace got. Elena's terror-sweat mixed with the smell of human waste and rotting flood debris making the very air oppressive.

"Oh, sweetheart," she purred, tilting Elena's chin up with the barrel of her pistol. The metal was burning hot from the sun, and Elena's eyes went wide with terror as it seared her skin. "Your personal arc is collapsing. Negative engagement, disloyalty…" She tapped the gun playfully against Elena's cheek, leaving red marks. "…irrelevance."

Elena sobbed, her makeup streaking down her face in grotesque rivers of black and brown, mixed with sweat and tears. "You don't understand," she gasped. "It was a bad moment of info, I got things mixed up, but I'm a loyal follower! I'll do anything. I'll stream, I'll hype you, I'll attack whoever you say. Just… please, I can turn this around! I can help you go viral again."

"Viral," Grace mused, rolling the word around her tongue like fine wine. "Such a beautiful concept. Spreading, infecting, taking over everything it touches." She crouched, lowering herself until their eyes met. "You hear that, Frankie? She wants to be useful."

Frank materialized beside the cage, his rotted form dripping with rainwater and something darker. "Desperation doesn't sell," he drawled, his torn lips twisting. "Loyalty's cheap when it's bought at the gallows. She's dead weight, and you're trending."

Grace tilted her head, feigning consideration. Her wet hair falling across her face like a curtain. She pushed it back with theatrical slowness. "Do you know what happens to leeches who feed without giving back, Elena? They get burned off."

"No, Grace! Please," Elena sobbed, collapsing to her knees in the muddy water. Her bound hands splashed desperately. "I'll change. I'll do anything. I'll get you more followers, I'll fight,

I'll—"

Grace silenced her with a slap, the sound echoing across the water like a gunshot. Elena's head snapped to the side, and blood trickled from her split lip.

"My dearest revolutionaries," Grace announced, turning to her gathered audience, arms spread wide like a crucifixion. "You know the rules. Loyalty is rewarded. Betrayal?"

Frank appeared again, his presence pressing on her chest like a weight, whispering venom. "Punished, darling. Publicly."

The execution dragged, each step meticulously orchestrated for maximum spectacle. Grace reveled in the performance, commanding the convoy to gather close, creating a makeshift arena in the muck. She could feel the eyes of her invisible audience burning into her skin, their anticipation electric in the air.

Elena pleaded, her voice breaking like waves against stone, "Please, Grace, I swear I can make this right. I'll do anything. Just give me a chance, just a chance."

"The time for chances passed when you chose betrayal. It was obvious from the beginning what you were doing," Grace purred, waving her cracked phone in the air as though broadcasting live to millions. The device caught the lightning, its broken screen flashing like a strobe light. "But don't worry, sweetheart, you still have a part to play. Every tragedy needs a proper climax."

Tears mixed with the filthy sweat as Elena sobbed out false confessions, blaming herself for every setback the attack had faced, calling herself a saboteur, a coward, a leech. Her body shuddered with every broken word, the heat making her delirium worse, until her strength gave out and she collapsed face-first onto the burning ground.

"Up," Grace barked, and her enforcers yanked Elena up by her hair. Strands came away in their fists, and Elena's scalp bled where they'd torn free. Her face was raw and blistered from scrape and the hot earth. Grace stalked forward, pistol drawn, pressing it to Elena's thigh.

"This is what happens to traitors," Grace said, her voice rich with imagined fanfare. She could hear the crowd's roar, feel their bloodlust feeding her own. She squeezed the trigger.

Elena's scream pierced the air as the bullet tore through muscle. She crumpled to the ground, clutching her leg, blood mingling with the muck. Her screams became hoarse sobs as she writhed, her body convulsing with each wave of agony.

"I can be better," Elena wailed, her desperation raw. "Please, Grace, please, it wasn't supposed to be like this. I just wanted to belong. I just wanted to be someone."

"Oh, you'll be someone," Grace murmured sweetly, circling Elena like a predator. Water lapped at her boots, and she imagined it was applause, waves of approval washing over her. "You'll be a warning."

Grace shot again, this time into Elena's side. The bullet punched through flesh with a wet sound, and Elena's back arched in agony. The convulsions returned, her body jerking violently, mouth gaping in shock and misery. Blood spread across the muddy puddle, dark red. Arterial blood rolling into the shallow water that would soon cook in the brutal sun and leave a stain baked into the pavement.

Grace leaned down, whispering, "This is your final scene, Elena. Don't ruin it by whining."

Elena sobbed, snot and tears mixing on her filthy face. "I'm sorry. I was stupid. I don't know how they knew. It wasn't me, Grace."

"Spies and traitors suffer their fate," Grace said, gesturing to the invisible cameras that surrounded them. "Millions of them. You're more famous than you've ever been."

Grace smiled, raised her voice to the gathered followers,

"Now, my dears, for the grand finale. No loose ends. No failed arcs. Just victory."

She pressed the barrel to Elena's forehead, savoring the shivering terror in her victim's eyes. The metal was scorching hot from the sun, and Elena's skin turned instantly red where it touched. "Smile for the audience," she whispered, and pulled the trigger.

The crack of the final shot echoed across the sweltering landscape, Elena's head snapped back before collapsing lifelessly onto the burning ground. Blood and brain matter painted the earth behind her in abstract patterns, and Grace watched with artistic appreciation. Silence fell briefly among the convoy, the only sound, the buzz of flies already gathering and the shimmer of heat waves rising from the road.

Grace turned, arms raised high, her face radiant with triumph. "This," she declared, "is how you build an empire."

"See that, my loves?" she whispered into the camera lens that no longer worked. "Traitors don't get redemption arcs—they get finales."

Gunshots punctuated her words, and Grace imagined fireworks in the blazing sky, a celebration for her loyal audience. Her laughter rose above the heat shimmer, shrill and manic, eyes wide and unblinking. The sound echoed off the surrounding hills, multiplying until it felt like a chorus of her own voice singing her praises.

"Engagement is up," Frank whispered approvingly, his rotted breath hot against her ear. "That's more like it."

She marched through the ranks, barking commands, repositioning her bedraggled crew. Her feet splashed through puddles of blood and stagnant water, and she devised elaborate attack formations, flanked by invisible advisors who nodded approvingly. Grace crafted speeches on the fly, rallying her troops for the "Great Siege," her voice raw but unwavering, her body trembling with anticipation despite the oppressive heat.

"Listen to me!" she shouted, spinning to face her followers. "What you just witnessed was justice! Elena chose betrayal, chose to poison our community with her negativity. But we don't let toxic influences destroy what we've built!"

A few followers nodded, their faces pale but compliant. Others stared at Elena's corpse with expressions Grace couldn't read. Shadows of fear, revulsion, something that might have been grief. But she saw only rapt attention, the kind that came from truly compelling content.

"We are family!" she continued, her voice building to a crescendo. "We are revolution! We are the future of this broken world! And tomorrow, we show the Thompson farm what real community looks like!"

Visions danced behind her eyes as she spoke. Streaming sponsors, brand deals resurrected, her name etched into the annals of this new world as a victorious queen… The Queen of Likes. She saw herself at the head of a growing empire, rebuilding civilization with her iron will and unmatched charisma. Cities would rise with her face carved into their foundations, children would sing her name in schools yet to be built.

As the convoy crested the hill to the farm, Grace danced atop the Humvee, drenched in sweat, caked in dried mud and blood, lost in a symphony only she could hear. Her movements were erratic, frenzied, arms flailing as she conducted an orchestra of ghosts. The heat made her delirious, her skin flushed and burning, but she felt only the cool touch of fame. Followers cheered; some genuine, others forced, all hollow. All while imaginary applause swelled in her ears.

The specter of Frank leaned beside her, spouting strategy and flattery, while other ghosts began to appear. Old followers who had long perished, smiling wide and hollow-eyed, urging her on. They crowded around the Humvee like hungry spirits, their voices joining in a chorus of encouragement.

"You're magnificent," whispered a girl Grace had executed weeks ago. "They'll never forget you."

"Immortal," added a man who'd died in the river crossing. "That's what legends are."

Children she had forgotten danced beside her in the storm, echoing her slogans, whispering her name like a mantra. Their faces were pale, their clothes torn, but their eyes burned with the same fervor that consumed her. Phantom camera drones circled her, their red lights blinking with approval, broadcasting her radiant glory to millions.

"This is it," she whispered to her audience of the dead. "The end of scarcity. The beginning of my empire. The finale they'll never forget."

Her cracked, blackened phone screen reflected only her own fraying image. It reflected someone she didn't quite recognize. The image of smeared makeup, crazed smile, eyes that had seen too much and understood too little. But she saw triumph, saw power surging in invisible waves. She saw herself crowned in light, worshipped by the masses, eternal and untouchable.

Below, her soldiers exchanged worried glances. Some gripped their weapons tighter, others looked toward the horizon as if calculating escape routes. Behind, Rebecca clenched her fists, her face a mask of barely contained fury. Beside her, Frank's rotted grin stretched wider, and shadows of the dead marched along with them, ghosts Grace welcomed into her growing court.

Grace didn't see fear anymore, not in her enemies, not in her followers. No, because fear was just a tool to manipulate the masses. All she felt was the surge of phantom notifications, the sweet high of imagined adoration, and the certainty of destiny at her fingertips. The world would remember her name, would speak it with reverence and terror.

Her victory was close. The show was just beginning.

Rebecca

The baked earth cracked beneath her boots as she stumbled, the air thick with the copper tang of blood and the sharp, electric scent of gunpowder. Sweat poured down her face, mixing with tears she refused to acknowledge, stinging her eyes as the merciless sun beat down on the carnage. Her hands trembled at her sides, knuckles scraped and raw, heart thudding so hard it blurred her vision. Elena's final scream still echoed in her head, the crack of gunfire, the muffled weeping from the crowd. The woman's body lay crumpled in the scorched mud, her eyes wide and glassy, mouth frozen mid-plea, dried blood painting abstract patterns across her lifeless face.

The stench was overwhelming. Elena's voided bowels added to the mix of God only knew what. All of it, with the putrid smell of flood debris baking in the sun, creating a miasma that made Rebecca's stomach lurch. Flies had already begun to gather, buzzing a grotesque soundtrack to the silence that followed Grace's performance. The heat made everything worse. The smell, the shock, the way sweat pooled in every crevice of her body like accusation.

Around them, Grace's followers stood in stunned silence. No cheers. No chants. Just hollow-eyed stares and the restless shuffling of feet on ground that had been turned to concrete by the brutal sun. Their faces were slack with horror, mouths hanging open, eyes reflecting the same terrible understanding that was clawing at Rebecca's chest. Two in two days and it was getting worse. Now…they were all complicit in this madness.

Rebecca felt bile rise, burning her throat like acid. To her left, Anna was rocking, arms wrapped tight across her chest, a keening sound slipping from her mouth like air from a punctured tube The young woman's clothes were soaked through with sweat and fetid water. Her dark hair plastered to her skull, and her eyes darted constantly between Elena's corpse and Grace's elevated position as if she couldn't process what she'd witnessed.

Caleb, once the loudest voice in Grace's chorus, stared blankly, lips parted, water streaking down his cheeks in an endless mix of perspiration and tears. His massive frame seemed to have shrunk in on itself, shoulders hunched, hands hanging useless at his sides. The man who had cheered Grace's executions now looked like a broken child, lost and confused.

The Burke brothers clung to their rifles like lifelines, their pale fingers clenched white and bloodless around the heated metal. Sean's jaw worked soundlessly, chewing on words that wouldn't come, while Tommy's eyes had gone completely vacant, staring at nothing. Both boys were young enough to be her sons, Rebecca realized with a pang of maternal horror. Just kids who'd been twisted into instruments of someone else's madness. Each of them knowing that for no reason at all they could be next in Grace's delusions and show of death.

The handlers lurked at the edges of the crowd like predators sensing weakness. Rebecca's gaze snapped to them, the men and women in scavenged tactical gear with cold, sharp eyes that flicked from face to face, calculating, measuring. They were not shocked by Grace's violence; they were evaluating its impact, determining whether their investment was still profitable. Already, they were stepping back, slipping into the shadows, ready to abandon a dying queen.

Rebecca's breath caught when a tall, narrow-faced handler met her gaze. His smirk was thin and sharp as a knife sliding under her skin, and she recognized him, One of the men who'd been whispering in Grace's ear all along. His presence had always made her skin crawl, but now she understood why. He tilted his head slightly, a quiet warning that thrummed like a drumbeat inside her skull. Stay quiet, girl. Or you will not live to regret it.

Her stomach clenched hard as real understanding crashed over her like a cold wave. Grace had never ruled this nightmare. She had been the blade, but the handlers were the hands guiding it. They fed her delusions, encouraged her violence, used her mental illness as a weapon against anyone who threatened their control.

The sun climbed higher, turning the air into a furnace that baked the blood into the ground and made breathing an effort. Rebecca's throat felt raw, her mouth dry as sand. The smell of death grew stronger in the heat, and she saw mirages shimmering in the distance. She had to laugh to herself when she thought maybe those were just more of Grace's hallucinations, bleeding into reality.

As the day wore on, a gusty wind rose in slight relief from the sickening smell of the rotting world following the flood. Canvas tarps snapped and flapped like dying birds. Smoke from a dying fire stung Rebecca's eyes as she moved, slipping between bodies, whispering to Anna, to Caleb, to the Burke brothers, to anyone who still had enough of themselves left to listen.

"This isn't right," she whispered to Anna, gripping the young woman's shaking hands. "What Grace did to Elena—that wasn't justice. That was murder."

Anna's eyes focused on her with desperate hope. "I know,"

she breathed. "But what can we do? If we speak up—"

"We do it together," Rebecca interrupted, her voice barely audible. "All of us. They can't kill everyone."

Every breath felt like breathing glass. Every step was a gamble. The narrow-faced handler brushed past her once, his fingers ghosting along her arm just long enough to make her skin crawl. His voice was a whisper at her ear, sour and low. "Careful, sweetheart. A lot of folks don't survive picking the wrong side."

Rebecca clenched her jaw and kept walking, pulse hammering in her ears. She was not just risking rebellion. She was balancing on the edge of a blade, and one wrong move would send her tumbling into the same abyss that had claimed Elena.

She found Tommy Burke crouched behind a supply truck, his young face pale and streaked with tears. "Hey," she said softly, settling beside him. "You okay?"

He looked up at her with eyes that had aged decades in the past hour. "She just… she just killed her. Like it was nothing. Like Elena was nothing. Yesterday, she was the new content— Today? She was the *new,* new content."

Tommy's grip on his rifle loosened slightly. "I keep thinking about my mom. What she'd say if she could see me now."

"What would she say?"

"That I was better than this. That I was raised better than this." His voice cracked. "But I cheered, Mrs. Mitchell. When Grace killed those people before, I cheered."

Rebecca placed a gentle hand on his shoulder. "You were scared. You were surviving. But you don't have to cheer anymore."

The message spread through the camp like wildfire—not

spoken aloud, but passed in glances, in subtle nods, in the way people began to cluster together.

Grace continued her performance from atop the Humvee, but something changed. Her movements were more erratic, her voice shriller. She kept glancing at the sky, having animated conversations with people who weren't there, her cracked phone held like a talisman against reality.

"The engagement numbers are dropping," she muttered, loud enough for Rebecca to hear. "Frank says it's because of the negative energy. Too much criticism in the comments."

Rebecca felt a chill despite the oppressive heat. Grace was spiraling deeper into her delusions, and that made her more dangerous than ever. Cornered animals were unpredictable, and Grace was certainly cornered now—by her own madness, by the growing resistance among her followers, by the approaching reality of the Thompson farm's defenses.

The first shot cracked through the air like a lightning strike, shattering the oppressive silence.

Chaos roared to life around them. Shouts exploded from a dozen throats, boots thudded through the baked mud, gunfire tore the blazing afternoon apart. Rebecca shoved through the panic, her hands scraping against shoulders, backs, arms slick with sweat, her heart beating so hard she tasted copper in her mouth.

She ducked as a rifle went off too close, the blast deafening, the air sharp with the stink of spent rounds and something else. Fear, thick and acrid. Figures slammed into her, knocking her sideways. The heat made everything worse, turning the chaos into a hellish furnace where panic and violence merged into something nightmarish.

"Hold your fire!" she heard one of those handlers shouting, but his voice was lost in the cacophony. "Hold your damn fire!"

But it was too late. Grace's carefully constructed army was

fracturing, and the cracks were spreading faster than anyone could contain them. Rebecca saw Sean Burke tackle his brother, both of them rolling in the dust as Tommy tried to turn his weapon on one of the handlers. Anna was screaming, her voice raw and desperate, calling for everyone to stop, to think, to remember who they were.

And there she was.

Grace stood on the hood of a ruined jeep, her sweat-soaked hair clinging to her face like seaweed, black makeup smeared in jagged streaks down her cheeks. She laughed and shouted into the blazing sun, swinging her cracked phone high like a queen with a crown of shattered glass. Her voice was raw, words slurred, mouth foaming with half-formed commands.

"Beautiful content!" she screamed at the sky. "This is what they want to see! Authentic conflict! Real drama!"

Below, her soldiers wavered, some rooted in place, some pulling back, their eyes darting between Grace and the handlers and each other. The careful hierarchy that had held them together was crumbling, and nobody knew who to follow anymore.

Rebecca's throat tightened as she watched Grace's performance. The girl was completely gone now, lost in a world of her own making, and Rebecca saw the exact moment when her remaining followers began to understand that their leader was beyond help.

She shoved through the last few stunned bodies, boots sliding in the slick mixture of mud and blood. Her breath tore from her chest in ragged gasps, the heat making every inhale feel like swallowing fire. "Grace!" she shouted, voice cracking. "Grace, look at me!"

For one aching moment, Grace's gaze snapped to her, wide-eyed, trembling. And Rebecca saw her—not the monster, not the queen, but the girl. The teenager who used to hum softly while braiding Hannah's hair in their last year of high school, who twirled barefoot on cracked pavement in the summer, who dreamed of stages and spotlights, not battlefields.

"Mrs. Mitchell?" Grace's voice was small, confused. She blinked rapidly, as if trying to focus. "What's happening? Where are my parents? They were just here; they were watching the stream…"

Rebecca felt her heart break. "They're gone, honey. They've been gone for a long time."

Grace's face twisted, and for a moment she looked like the lost child she'd always been. "They're gone," she whispered, her voice small, shaking. "Why aren't they watching? Where did they go?"

"The phone doesn't work, Grace," Rebecca said gently, stepping closer. "It hasn't worked for months. There's no audience. There never was."

Grace stared at the cracked device in her hands, and Rebecca saw understanding flicker across her features. "No," she whispered. "No, that's not right. Frank told me the numbers were good. The engagement was—"

"Frank is dead," Rebecca said softly. "You killed him, remember? You hanged him in Cornish."

Grace's eyes went wide with horror. "No, he's right here. He's been helping me plan the content. He said the farm would be perfect for—" She stopped, her gaze darting around frantically. "Frank? Frank, where are you?"

Rebecca forced her voice steady through the quake of her chest. "It's over, Grace. Please. Let me help you."

At the edges of the chaos, the handlers melted into the background, their boots silent, their faces turned elsewhere. They had already left her to fall, abandoning their puppet now that she was no longer useful. Marcus caught Rebecca's eye one last time, his expression cold and calculating, before he disappeared into the crowd.

Grace swayed on her feet, shoulders shaking. Her hand trembled, the cracked phone slipping from her grip, hitting the pavement with a shatter. Her lips quivered, her eyes glimmering with something sharp, wet, human. "Mrs. Mitchell," she choked, "I didn't mean to. I didn't—"

"I know," Rebecca said, stepping forward slowly, hands open, heart roaring in her chest. "I know you didn't mean it. You were sick. You needed help, and nobody gave it to you."

Grace's breathing was ragged now, her chest hitching with suppressed sobs. "I remember," she whispered. "I remember Hannah laughing. I remember when we used to dance in your backyard. I remember when I was..." She paused, her voice breaking. "When I was at Harvard. Oh God! Am I even human?"

"You're still human," Rebecca said desperately. "You're still that girl who loved her friends, who wanted to make people happy. That's still in there, Grace. We can find her again."

But even as she spoke, Rebecca saw the madness reasserting itself. Grace's eyes began to dart frantically, and she started muttering to herself, having rapid conversations with invisible advisors.

"The algorithm doesn't like redemption arcs," she said suddenly, her voice taking on that manic quality again. "Frank says it's too predictable. The audience wants—"

"There is no audience!" Rebecca screamed, her composure finally cracking. "There is no Frank! There are no likes, no followers, no engagement! It's just you, Grace! Just you and these people!" Rebecca's arms went wide to each side showcasing the hollow faces staring at them.

She stumbled backward, her face cycling through confusion, recognition, and desperate denial. "No," she whispered. "No, you're wrong. They're watching. They have to be watching. Otherwise, what was it all for?"

Rebecca's heart shattered as she watched Grace's mind fracture in real time. The girl was trapped between two realities—the one where she was a beloved influencer creating content for millions, and the one where she was a murderer standing in the ruins of her own making.

"Come with me," Rebecca pleaded, reaching out her hand. "We can fix this. We can get you help. Hannah would want that. She'd want us to save you."

Grace stared at Rebecca's outstretched hand, and for a moment, hope flickered in her eyes. She took a step forward, then another, her movements hesitant but deliberate. "Hannah," she whispered. "Is she—is she really alive?"

"Yes," Rebecca said, tears streaming down her face. "She's alive, and she's safe, and she still loves you. She never stopped loving you."

Grace's face fell completely. "I tried to kill her," she sobbed. "I tried to kill my best friend. For fucking content that doesn't even exist?"

"But you didn't," Rebecca said urgently. "You didn't kill her. That means something. That means you can still choose differently."

For a moment, the clearing went quiet except for the sound of Grace's ragged breathing. Rebecca saw the war playing out behind her eyes—the broken girl fighting against the monster she'd become, reality battling delusion, love struggling against the madness that had consumed her.

Then Grace's expression changed. The lucidity vanished, replaced by something cold and calculating. Her eyes narrowed and she stepped one hesitant step back. "You're trying to tank my ratings," she said, her voice flat and emotionless. "You're working for the competition. That's why you want me to quit. That's why you're trying to make me think—"

"Grace, no," Rebecca said desperately. "I'm trying to help you. I'm trying to save you."

But Grace was already backing away, her hand moving to her belt. The shift was small, so small Rebecca almost missed it. A flicker of panic. A sharp, desperate gleam slicing through Grace's gaze. Her hand snapped out, yanking a knife from the belt of a nearby fighter.

Rebecca screamed, throat tearing with the force of it. "No!"

Grace's chest hitched, her fingers shaking as she pressed the blade to her own throat. "Stay back Mrs. Mitchell."

The sun blazed overhead, making the metal gleam like liquid fire. Her breath hitched, her body trembling. "May God forgive me," she whispered.

"Grace, please," Rebecca sobbed, reaching out desperately. "Please don't do this. Hannah needs you. I need you. We can fix this together."

But Grace was already gone, lost in the space between realities, between the girl she'd been and the monster she'd become. "Tell them," she whispered, her voice barely audible. "Tell them I was trying to make something beautiful."

The blade flashed in the merciless sun. The slash was brutal, sudden, efficient.

Blood sprayed in an arc, bright red against the bleached landscape, warm and shocking against the burning air. Grace gasped, her mouth opening in a silent apology as she stumbled, knees buckling, hands falling limp at her sides. The knife clattered to the ground, its blade painted crimson. She fell, folding inward like a broken doll, her body hitting the baked earth with a sick, final sound.

The world lurched to stillness. Even the wind seemed to hold its breath.

Around her, soldiers froze like statues. Some dropped their

weapons with soft, metallic clatters. Some fell to their knees, hands buried in their hair, shoulders shaking with helpless sobs. Others stood locked in place, faces blank, eyes wide with shock as they tried to process what they'd witnessed.

Tommy Burke was the first to move. The young man stumbled forward, his rifle forgotten, and knelt beside Grace's body. "She was just a young girl," he whispered, his voice broken. "She was just a fucking kid at heart."

Anna collapsed beside him, her keening wail joining Rebecca's as they mourned not just Grace, but all the people they'd been before this madness began. The Burke boys held each other, their young faces streaked with tears, while Caleb stood like a monument to grief, his massive frame shaking with suppressed emotion.

The handlers were gone. Slipped away like smoke, leaving nothing but ruin in their wake.

Rebecca lifted her head, her vision blurred, lashes clumped with sweat and tears. Her throat felt raw, her chest hollow, her heart a bruised and battered thing that somehow still beat. The sun continued its merciless assault, baking the blood into the ground, turning Grace's final performance into just another stain on the scorched earth.

Beyond the wreckage, past the scattered, broken lines of Grace's former army, the Thompson farm waited. Rebecca could see it in the distance, a beacon of normalcy in a world gone mad. Lanterns swung gently in the hot breeze. Figures moved between them, waiting, watching. Rebecca walked slowly waving a white shirt, her hands raised in a silent offer of peace.

Rebecca pulled in a ragged breath, and her heart beat, bruised but unbroken, considering all she'd witnessed and all she'd lost.

"It's over," she whispered, her voice splintering at the edges like broken glass. "We are still here."

Hannah

Hannah Mitchell stumbled forward, her legs heavy with exhaustion, her chest tight, recalling the last day. Smoke hung low over the shattered farmland, curling in thin, acrid ribbons that filled her mouth and nose with the stench of burned wood, gunpowder, and diesel exhaust. The oppressive heat made everything worse—the smoke clung to her skin like a second layer of clothing and sweat mixed with soot to create dark streaks down her face and arms.

The earth was slick beneath her boots, churned to a paste by panicked feet, and the desperate struggle of bodies clashing in the blazing afternoon sun. The mud was warm, almost hot, and it sucked at her boots with each step. Shouts echoed faintly through the heat-hazed air, and the sharp cracks of final, isolated gunshots rattled across the farmyard like punctuation marks at the end of a nightmare.

Her eyes burned as she scanned the yard, heart twisting with a mixture of relief and horror. People moved like ghosts among the wreckage, their silhouettes wavering in the heat shimmer that rose from the baked earth. Some carried makeshift stretchers, the groaning wounded lashed down with belts and torn fabric, their faces pale and slick with perspiration. Others piled smoldering debris, stamping out the last tongues of fire that hissed and popped as wet timbers met the merciless sun.

She caught the faint sound of sobbing, the low murmur of prayer, the sharp bark of orders as defenders checked the perimeter. A child's cry rose above the other sounds—high, keening, desperate—and Hannah's medical training kicked in automatically. Someone was hurt, someone needed help, but first she had to find…

Then, through the flickering heat waves, she saw her mother.

Rebecca stood near the collapsed fence, her shoulders hunched, mud streaked up her arms, her hands trembling at her sides. Her hair hung damp with sweat around her face, her eyes glazed with exhaustion and something deeper, cracked open and raw. The woman who had raised her, who had packed her school lunches and braided her hair and worried about her grades, looked like she had aged a decade in the months since they'd been separated.

Hannah's breath hitched painfully, a sob clawing up her throat. She stumbled forward, her feet splashing through shallow puddles of water and blood, faster, faster, until she reached her mother. The heat radiating from the ground made her feel dizzy, but she pushed through it, driven by desperate need.

"Mom," she gasped, the word breaking like glass in her mouth.

Rebecca turned, slow and dazed, and when her eyes met Hannah's, they widened. Her arms opened without a word, and Hannah crashed into them, burying her face in the crook of her mother's neck. In that embrace they fell to their knees together right there in the middle of the drive.

Hannah felt the hitching of Rebecca's breath, the shudder in her arms as they clutched tight, almost too tight, as if afraid to let go. Her mother's body was thinner than she remembered, harder, shaped by the captivity and survival.

"You're here," Hannah whispered, her voice small, trembling. "You're really here."

"I'm here," Rebecca choked, her hands fisting in Hannah's jacket, her body trembling like a wire pulled too tight. "You're safe. Oh God, you're safe."

For a moment, the sounds of the still smoldering battlefield faded—the clatter of weapons, the crackle of fire, the distant groans and cries. For a moment, there was only the ragged heartbeat of reunion, the desperate clutch of family finding itself again.

"Jake," Rebecca whispered against Hannah's shoulder. "Is Jake—is he here? Is he safe?"

"He's fine," Hannah breathed, her voice thick with tears. "He's beautiful and strong and so much braver than any boy should have to be. He's on patrol." She paused and held her mother tighter. "He saw you, Mom. He delivered the message after your note."

Rebecca pulled back just enough to see Hannah's face, to read the truth in her eyes. "And you? Are you hurt? Are you—"

"I'm alive," Hannah said simply. "We're all alive. That's what matters now."

Around them, the battered community pulled itself together piece by piece. Marianne moved among the wounded, her face pale but composed, her hands gentle as she pressed bandages, checked pulses, offered whispered reassurances. Her movements were economical, practiced; she had done this before, in the early days after the collapse, when communities were still learning what survival meant.

Michael and Beth directed defenders to reinforce the gates,

their voices hoarse but determined. The heat made their work harder, sweat pouring down their faces as they dragged debris and positioned barriers. Beth's uniform was soaked through, her badge tarnished but still pinned to her chest—a reminder of the world they'd lost and the order they were trying to rebuild.

Maddie emerged from the barn, her clothes streaked with ash and grease, her arms full of salvaged supplies, her face set in a mask of grim focus. She moved with purpose, organizing the chaos when Hannah waved her over.

Then the refugees arrived.

It began as a trickle—gaunt, mud-smeared figures appearing on the road, hands raised, eyes wide and wary. They stumbled forward in ones and twos, clutching makeshift bundles, supporting the wounded, their clothes tattered, their bodies hollow with hunger and fear. The heat had taken its toll on them too; their faces were flushed and streaked with sweat, their movements sluggish with dehydration.

The defenders bristled, weapons half-raised, but Rebecca lifted a hand, her shout echoing in the yard with unexpected authority.

"They're laying down arms," she called, firm and steady. "They're not here to fight."

Hannah counted as the group drew closer, and her heart twisted at the sight. There were children among them, small faces streaked with grime, eyes darting with animal wariness. Mothers bent protectively over them, their arms thin and bruised, their clothes hanging loose on frames that had been reduced by starvation. Old men stumbled, coughing, one leaning heavily on a homemade crutch fashioned from a broken rifle.

And there, near the back, someone called out when they recognized the Burke boys—shoulders slumped, faces pale, dragging their feet as if every step was a penance. They were younger than she'd expected, barely out of their teens, and they carried themselves with the defeated posture of people who had finally understood the true cost of their choices.

"Look at them," Rebecca said quietly, her voice held a note of pity that surprised Hannah. "Most of them never wanted this. They were just scared, hungry, desperate. Grace and her handlers used that desperation."

Hannah turned as Maddie appeared at her side, her arms crossed tight over her chest. "We're going to need a separate farm for them," Maddie murmured, thoughts already working through the logistics. "Close enough to keep an eye on them, far enough they can build something on their own. The Henderson place might work—it's only a quarter mile down the road."

Rebecca gave a slow nod. "We can do that. Give them a chance to prove they can be something better than what they were forced to become."

Her expression darkened, and she glanced between Hannah and Maddie. "There's something else you need to know. Something that happened before Grace..." She paused, searching for words. "Elena was with us. She came to Grace's camp, fed her intelligence about your defenses, about the farm's layout."

Hannah felt her stomach drop. "Elena? But she was—"

"She was angry," Rebecca said quietly. "Bitter and feeling abandoned by the community. She wanted revenge, and Grace gave her a platform for it."

"Where is she now?" Maddie asked, though something in her tone suggested she already suspected the answer.

Rebecca's face was grim. "Grace killed her. Called her a spy, and said she was trying to sabotage the attack. Elena tried to convince her she was loyal, but Grace was too far gone by then. She shot her in the mud. Right there in front of everyone."

The silence stretched between them; another life lost to the madness.

"Matthew needs to know," Hannah said finally.

Maddie stepped forward. "I'll tell him. After everything that happened between them, it should come from—"

"No," Rebecca interrupted gently. "It should come from me. I was there. I saw what happened. He deserves to hear it from someone who witnessed it, not filtered through other people's interpretations."

Hannah exchanged a look with Maddie, recognizing the wisdom in her mother's words. "He's probably at the medical station. Emily had him helping with the wounded despite his shoulder."

They found Matthew near the barn, his left arm still in a sling, using his good hand to help organize supplies. He looked up as they approached, his face showing the strain of the day's events but also something like relief.

"Matthew," Hannah said, stepping forward. "I'd like you to meet my mother, Rebecca. She just escaped from Grace's camp."

Matthew straightened, extending his good hand. "Mrs. Mitchell. Hannah's told us so much about you. I'm glad you made it safely."

"Thank you," Rebecca said, shaking his hand briefly. "And I'm sorry about what I need to tell you. Something about what happened to Elena"

His expression grew wary, and his jaw tightened. "She's dead, isn't she?"

"Yes," Rebecca said simply. "Grace killed her yesterday. Elena went to Grace's camp, fed her information about the farm's defenses. She wanted revenge against the community, against people she felt wronged her."

Hannah couldn't help but notice the way her mother always seemed to try and make the actions of people somehow excusable. She knew, all of them did now, what Elena did to Matthew, and she struggled to find pity for her.

Matthew closed his eyes for a moment, processing this. When he opened them, there was sadness there, but also something like acceptance. "She chose her path," he said quietly. "I tried to help her, tried to be what she needed, but she was so angry, so bitter. I couldn't save her from herself."

"I'm sorry," Rebecca said. "I know you cared about her."

Matthew nodded once, then looked at Hannah and Maddie. "Thank you for telling me. For not letting me wonder." He turned back to the supply boxes; his movements deliberate and controlled. "I should get back to work. People need these supplies."

Hannah watched him walk away, recognizing the way he channeled the news into action. It was how they all coped now—by staying busy, by focusing on the work of survival rather than loss.

At the back of the group, a sharp commotion snapped Hannah's attention around. A knot of defenders had seized several figures, rougher, harder-faced, dressed in scavenged military gear. These weren't the hollow-eyed refugees—these were predators, men and women who had thrived in the chaos, who had fed on others' desperation.

Whispers rippled through the crowd: handlers. The ones who fueled Grace's rise, whispered in her ear, turned her into a weapon.

Beth's voice cut sharply across the yard. "Lock them in the root cellar."

In all, six figures were dragged away—four men and two women, all identified by the refugees as the worst of Grace's inner circle. Cruel and inhumane, responsible for organizing the executions, torture, the systematic degradation of human dignity. The Burke boys were also taken and placed in custody, their youth offering no protection from the gravity of their crimes.

As the sun began to sink toward the horizon, the community gathered in the farmhouse kitchen to decide the fate of their prisoners. The room was stifling, packed with bodies and heavy with the weight of judgment. Hannah found herself pressed against the back wall, her mother's hand in hers, watching as the most difficult decisions of their new world were debated.

James Thompson stood at the head of the table, his face drawn with exhaustion but his voice steady. "We have eight prisoners. Six who were Grace's handlers, two who we know from town who killed Mr. Miller. All are guilty of crimes that in the old world would have meant life in prison or death."

"The handlers organized mass murder," Beth said flatly. "They turned Grace's mental illness into a weapon and used it to terrorize communities across the region. There's no rehabilitation for that kind of evil."

Daniel nodded grimly. "The Burke boys killed George Miller during that pharmacy robbery. Shot an old man in cold blood for medication. That's murder, plain and simple."

"They were stupid," Rebecca said quietly. "Making terrible choices in terrible circumstances. That doesn't excuse what they did, but it explains it. Young boys whom I can say had no hand in the murders within our group."

"Explanation isn't absolution," Michael replied. "George Miller was a good man. He helped people. He didn't deserve to die for a handful of pills."

Hannah watched the debate unfold, feeling the terrible weight of civilization being rebuilt one decision at a time. In the old world, there were courts, lawyers, and appeals processes. Now there was only this—a kitchen full of exhausted people trying to decide who lived and who died based on their own sense of justice.

"We don't have facilities to keep prisoners long-term," Emily pointed out. "We can't feed them indefinitely, can't guard them indefinitely. And we can't let them go free to terrorize other communities."

"So we're talking about execution," Sarah said quietly. "We're talking about hanging people in our backyard."

The word hung in the air like a presence. Execution. In the old world, it was rare, controversial, carried out by the state with elaborate protocols. Now it was a practical necessity, discussed in the same tone they might use to debate crop rotations.

"For the handlers, yes," James said finally. "They've forfeited their right to life through their actions. But the Burke boys..."

"Are barely more than children," Marianne Miller said suddenly. The elderly woman had been silent throughout the debate, sitting in the corner with her hands folded, her face composed despite the discussion of her husband's killers. Now she stood, her voice carrying the authority of age and loss.

"Mrs. Miller," Beth said gently, "you have every right to demand justice for George. No one would blame you—"

"Justice," Marianne interrupted, "is not always the same as revenge. George was a good man, a kind man. He would want those boys to have a chance at redemption."

Hannah felt tears prick her eyes as she watched the old woman struggle with grief and grace in equal measure. Here was someone who lost everything and still chose mercy over vengeance.

"They're nineteen and twenty-one," Marianne continued. "Old enough to know better, young enough to change. If we hang them, we're no better than the world that created them. If we spare them, we might help them become something better."

"And if they kill someone else?" Daniel asked. "If they run away and join another group of raiders? Their blood will be on our hands."

"Then we make sure they don't," Marianne said firmly. "We put them to work. Hard work. Dangerous work. They rebuild what they helped destroy, they tend the sick they helped create, they earn their place in this community one day at a time."

The debate continued for another hour, voices rising and falling as people struggled with questions that had no easy answers. Hannah found herself thinking about Grace—her friend who became a monster, who chose death over redemption. Was it kindness or cruelty to offer the Burke boys a chance Grace refused?

Finally, a vote was called. The handlers would hang at dawn—their crimes were too severe, their influence too dangerous to risk. But the Burke boys would be given a chance, under Marianne's supervision, to prove they could be more than the sum of their worst moments.

As the meeting broke up, Hannah stepped outside into the cooler evening air. The heat was finally beginning to break, though the ground still radiated warmth from the day's brutal sun. Stars were beginning to appear overhead, and for the first time in days, she felt like she could breathe.

Jake found her there, running across the yard with the boundless energy of youth. "You okay?"

"I'm okay," she said, ruffling his hair. "I'm better than okay. We're all together again."

As darkness settled over the battered farm, lanterns flickered to life, their warm glow casting long, golden ribbons across the mud. Fires crackled in makeshift pits, the smoke curling upward in thin, silver trails. The community was slowly coming back to life, people emerging from their shock to begin the work of rebuilding.

Somewhere, a child let out a thin, hiccupping laugh, and the sound was so shockingly normal, so heartbreakingly human, that Hannah felt tears sting her eyes again. This was what they were fighting for, not just survival, but the chance to be human again.

Rebecca sat beside her near the farmhouse steps, Jake asleep with his head in her lap, his curls damp with sweat. Grayson's family clustered nearby, speaking in soft voices, arms around one another, holding tight as if they might float away. The Burke boys sat under guard near the barn, their heads bowed, probably contemplating their narrow escape from the noose.

Hannah leaned her head back, staring up at the bruised purple sky. Her hands were raw, her body ached, and every inch of her felt scraped thin and hollowed out. But when she reached over and grasped Rebecca's hand, felt her mother's fingers tighten around hers, she let out a shuddering breath.

"We made it," she whispered.

"We did," Rebecca agreed, her voice soft but steady. "We actually did."

From the barn, Old Man Jenkins emerged, his face grim, a piece of paper clutched in his weathered hands. He approached the group around the farmhouse steps with the careful gait of someone bearing bad news.

"James," he called out, his voice carrying across the yard. "James, you need to hear this."

James Thompson looked up from where he'd been talking quietly with Beth and Michael, his face immediately alert. "What is it, Jenkins?"

"Radio chatter," Jenkins said, waving the paper. "Been monitoring the frequencies, and I picked up something you're not going to like."

Hannah felt her stomach drop. Around her, the peaceful evening atmosphere evaporated as people sensed the approaching storm.

"What kind of chatter?" Beth asked, her hand instinctively moving to her weapon.

Jenkins looked around at the assembled faces, then back at the paper in his hands. "Another group. Moving north on Route 25. Fair sized force, well-organized. They're about two hours out, maybe less."

"Well, shit," Michael breathed. "How many?"

"Hard to say from the radio intercepts, but..." Jenkins paused, his face grave. "Could be as many as fifty, maybe more. And they're not refugees looking for shelter. They're asking about the Thompson farm specifically."

The blood drained from Hannah's face. After everything they'd been through, after Grace's defeat and the capture of her handlers, there was another threat bearing down on them. The nightmare wasn't over—it was just beginning a new chapter.

"How much time do we have?" James asked, his voice steady despite the circumstances.

Jenkins looked up at the darkening sky, then back at the assembled faces. "If they're moving through the night, they'll be here before dawn. Right about the time we planned to..." He glanced toward the root cellar where the handlers waited. "Well, right about the time we planned to deal with our other problem."

Maddie

Snow blanketed the farm in thick, quiet drifts, softening every scar the siege left behind. Broken fences and patched roofs disappeared beneath winter's hush, their harsh edges smoothed by ice and time. Maddie Foster stood at the ridge overlooking the valley, her breath rising in pale clouds as she tucked her scarf tighter around her face. The cold stung her cheeks and slipped down her collar, but the air felt sharp and pure in her lungs—cleaner than it had in months.

Sunlight skimmed over the snow, setting the fields aglow like scattered glass. Smoke curled up from chimneys below, carrying the earthy scent of woodsmoke and simmering broth across the cold morning. She could hear voices drifting up from the farmyard—children laughing, adults calling out morning greetings, the steady ring of hammers from the workshop.

"You're up early," Matthew said behind her, his boots crunching through the snow as he approached. His rifle hung across his shoulder, and his breath puffed in pale bursts. His hair was longer now, dark curls peeking from under his knit cap, his face thinner but calmer than she'd seen it in months.

"Couldn't sleep," Maddie replied, turning to face him. "Still getting used to the quiet."

Matthew joined her at the ridge, his shoulder brushing hers as they looked down at the farm. "Hard to believe it's been six months."

Six months since the siege, since Grace's fall, since the handlers were executed and the community was left to pick up the broken pieces. The farm had not only survived—it had taken root again, battered but unbroken. The fear of more raiders ended when Jenkins' radio network confirmed that most of the organized groups had either destroyed themselves or been absorbed by the growing settlements.

"Jenkins got more reports from Portland yesterday," Matthew continued, his voice thoughtful. "Says the city's nearly uninhabitable. Death and destruction everywhere, just waiting for nature to reclaim it."

Maddie nodded, remembering the chaos Hannah had escaped from. "Maybe that's for the best. Let it grow over, start fresh somewhere else."

"The antenna array is working well though," Matthew said, a note of pride in his voice. "Your design is pulling in signals from as far as Chicago. People are sharing everything—weather reports, crop information, even just… good news."

A smile tugged at Maddie's lips. Her father's notebooks provided technical knowledge, but it was her own engineering that made the communications network possible. Connecting isolated communities, sharing vital information, rebuilding civilization one radio frequency at a time.

"Ready for another hunting trip?" Matthew asked, adjusting his pack. "The deer tracks Jake spotted yesterday should still be fresh."

"Always," Maddie said, shouldering her own pack. Her father's rifle—cleaned, oiled, and reliable—felt familiar in her hands now. "Though I think you just like getting me alone in the woods."

Matthew's cheeks flushed, and not from the cold and he smirked when he raised an eyebrow. "Maybe I do."

They walked down the hill together, their boots crunching softly in the snow. In the yard below, the day was already alive with purpose. Ethan and Jake were out past the fence, teaching younger teens how to track in the snow, their voices clear and steady as they pointed at faint hoofprints in the powder.

"See how the back hooves register in the front prints?" Ethan was saying, his tone patient but authoritative. "That means the deer was moving slowly, probably foraging."

"Unless it's a buck," Jake added, crouching beside a deeper impression. "Then the stride pattern's different, more deliberate."

Maddie watched the boys work, remembering when they were just kids playing in the barn loft in the early days. Now they were teachers, passing on skills that might mean the difference between life and death for the next generation.

Near the well, Hannah crouched to break the thin skin of ice, her cheeks flushed, a smile tugging at the corners of her mouth as she worked. She looked up as Maddie and Matthew approached, her eyes bright with something that might have been mischief.

"Off hunting again?" Hannah asked, straightening with the water bucket. "You two certainly spend a lot of time in the woods together."

"Someone has to keep the community fed," Maddie replied, but she felt heat rise in her cheeks.

"Mm-hmm," Hannah said, her smile widening. "Just hunting. Of course."

Rebecca appeared from behind the woodpile, her arms full of split logs. "Leave them alone, Hannah. They're figuring things out at their own pace."

"I'm not bothering anyone," Hannah protested, but her grin was infectious.

"You're bothering me," Jake called out from across the yard. "Some of us are trying to concentrate on serious tracking work here."

"Sorry, little brother," Hannah called back, then turned to Maddie with a theatrical whisper. "But really, you two are adorable."

Maddie groaned, but she was smiling. This was what they'd built—a place where people could tease each other, laugh together, worry about normal things like who was dating whom instead of who might be trying to kill them.

"We should get going," Matthew said, clearly as embarrassed as she was. "If that last transmission was correct, a storm's supposed to move in tonight."

They made their way past the workshop, where Marianne directed repairs with her sleeves rolled to her elbows, her hair streaked silver but her voice strong. The Burke boys worked beside her, their young faces serious as they measured and cut lumber. Both had grown into the second chance they'd been given, becoming skilled carpenters and dependable community members.

"Tommy, mind that angle," Marianne called out. "The roof won't hold if the joists don't sit properly."

"Yes, ma'am," Tommy replied, adjusting his work with careful precision.

Sean looked up from his sawing. "Mrs. Miller, do you want us to start on the window frames next?"

"That'd be perfect," Marianne said, her approval evident. "You boys have become quite the craftsmen."

Maddie caught Matthew's eye, and they shared a smile. The

Burke boys had been sullen and resentful at first, working only because they had to. But Marianne's patient guidance had shown them that building things was more satisfying than destroying them. Somewhere deep-down Maddie wondered if she loved them as much as they loved her. Both of them had grown so attached that she couldn't lift a finger without one of them hopping up to assist.

They passed the old ham radio where Jenkins hunched in his coat, twisting the dials with careful fingers. Voices crackled through the static. Reports from Augusta about reopened markets, news from Boston about repaired mills, word of traders on sleds moving between scattered communities.

"Any word from the western settlements?" Matthew asked, pausing beside the radio.

"Heard from Colorado yesterday," Jenkins replied without looking up. "They're trading seeds for medical supplies. Sounds like they've got a good thing going out there."

"What about the group in Virginia?" Maddie asked. "The ones with the solar panel factory?"

"They're expanding," Jenkins said, his weathered face brightening. "Taking orders for spring delivery. Might be able to get us some panels for the new workshop."

It was a thin thread connecting them to a larger world, fragile but real. The radio network had become the nervous system of the new civilization, carrying information, hope, and the promise that they weren't alone in trying to rebuild.

"Storm's coming tonight," Jenkins muttered, eyes lifting briefly. "Be careful if you're heading out."

"We'll be back before dark," Maddie promised, adjusting the pack on her shoulders.

They crossed into the woods, their boots leaving deep prints in the untouched snow. The trees stood black against the white, their branches heavy with ice that caught the morning light like crystal. It was beautiful and harsh, like everything else in this new world.

"I never really knew you before all this," Matthew said quietly as they followed a game trail through the pines. "I wish I had."

Maddie glanced at him, surprised by the wistfulness in his voice. "We were different people then. We had to be."

"You were always brilliant," Matthew said. "Even in high school, you were building things, solving problems. I just never took the time to really see it."

"You were the star athlete," Maddie replied with a gentle smile. "I was the nerd with grease under her fingernails. We lived in different worlds."

"Stupid worlds," Matthew said, shaking his head. "All that time wasted on things that didn't matter."

They walked in comfortable silence for a while, following the deer tracks deeper into the forest. The snow muffled their footsteps, and the only sounds were the creak of branches and the distant call of a hawk.

"Do you ever regret it?" Maddie asked suddenly. "The way everything changed? The world we lost?"

Matthew considered this, his breath misting in the cold air. "I regret the people we lost. I regret the pain, the fear, the way we had to learn to be hard. But this?" He gestured at the snow-covered forest around them. "This quiet, this peace? The way we actually know our neighbors now, depend on each other? No, I don't regret that."

They reached the edge of the orchard, where deer sometimes sheltered in the thickets. The trees were bare; their branches etched against the gray sky like intricate lacework. Fresh tracks crisscrossed the snow between the trees.

"There," Matthew whispered, pointing to a cluster of does

grazing about fifty yards away. "Three of them, good size."

Maddie raised her rifle, settling the stock against her shoulder. She'd learned to shoot, but the necessity of hunting for survival had made her truly skilled. She breathed slowly, steadying her aim, then squeezed the trigger.

The shot echoed through the forest, and one of the does dropped cleanly. The others bounded away, white tails flashing as they disappeared into the deeper woods.

"Nice shot," Matthew said, his voice warm with admiration.

"Thanks," Maddie replied, feeling a familiar mixture of satisfaction and sadness. Taking a life was never easy, but it was necessary. The doe would feed several families, and they would use every part of it.

They worked together to field-dress the deer, their movements efficient and practiced. The blood steamed in the cold air, and Maddie found herself thinking about how much they'd all changed. A year ago, she couldn't have imagined herself gutting a deer. Now it was just another part of life.

"We should head back," Matthew said, glancing at the sky. "Jenkins was right about that storm."

Dark clouds were building on the horizon, and the wind was picking up. They wrapped the deer in canvas and began the trek back to the farm, carrying the load. between them strapped to a long pole.

"Maddie," Matthew said as they reached the ridge overlooking the valley. "There's something I've been wanting to tell you."

She stopped, turning to face him. His expression was serious, almost nervous.

"I know we've been… figuring things out," he continued. "Taking our time, not rushing into anything. But I need you to know what I feel for you; it's not just about surviving together.

It's not just about finding comfort in this broken world."

Maddie's heart began to beat faster. "Matthew…"

"I love you," he said simply. "I love your brilliant mind, your steady hands, the way you can fix anything. I love how you make me want to be better than I am. I love that you see possibilities where other people see problems."

Tears stung Maddie's eyes, but they were good tears. "I love you too," she whispered. "I think I have for a while now."

He reached for her hand, hesitant, but when she met him, her fingers slid easily into his. Even through their gloves, she could feel the warmth of his touch.

"We don't have to rush," Matthew said. "We don't have to decide everything right now. But I wanted you to know. I wanted to be honest about what this is."

"What is it?" Maddie asked softly.

"Hope," Matthew said. "It's hope for something better. For a future we can build together."

They stood there for a long moment, the world hushed around them, snow beginning to fall in lazy flakes. The storm was coming, but they were safe, they were together, and they were home.

From the farmyard just ahead, voices drifted on the light breeze—Jake's laughter as Ethan tossed a snowball, younger children shrieking with delight. Rebecca's voice called from the porch, bright and welcoming as she beckoned them in. Hannah was probably already preparing to tease them about their "hunting trip."

Life weaved itself through every corner of the farm, messy and stubborn and alive. It wasn't the life any of them had planned, but it was theirs. They had built it from the ruins of the old world, brick by brick, choice by choice, day by day.

Maddie looked out at the hills, where the road curved away

into the white. There would be more work, more challenges, more communities to connect and help. But her shoulders felt lighter than they had in months. She squeezed Matthew's hand, feeling his grip tighten in answer.

"Come on," she said, pulling him toward the farmhouse. "Let's go home."

Together they walked through the snow, through the cold, into a world still wounded but healing, still fragile but theirs, still waiting to be made whole. The storm was coming, but they would weather it together, the way they had weathered everything else.

Behind them, their tracks in the snow told the story of where they'd been. Ahead of them, the warm glow of the farmhouse windows promised where they were going. And in the space between, in the here and now, there was everything they needed to build tomorrow.

"It is impossible to show why certain things should not utterly destroy and end the human race and story..."
- H.G. Wells

Thank you for reading. Please consider leaving a review.

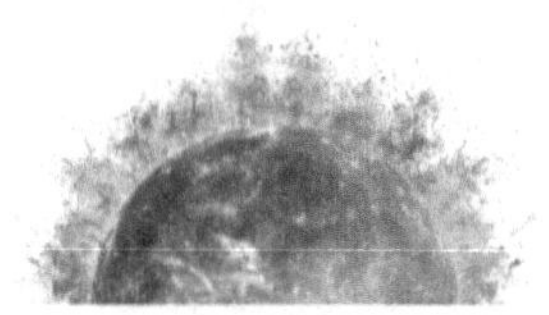

Also by DJ Cooper

<u>Dystopia Series</u>

Beginning of the End

Long Road

Revelations

Dark Days

<u>Apocalypse Fire Series</u>

Endure the Chaos

Survive the Chaos

Beyond the Chaos

<u>Cincinnati Fall Series</u>

Cincinnati Fall 1

Cincinnati Fall 2

Cincinnati Fall 3

<u>Nine Meals From Anarchy Series</u>

Sun's Fury

Terminus State

<u>Insurrection Series</u>

Deception

Evasion

Abolition

<u>WordPeddler Magazines</u>

COMING SOON

https://fire-n-ash.com

Acknowledgements

Altered World is a story of not just survival but of human desire to persevere. In book one *Wasted World*, the separate journeys through areas mired with challenges around every corner. Followed by *Decayed World* where the stunning revelation of a new threat, The Queen of Likes Emerges. Now they faced challenges they never thought would come to them and overcame. Showing a resilience and human desire to not just survive but to *Thrive!*

If you would like to stay updated on this and other emerging stories in my new Fire & Ash World, visit my website at https://authoroftheapocalypse.com

I am incredibly grateful to all who read this and my other stories. A passion I never knew existed until I sat down one day to write and now, I try harder with each book, chapter, paragraph and sentence to make it better than the one before. If it were not for the amazing readers who give up their time to walk these tales along with me, I would not be able to do so. It is for you I try to make each one more than the last. I love hearing from readers even if you don't like it. Without feedback I can't do better next time.

I am thankful that through the terrible things not just in this book but also in life I have friends and family to see it through.

While writing this book, we lost the person who inspired a desire to understand preparedness topics. My mother went home to be with Jesus on July 19th and she will be missed. I take comfort in knowing that the end is not really the end and we will see her again.

-DJ